SATE

The Burn Duet

LOREN LEE

Contents

Sate

To my fellow black sheep: fitting in isn't all it's cracked up to be. Just because your path doesn't look the same as everyone else's doesn't mean you're going the wrong way.

Stay weird, babes.

———————————————

Trigger Warnings

———————————————

Dear reader, Sate deals with some pretty heavy stuff. Please read the trigger warnings and protect your mental health.

- Stalking
- Murder
- Age Gap
- Attempted suicide, anxiety, depression
- Open door MFM scenes, some explicit (you're welcome)
- Why choose

If you are considering harming yourself, please contact the National Suicide Prevention Hotline by texting or dialing 988. Someone is available 24-hours a day to help. Alternatively, you can reach out to a friend or call a family member. Whatever it takes. Just remember, whatever lies your brain tells you about how no one wants to be there for you are not true. Believe me. You are loved. You are valuable. You are important.

Playlist

1. All My Friends - Dermot Kennedy
2. And so it Begins - Klergy
3. Blood Sport - Sleep Token
4. Boiling Water - little hurricane
5. BOYTOY - Halle Abadi
6. Can't Help Falling In Love - DARK - Tommee Profitt, brooke
7. Cardigan - Taylor Swift
8. Climb - ADONA
9. Cold Cold Cold - Cage The Elephant
10. Cringe - Matt Maeson
11. Dangerous Game - Klergy, BEGINNERS
12. Darkside - Oshins, Hael
13. Dark Things - ADONA
14. Descending - Sleep Token
15. Devil Devil - MILCK
16. Devil's Playground - The Rigs
17. Dirty Hands (Gone Mad) - Kendra Dantes

18. Dug My Heart - BØRNS
19. Emergence - Sleep Token
20. Enjoy The Silence - Ki:Theory
21. Fallout - UNSECRET, Neoni
22. Flesh and Bone - Black Math
23. Gimme Shelter - The Rolling Stones
24. Good in Goodbye - Madison Beer
25. Grave Digger - Matt Maeson
26. Hide and Seek - Klergy, Mindy Jones
27. Holding Out for a Hero - Nothing But Thieves
28. How Villains Are Made - Madalen Duke
29. idfc - blackbear
30. I Found - Amber Run
31. In Flames - Digital Daggers
32. In the Shadows - Amy Stroup
33. It Works Itself Out - Half Moon Run
34. Jaws - Sleep Token
35. love and hate - Camylio
36. Man or a Monster (feat. Zayde Wolf) - Sam Tinnesz
37. No Good - UNSECRET, Ruelle
38. Pushing Me Away - Linkin Park
39. Rebels - Royal Cinema
40. Santeria - Sublime
41. Scars - Boy Epic
42. Smells Like Teen Spirit - Saint Mesa
43. Snow On The Beach - Taylor Swift, Lana Del Rey
44. Take Me to Church - MILCK
45. Throne - Saint Mesa
46. Use Somebody - Kings of Leon

____

Prologue

____

Astrid. January. Hank Turner is dead.

MY PHONE RANG, JARRING ME OUT OF A RESTLESS SLEEP. I could barely open my eyes, and when I rolled over to grab my phone off the nightstand, the numbers on my clock cheerfully informed me in glowing blue that I'd only just climbed into bed two hours prior. I shook off the grogginess, noting the ringtone was one I'd assigned to my best friend, Imogen. If she was calling me this early in the morning, something must be wrong.

I sat up against my pillows and swiped my finger across the screen to answer. "Hey, babe, what's wrong?"

The only sound coming from the other end of the line was a sniffle. "Gen? Gen, what's wrong?"

I heard her take a deep breath before she responded. "Astrid, I...don't know how to tell you this, but...he's gone." Her voice sounded...off. I could tell she was upset, but something about her tone set off warning bells in my head.

"What do you mean, 'gone'? *Who's* gone?"

She continued almost like she hadn't heard my question, and the more she spoke, the more confused I got. "I didn't want to tell you like this, over the phone, but I didn't want you to hear it from someone else..." It sounded like a speech she'd rehearsed. Something was definitely off.

"Imogen, what are you trying to say to me right now? *Who* is gone?" I repeated.

"Hank, As. Hank is gone. I really can't say anymore right now. I'll let you know as soon as I've made some arrangements but I need you to pass the word along to your folks and see if someone can keep an eye on the house until I can come back and get it cleaned out. It might be a while, but I'll take care of it eventually."

I gasped, my hand flying up to cover my mouth. My face went numb, frozen in shock and grief, but I forced myself to respond. "Gen, oh my god, Gen. Hank is... how the fuck are you so calm right now? What is going on, Imogen? I don't understand...*how*? How did this even happen?"

Imogen coughed roughly on the other end of the line before she responded. "I know none of it makes any sense to you, As, and I promise I'll explain as much of it as I can, but I just can't right this second. I need to make some calls and start getting his affairs in order." She sounded so matter of fact. Was she in shock? I could tell she was upset, but there was something else there too. I'd known my best friend long enough to know when she wasn't giving me the whole story, and my radar was in overdrive.

"God, baby, I'm so fucking sorry, is there anything you need me to do aside from getting the house covered until you can get back here? Do you need me to come there? I hate the idea of you going through this without me by your side." I could feel my throat trying to close around a sob but tried to focus on what she needed and not my own grief.

"I'm okay for right now, I promise, but let's talk in a couple of days and I'll let you know if I need you to come. I always want you here with me, you know that, but the guys haven't left my side since it happened. Don't worry too much, I'm not alone."

I sniffled, a little hurt, but tried to set my feelings aside. "Okay, babe. Call me if you need anything. I love you, Gen. Never forget that."

"Love you too, As. Always. I'll call you soon." And then she was gone, and the silence was my cue to fall apart now that I wasn't trying to be strong for her.

I laid back and rolled onto my side, wrapping myself around my pillow. My initial shock gave way to grief in the amount of time it took to let my phone drop onto the bed. There was a lump in my throat that I couldn't seem to breathe or swallow past. I was suffocating under the weight of the news Imogen had just shared.

My heart...*ached*.

Not only for Imogen—who'd just lost her father, the only family she had in the whole world—but for me.

Hank Turner had been a father figure to me since I was seven years old, when I became attached at the hip to his only daughter. She and I had grown up more like sisters than friends, and I'd always looked to their relationship as the example of what family *should* be. My experiences with my own family hadn't come close to the connection they'd shared.

The all-encompassing sense of loss from knowing Hank was no longer out there in the world left me reeling and rootless. I knew that Imogen had support from Auley and Key, the two men who had come into her life in a surprising turn of events recently, and I was so glad she wasn't alone in her grief. But, as I curled up in a ball underneath the covers of my bed and cried into my pillow, I wondered, *who would comfort me?*

It was undeniably selfish but I wished that, just once, someone could be there to wipe my tears as I felt myself floating adrift, soaking my pillow until I fell back into an uneasy sleep.

Part I

All this time, I've felt like a failure to you, but we failed each other, didn't we? The weight was never all mine to carry.

1

Astrid

November. Diverge

I slammed the door to my Scout, leaving it parked in front of the administration building.

It was early enough that the campus looked more like a ghost-town than a bustling hub of higher education. I hurried up the sidewalk into the relative cool of the building in front of me and smiled as I greeted the girl sitting behind the desk.

"Hi, I'm Astrid Scott, I'm here to see Dean Alverson."

She skimmed her finger over the calendar in front of her before nodding, gesturing to the chairs lined against the wall. "Have a seat, and I'll let him know you're here."

I opted to stand by the window instead, nervous energy making me too fidgety to sit. I looked out onto the lawn that wrapped around the building as I waited. I turned away from the view as footsteps approached from the hallway, and I couldn't help but grin when my advisor rounded the corner with a jumbo cup of coffee clutched in his hand and a warm smile for me.

"Ms. Scott, a pleasure to see you as always. Come on, follow me to my office and you can tell me what brings you to see me today." With that, he spun on a heel and began striding toward his office just down the hall. The spring in his step belying his head of silver hair.

When we reached his office and settled into our chairs, he leaned back, coffee cup resting on his stomach. "Not that I was upset to see you on my schedule first thing this morning, but I can't help but wonder what brings you in to see me again so soon after our last appointment?" His white eyebrows gathered together between his eyes with apparent concern.

I chewed on my lip for a moment before I answered, trying to find the right words to explain why I was there. His slightly rheumy blue eyes never seemed to judge, something I always appreciated about him.

"I just don't think I *fit* here. I know what you said last time, about giving it time, but I feel like I'm always on the outside looking in. Everyone else seems to have their shit together." I paused as my eyes widened at my slip of the tongue. "Sorry for the language, sir."

Dean Alverson chuckled. "Young lady, I assure you that's not the first, nor the worst, four-letter word that anyone has uttered in this room. I'm fairly hard to offend at my age."

My cheeks pinkened in embarrassment, but I carried

on. "I've just always had a hard time forcing myself to fit in places, even when everyone in my life is telling me that's where I belong. I don't have any idea what I want to do with my life, but my gut keeps telling me that I'm not going to figure it out here, locked in a stuffy classroom learning how to compose 'business-like' emails."

He studied me thoughtfully for a minute before he leaned forward, placing his cup of coffee on the coaster next to his keyboard and leveling me with a kind, but direct, look. "I'd like to ask you a question, and feel free to tell an old man to mind his business, but is there anywhere you ever *have* felt like you belonged?"

Unbidden, I felt the burn of tears behind my eyes and I blinked furiously to try and dispel them. I met his stare, knowing by his sympathetic expression that he could see the unshed tears I was unable to hide, though he was kind enough not to acknowledge them.

"No, sir," I whispered.

He nodded, as if that was exactly the response he'd expected. Pausing, he tapped his finger against his chin until he found the words to speak again. "And what do you think would happen if you walked out this door today and took a leap? No plans. No curriculum. No expectations. Do you think you'd eventually find your place, Astrid? Or would you languish in the world if the structure of higher education wasn't there to push you forward?"

I looked over his shoulder, out the double-paned windows behind his desk. It was a crisp and beautiful day and I could just barely see the peak of the Sundial Bridge in the distance. I pictured myself crossing over it with no destination in mind, nowhere to be, and a smile crept onto my face.

"I think that maybe I would find my place, sir. Eventually. I've never been given the chance to see what would happen if I were the one steering my life, apart from everyone else's expectations and demands."

He leaned forward to rest his elbows on the desk in front of him, smiling at me with a kinder expression than I'd learned to expect from most authority figures.

"Then I think you have your answer, my dear. The notion that everyone must walk the same path in order to achieve success is as outdated as my wardrobe is, but please never tell my wife I said that." He paused the way he always did before saying something profound, and I sat straighter, giving him my full attention. "Astrid, it's okay to find your own path. And it's okay if it looks nothing like anyone else's. And it's okay if you stumble along the way, as long as you get back up. That's the difference between failure and success as far as I can tell."

My eyes continued to burn as the tears began to overflow and I absorbed what he'd said. "You've been so amazing to me, sir. I almost want to stay just so that I can still come see you and talk about life."

He gave me a rueful grin. "Well, I have been known to have a coffee in places other than this office from time to time. Don't despair. You might just run into me when you least expect it."

I grinned at him through my tears. "I'll count on it, sir."

He stood and made his way around his desk,

offering me his hand to shake. "It has been a delight to get to know you, Astrid Scott. Something tells me that you are going to lead an amazing and colorful life. I hope to have the privilege of catching glimpses of it from the sidelines."

I rose from the chair in front of his desk before ignoring his outstretched hand and throwing my arms around him, offering a hard squeeze. Unbearably sad that I might never see him again, but so grateful to have had someone like him there for me at that moment.

He patted my back awkwardly before speaking. "Now that's settled. What say you go knock 'em dead?"

I stepped back, nodding, and swiped my fingers under my eyes. "Thank you, sir. You'll never know how much your words have meant to me. Next time we see each other, I'll buy you a coffee and tell you all about it."

He beamed. "You've got a deal, Ms. Scott." He offered me one last grandfatherly smile and nodded toward the door. "Now, run along, I've got other students to meet with today and hopefully I won't convince any of them to give up higher education or I'll be out of a job before I know it."

Back in the parking lot, I climbed into the Scout and sat for a minute, feeling inexplicably light somewhere in the vicinity of my soul. The possibilities in front of me were limitless. And slightly terrifying. But the feeling of anything being possible was one I'd grab onto with both hands. I knew it wouldn't stay with me forever, so I'd savor it for as long as I could.

I smiled and cranked the old truck, enjoying the rumble as the engine turned over. Maybe, before I took on the world, I'd grab a coffee. After all, if I was going to start a whole new life, I'd need caffeine. Right?

2

Liam

November. It's a Small World After All

WHEN I DEBOARDED AT LOGAN INTERNATIONAL, MY GUT told me yet again that I could be making the stupidest decision I'd made in memorable history. Like, the kind of mistake that could have big consequences for me in the long run.

The problem was, I didn't see any other way to get the funding I needed to open my club. I'd invested every bit of personal savings I had to get it up and running, but I needed more and the nature of the business meant that most *traditional* means of getting a business loan were not available to me. At this point, if I couldn't convince the Organization to help me, I was at risk of losing everything I'd ever worked for.

I stood at the baggage carousel and watched bags from all over the world circle round and round, losing track of time until an airport employee nudged me, gesturing to the one bag that hadn't been claimed from our flight. "That yours?"

I snapped to, nodding gratefully. "It is. Thanks, man." I stepped forward and grabbed the handles of my duffle, slinging it over my shoulder before I turned and surveyed the various exits, wondering which one my ride would be waiting at.

I pulled my cell out of my pocket and realized I hadn't switched it off airplane mode. When I did, several notifications popped up—which I ignored—but there was one from ten minutes prior indicating my ride was here and where to find them.

I ignored the feeling of foreboding that was slowly increasing pressure in my chest and made my way outside to see a kid who couldn't have been older than eighteen leaned up against an old Chevelle with a hastily made cardboard sign clasped in his paws. It read L. Asbury, and—I shit you not—it had a little smiley face drawn next to it.

That probably would have made me laugh under different circumstances, but I couldn't forget who had ordered this car for me. Who I was heading to meet. Something told me that smiley face was his own special touch, not something that had been ordered by Merebitch.

As I approached, he surveyed me in my nicest denim, freshly polished boots, and a button down. It was the closest thing in my closet to business casual, yet somehow I felt like this little shit was judging me for it.

"Liam Asbury?" he asked with his head tilted to the side like an inquisitive puppy. I decided that's exactly what he reminded me of. A puppy. How the hell did such a young kid get mixed up with these people?

"That's what my mother calls me." I gestured to the trunk, and he rounded the back of the car to pop it open for me.

When I'd deposited my bag inside and slammed the lid, he waved toward the front of the car. "Front seat, back seat, doesn't make a difference to me, man, but I'm no chauffeur so you can get your own door."

I raised a brow at him. "I'm shocked to discover this isn't your calling in life."

He just rolled his eyes and circled to the driver's door, not waiting to see which option I'd choose. After a moment of deliberation, I opted for the front seat. I guessed the smiley face didn't mean we were going to be besties. *Aw.*

Once I was inside with the door pulled shut behind me, he tossed a black bag in my lap before cranking the old muscle car. I groaned. "You gotta be fucking kidding me."

"Look, man, I don't make the rules. And you don't have to put it on right now. In fact, I'd rather you didn't. Even in Boston, people might look twice at a man riding down the expressway wearing a hood. I'll let you know when you need to put it on."

I stood with my back to a wall, biding my time where my driver had placed me with a cautionary word of advice. "Don't take that hood off 'til they tell you. Safer that way."

His retreating footsteps told me he'd abandoned me to whatever fate my idiotic life choices had brought me to.

"Mr. Asbury, I presume?" a feminine voice inquired, and I raised a hand to the bottom of the hood I wore, pausing before I lifted it. "By all means," she continued, "let us see our new business partner in the flesh."

I had to squint my eyes for a moment once I'd removed the hood, so it took a moment to register, but I did my best to curb my surprise when I responded. "Liam, please. Mr. Asbury was my mother." I waited a full five seconds for her face to crack and show she had a sense of humor, but she just continued to stare at me without a single twitch in her expression. "Tough room," I muttered.

She simply turned her chair with a flick of her wrist and gestured for me to follow. "If you're quite done, it's best not to keep him waiting."

Two hours later, my barely post-pubescent driver had collected me from my meeting, gestured to the hood I'd tucked into the back pocket of my jeans, and dropped me unceremoniously at my hotel a half hour later. I suspected he'd circled the same block several times in an attempt to throw me off, but I honestly didn't care enough about where their "headquarters" were to try and puzzle it out. If he had orders to take me to my hotel via some convoluted route, far be it from me to point out that I wasn't a complete fucking idiot.

I grabbed my bag from the trunk and he was pulling away as soon as I slammed the lid.

"Aw. Guess we're not gonna hang out then, and here I thought we'd made so much progress."

I turned toward the entryway and the doorman did an admirable job of pretending he hadn't just heard me talking to myself as he opened the door for me. He indicated the formidable front desk just inside and to the left of the lobby.

I stepped up to the first computer. "Checking in." I slid my ID across the counter to the attractive brunette on the other side and pulled my shoulders back, trying to release some of the tension that had been growing between them for the past twenty-two hours. She smiled a plastic smile and examined my ID before sliding it back to me. She punched a few keys on her computer before turning to the keycard machine behind her.

She turned back and offered me an envelope and another one of those smiles. "We hope you enjoy your stay at the Mandarin Oriental. Our staff is on call twenty-four hours a day. Should you require anything during your stay, just pick up the phone in your room and press nine."

I took the proffered envelope with a tired smile. "Thank you. Could you recommend somewhere close by that I could grab a beer and relax? I know, it being the holiday and all, there might not be much open."

"Of course, sir. Our bar will be open until ten o'clock tonight, but if you'd prefer to go somewhere outside the hotel, might I recommend Abe and Louie's. They have a spectacular mixologist on staff and are open this evening for special holiday hours. I think you'll be pleased."

I offered her a salute and grabbed my bag from the floor at my feet, turning toward the elevators. Once inside, I pulled up the restaurant she'd recommended. There was no reason to explain to her that I didn't want to settle at the hotel bar and be so easily accessible to the people who had put me up here for the night.

Freshly showered, but not shaved, and in clean clothes, I felt substantially more human. I pulled my jacket out of my duffle and shook it a few times before I decided there was no help for the wrinkles and slid it on. Now that the sun had gone down, Boston in November had me shivering in a way that I rarely ever did in Redding, but I conceded that might just be nerves.

Outside the doors, past the stoic doorman once again, I took a left and found my destination less than a block down. The light spilling from inside was warm and inviting, and I was relieved when the hostess informed me that seating at the bar didn't require a reservation. I crossed the room and claimed the last open spot, conveniently in a corner so I could place my back against the wall and observe the room around me while I waited for the bartender's attention.

I did a double-take when I recognized someone seated at a nearby table. I looked away and then looked back and, this time, his dark gaze was narrowed on me. I lifted a shoulder and mouthed, *"Small world?"*

He just shook his head almost imperceptibly and promptly looked away, returning his attention to the pretty blonde sitting across from him. I was forced to change my focus when the bartender cleared his throat across from me, so I placed an order for a Guinness and an order of shepherd's pie, chuckling to myself even if no one else got the snub.

With my order placed and a cold Guinness in front of me, I surreptitiously studied the occupants of the table across the room. Noting the contradictory body language of almost everyone at the table, except for my associate, that was. *He* appeared quite relaxed. One of my ex-girlfriend's books would have called him insouciant.

What? I occasionally read them with her. For the plot.

As my plate of delicious Irish fare appeared in front of me, a commotion from the table in question drew my attention again. The girl slid her chair back abruptly, spoke a few angry words as she tossed her napkin down, and turned to leave. Leaning down to kiss one of the men on the cheek on her way out. As she passed right by where I was sitting, a kernel of recognition teased the back of my brain. I'd seen this girl some-where before.

But where?

The witching hour found me lying in the hotel bed staring at the ceiling, wishing I'd had three or four beers instead of just the one, so that maybe I'd be happily unconscious right now instead of inspecting the tray ceiling in my hotel room.

I wasn't usually an insomniac, but lately I'd been having an increasingly difficult time sleeping. I attributed it to the absolutely poor life-choices I was making, despite the fact that I couldn't come up with an alternative. I kicked my legs a couple of times, attempting to get my body to relax, before I flopped over onto my stomach and rested my chin on my pillow. I needed a distraction. Something for my mind to focus on that didn't have to do with my current predicament.

Like a gift from the insomnia gods, the face of the girl from the restaurant earlier popped into my brain. Where had I seen her before? I'd definitely never dated her. Too young. And none of my friends had that good of taste, honestly, so I was pretty sure that wasn't how I knew her.

Just as I started to drift back off, a mental image of the two girls from the concert last summer popped into my head and my eyes sprang open.

No fucking way. What were the odds that it was the same girl?

I laid there, wide awake again, doing my damndest to recreate her face in my mind, and finally decided it really was the same girl. Her eyes were such a striking shade of blue that it would be hard to mistake them. It was wild to even consider that I'd seen her months ago halfway across the US, and now, here she was again in

Boston, *and* with a known associate of the criminal organization that I'd just aligned myself with.

I filed the information away, not sure when or how it might come in handy, but trusting that there was no such thing as a coincidence.

3

Liam

Last Summer. Happenstance

Red Rocks Amphitheater

"Come on, Gen! We're gonna miss the opener!"

I stepped back quickly before I got mowed down by the brunette pushing past me with a blonde in tow. She was pulling so hard I could see a grimace on the blonde girl's face, and I wondered if she was about to wind up with a dislocated shoulder.

The blonde winced as they passed me and she mouthed, *"So sorry!"*

I just laughed and tipped my beer at her, shaking it off. Once upon a time I'd been that young, and, even now, I still got pretty excited when I had a chance to see one of my favorite acts play live. This night was no exception, though my enthusiasm was overshadowed by the heavy things weighing on my mind.

Before I could turn away, I saw something lying on the ground at my feet—one of those tiny leather ID holders that girls sometimes carried. It was smart not to carry a purse in a crowd like this, I supposed, but that only helped if you managed not to drop it on the ground. I reached down and picked it up, recognizing the brunette in the photo and immediately began scanning the crowd in front of me to see if they'd made it all the way to the front yet. I glanced back down at it, noting her name, Astrid James Scott, and the year on her ID jumped out at me. Fucken hell. She was just a baby.

I spotted my quarry down near the stage and began making my way toward them. When I caught up to the blonde who was still being towed forcibly by her friend, I reached out and tapped her on the shoulder, causing her to jerk her head in my direction, already defensive.

I put my hands in the air. "Whoa. Sorry for getting in your bubble, but your friend dropped her wallet back there." I held it out in explanation, trying to make myself as small and non-threatening as I could in an attempt to ease her anxiety.

She blew out a relieved puff of air and offered me a genuine smile. "Thank you so much!" She pulled her arm to get her friend's attention before she spoke again. "As, you dropped your wallet, babe. Say thank you to this nice man for giving it back and not being a creep."

The brunette widened her eyes and took the wallet from her friend, offering me her own smile and a little eye roll. "Gah, I'd lose my ass if it wasn't attached. Thanks, man!"

I offered them both a salute and a smile. "No worries, glad I could help. Enjoy your night."

I retreated to the VIP section and headed toward one of the spots that had been reserved for us, grabbing a fresh beer from the bartender along the way. These days I much preferred to catch my shows while seated, with a cold beverage in my hand.

When I heard the first guitar notes of "Grave Digger" kick off a few minutes later, I couldn't stop the chills that spread over me. The tune was unmistakable and fucking epic, if you trusted my judgment about it. Which you totally should. I had excellent taste in music.

I hoped my two young friends had found their way to the front of the crowd and managed to hold onto their stuff in the process. The next guy might not be so nice.

When I plopped down onto one of the rows, leaning back onto my elbows and stretching my legs out a bit in front of me, I heard a sharp whistle from behind me. I turned to look and grinned from ear to ear, waving my buddy down to join me.

"What's up, fucker?" My best friend Luke grabbed onto my shoulder and shook me within an inch of my life.

"I'm too old for shaking baby syndrome, hands off, asshole."

He just laughed good-naturedly and settled down next to me, taking a moment to enjoy the chorus of one of our favorite songs. "Ahh, this is epic. Thanks for the invite, buddy!"

I waved him off. "Who else would I invite? Didn't you know you're my only friend?"

He snorted without looking away from the stage. "Shut up, idiot."

I just laughed and leaned forward, draping my arms over my knees as Matt Maeson launched into his second song of the night. Another banger. Obviously this was going to be a killer set, and I was glad I hadn't skipped it.

4

Meredith

November. The Villain

"CHECK ON OUR WAYWARD EMPLOYEE, I WANT A STATUS *update on what's taking so fecking long and I want it now."*

"Yes, sir," I replied. "I'm on it." I hit the red button on my phone multiple times, ensuring it was well and truly disconnected before I allowed myself to growl out loud, grinding my teeth painfully.

I'd fought my way up the ranks to get where I was at Dearil's right hand, but it was all out of strategy, not any deep sense that Dearil was a good leader worth following. In truth, he was a barely functioning toddler with anger issues and a lack of impulse control. The fact that he'd landed himself as the head of the Organization on US soil was a matter of great speculation throughout the ranks, and with good reason. It was my job to quell any talk against him if I came across it, but I had the same questions and suspicions that everyone else did. So, despite the fact that he was a dick who most likely murdered his own brother to climb the ranks on the back of his still cooling corpse, I aligned myself with him when the opportunity struck.

I knew our association wasn't making me any friends with my colleagues, but I'd given up on making friends long ago. Now? Well, now I just wanted the power and respect that I'd been granted as an active agent for the Organization before my accident. Back then, no one cared if I was a woman, because I was a carefully honed weapon. Now I had to fight not to be dismissed because of my gender or my physical limitation. Neither my vagina nor my shattered L3 vertebrae had any effect on my ability to do my job with ruthless precision. However, both had, at one time or another, rendered me virtually invisible to the higher-ups. Dearil was the first one in a position of power who didn't dismiss me outright. I'd have been flattered if I hadn't known full well that it was because no one else could stand to work with him so closely.

Regardless, I'd built a reputation for myself since I'd become his right hand person, and it had served me well so far. People *saw* me now, and they respected me even if they didn't like me.

Fuck being liked. It was overrated.

I pushed back from my desk, using my right hand to turn my chair away from it and toward the kitchen. If I was going to call a known assassin before daybreak and issue threats, I needed to do it with a hot cup of tea in my hand.

The ringing stopped abruptly when the line connected and the man I was trying to reach answered with a growl. *"What!?"*

"We'd like a status report, *boy*, and a bit less of the attitude before we remind you how respect is taught within our organization." I prided myself on keeping my voice level, cold.

I heard material rustling abruptly on the other end of the line before he responded, his tone slightly more respectful. *"I'm doing reconnaissance. I'll have more information soon. This isn't something I can rush or she'll see me coming a mile away."*

I made note of his location via the tracker in his phone and entered the information into my laptop for further investigation. "See that you do. We don't like to be kept waiting, *ya ken?*" That last was a thinly veiled threat, and I didn't worry that it would miss him. Key was, everything else aside, quite clever, and I knew he understood the precarious position he was in working for the Organization. We had leverage over him. We'd never had reason to use it before, but something told me that this circumstance might be different.

"Understood. I'll be in touch." He ended the call, and I placed my phone down on the desk next to my laptop, opening up the mapping software. It may serve me well to know exactly where Mr. Mackintosh was laying his head of late.

I heard footsteps as I was doing some digging into Key's location, and I tilted my head to the side as warm lips slid over the pulse point on my neck, bringing chill bumps to the surface of my skin. A sexy voice, rough with sleep, greeted me. "You're up early, babe. Couldn't sleep?"

I turned, studying him in his drawstring pajama bottoms and bare chest, yawning and rubbing his hand over his pecs as he waited for my response.

"Work," I answered. "The boss has no concept of work-life balance. You know how it is."

He nodded before making his way sleepily into the kitchen, grabbing the coffee pot and carrying it to the sink to rinse. "Did you already have your tea?"

I lifted the mug from the other side of the desk and gestured with it. "But thanks."

"Sure, babe, I'm gonna start this and then go grab a shower. I've got to go get set up for the science fair this morning, so I'll have to run in a few, but I'll be back for dinner. Want me to bring Pad Thai?"

I grinned, loving that he knew exactly the way to my heart. "Extra hot?"

He chuckled on his way back toward the bedroom. "Is there any other kind?"

5

Liam

November. Insurance

AFTER ISSUING A NOT-SO-SUBTLE WARNING, THE CITY coordinator hung up, leaving only the sound of a dial tone.

"Ah, fuck off, ya asshole," I muttered angrily as I slammed down the phone and rocked back in my office chair behind my desk, running my hands through the unruly blond mop on my head and tugging the ends in frustration.

"Everything okay, boss?"

I looked up to see one of my newest, and best, hires leaning on my office door.

I grinned at her, trying to disguise my stress. "I've got it all under control, nothing to worry about." I slid back and stood, leaning left and right to crack my spine from where I'd been hunched over my desk for too damn long. "What's up, did you need something?"

I studied my bartender as she tilted her head at me, clearly not buying my brush off, but Rae was a pro and I knew she wouldn't push for details if I didn't offer them. Her shoulder-length blonde hair curled around her face, accentuating the tattoo that wrapped around her neck like a collar. That, combined with her uniform of a tight black vest worn without a shirt underneath, revealing even more ink spilling down her arms and across her chest, gave her the look of a punk rockabilly badass. If I wasn't *all the way* against fucking my employees, she would absolutely be my type. She was edgy and gorgeous and far smarter than I was, undoubtedly. I'd recently decided to make a habit of surrounding myself with women that could take me on in a battle of wits and she was no exception.

"We're out of vodka. Which is problematic, ya know, seeing as how we're a bar, which people generally presume is going to be in a position to serve them the alcoholic beverages of their choice." Her eyebrow was raised at me, and I snorted. This smartass.

"I'll get an order in tonight. Offer them gin and give them a discount."

Rae rolled her eyes at me and offered a one-finger salute before she turned on a heel to head back out front.

I could hear her muttering under her breath before she turned the corner. "This Philistine thinks all clear liquors are the same. Why do I even bother?"

I slumped back in my chair and once again rested my head in my hands. I needed to figure out how to get the city off my damn back about the "nature" of my business, and *then* I needed to hire someone to keep this place stocked and running like a well-oiled machine. My strengths tend to lie elsewhere, it seemed.

A ding on my laptop drew my attention and I cursed under my breath again when I saw who it was from.

To: Liam Asbury
From: Meredith Cairn
Subject: Your abject failure to comply

Mr. Asbury, please be aware that compliance with our agreement is mandatory, despite any issues you may be encountering with your local city government. We are unconcerned with any excuses you have provided thus far and expect that you will find a way to resolve this issue in a timely manner. If your business doesn't remain a viable partner for our organization, we will be forced to terminate your contract and collect any unpaid debts immediately by whatever means we see fit.

Rest assured, Mr. Asbury, you do not want that to happen.

. . .

```
Warmest regards,
   Meredith Cairn
```

"*Fuuuuuuuck.* Warmest regards, my ass. You wouldn't know warm regards if they crawled into your frigid cunt and took up residence there," I muttered under my breath and cracked my neck, opting not to respond to the email until I'd come up with some sort of solution to my problem.

If I couldn't get the city off my back, they were going to pull my business permit and I'd have to shut down and *that* would likely end up with me being fitted for a pair of cement shoes.

I didn't just need a solution, I needed an insurance policy.

____

6

Astrid

____

November. Strangers

THE DOOR TO MY FAVORITE COFFEE SHOP LET OUT A LOUD
squeak as I opened it, the bell jingling over my head. I
stepped inside and was immediately enveloped in the
scent of chocolate, cinnamon, sugar, and, most impor-
tantly, the fuel on which my body ran: coffee.

I got into line at the counter, leaning around the man
in front of me to look at the pastries that were on
display, deciding immediately that a chocolate croissant
would go perfectly with my coffee. With that sorted, I
straightened, noticing the man standing in front of me
had turned and was giving me an amused look out of
the corner of his eye, a grin curling up one side of his
mouth.

I shrugged and offered him my most serious expression. "Sorry if I got in your bubble. But it's really impor-

tant to choose wisely. I can't wait until I get to the counter to pick my pastry, I might panic and order the wrong thing."

He cocked a brow, turning fully toward me. "Panic? Pastry panic?"

I nodded emphatically. "Oh yes. It's tragic. And then you have to live with your decision, watching as someone else walks away with the treat that you *should* have ordered, but didn't. Because you panicked."

He nodded slowly. "Hmm. Sounds serious. Now you've got me worried. I was just going to order the first thing that popped into my head, but maybe I should be a bit more intentional with my choice. I wouldn't want to live with regret, after all."

I nodded sagely. "Ah, yes. The pastry regret. I wouldn't wish it on my worst enemy."

He turned back toward the case, giving its contents an intense look before he looked back at me over his shoulder. "Don't suppose you'd be willing to help? Now that there's so much pressure, I find that I'm having a hard time choosing."

I laughed. "My best friend would say, you shouldn't ever have to choose, but that has less to do with sugary treats than it does with other more...*visceral things*."

His eyebrows rose toward his tousled hair and he coughed a bit. "Now *that* is a story I need to hear. What say you help me choose from these delectable options, and I'll buy yours in return? Then you can join me at that little table over there in the corner and tell me all about it while we eat."

I cocked my head for a minute, studying him. He didn't *look* like a serial killer. And it wasn't like I was going to *go* anywhere with him. "Okay, pal, you've got a deal."

He grinned and waved his hand in front of him in line. "In that case, ladies first."

He shifted around on the tiny cafe chair for a few minutes as I watched him with my eyebrows raised, trying not to laugh at his attempts to fold himself into it.

"Everything okay over there?" I quipped.

He mock glared at me before he gave up and snagged a bigger chair from a neighboring table and settled onto it with a huff. "It's not my fault these chairs are made for children and child-sized women. I don't fit!"

I laughed out loud before picking up my coffee and blowing across the surface. "You picked the table, pal. There are giant chairs over there in front of the fireplace that would have suited you better, in case you didn't notice."

He leaned around me a bit to study the chairs in question before he shrugged. "This table's private."

I raised my brows again. "And we need privacy? I usually require more than a chocolate croissant and a coffee before I consider doing anything that requires privacy."

He smirked. "I knew when you leaned around me

and made that humming sound low in your throat when you spotted those"—he gestured at the croissant in my hand—"that if I could talk you into joining me for coffee, it would be a conversation best had in a private corner."

7

Liam

Serendipity, You Say?

WHEN I SAW HER WALK INTO MY FAVORITE COFFEE SHOP, IT was like I'd been struck by lightning. Immediately, the seeds of a completely crazy plan began to come together, and I couldn't believe the dumb fucking luck I would run into her after what I witnessed when I was in Boston. Shit like this didn't happen unless the universe was just *trying* to throw you a bone. No way was I going to pass it up.

I watched her take a giant bite out of the chocolate croissant in front of her, grinning at the bit of chocolate that remained at the corner of her mouth when she paused and caught me staring.

"Are you perving on me eating a pastry? 'Cause that's not assuaging any of my stranger danger instincts." She raised a brow at me and took a sip of her coffee, her tongue peeking out after she swallowed to remove the bit of chocolate before I could do something even creepier like reach out and swipe over it with my thumb.

I put both hands up in front of me, leaning back in my chair to give her some extra space. "No perving at all, just appreciating a woman who's not scared to enjoy her food."

She wrinkled her brow at me, looking truly perplexed. "What decade are you living in where women don't enjoy food?"

I thought back to the last woman I'd dated, and the fact that she'd only ever ordered salad when we went out, before I answered her honestly. "I think it's more the type, not the decade."

She grimaced. "I think you need to revamp your type then, friend." Then she grinned before she took another savage bite out of her pastry, sighing in obvious enjoyment as it hit her tongue.

I chuckled, acknowledging she was probably right. "Agreed. I'll try to do better going forward."

She nodded, like her work there was done, before she continued. "So, aside from an abnormal obsession with watching women who like to eat, why did you lure me into this corner?"

I straightened in my seat, cutting my eyes to the tables closest to us, before I returned my attention to her. "I've seen you before, did you know that?"

She narrowed her eyes. "You stalking me, pastry boy?"

I tilted my head back, laughing outright. "Would I actually tell you if I was?"

She shrugged. "You might. Or you might lie, but I'm a pretty good judge of character, so I think I'd know if you lied to me." Her unwavering blue gaze seemed to cut right into me as she leveled me with it.

"Fair enough. No, I'm not stalking you. To be honest, I'm a little offended that you don't remember meeting me before."

She narrowed her eyes, studying my face intently before she shook her head. "I've got nothing, pastry boy, where did we meet?"

Again, I couldn't contain my laughter. I found myself truly enjoying her direct, no bullshit, way of addressing me. I felt a twinge of conscience at the spur of the moment decision I'd made to "use" her, but consoled myself with the knowledge that I wouldn't actually ever do anything to *hurt* her. I just needed her to be my insurance policy.

Just in case.

I reminded her. "Last summer at Red Rocks. You dropped your wallet and a chivalrous stranger returned it to you? That jog your memory at all?"

She made a little *O* out of her mouth as she looked at me with fresh eyes. "Holy shit. When they say it's a small world they really aren't joking, are they?"

I laughed. She wasn't wrong. I plowed forward, mentally committed to my evil plan, hoping that she wouldn't see right through me the minute I opened my mouth. "I know this is going to sound crazy, but you don't happen to need a job, do you?"

She stiffened in her chair, her expression no longer teasing. "Pastry boy, you just slid back into the creepy realm again. You don't even know me, why the fuck would you offer me a job?"

I leaned forward and offered her my most earnest expression. "I have a good feeling about you and my gut very rarely leads me wrong in these cases. I need help at my club, and here you are. It's gotta be serendipity, don't you think?"

Again, she raised a brow at me but the suspicious look in her eyes eased up a bit, leaning more toward teasing. "A club, huh? Well, that sounds shady AF. Please, say less." She rolled her eyes at me, draining the last of her coffee before she set the cup back on the table between us. "As it happens, I do find myself at loose ends at the moment and gainful employment wouldn't be amiss." She stood up and grabbed her bag, draping it over her shoulder before she narrowed her eyes at me once more. "Will I have to take my clothes off or do anything that will get me arrested?"

I felt my face split into a relieved grin. "First, not unless you want to. And second, not as long as everyone does their job." I winked at her and gestured to the door. "How about a tour before I tell you more?"

I glanced in my rearview mirror periodically as I led the way to the industrial area of town, making sure she was still following, and, despite her valid suspicions, she never lagged more than a car-length behind my Porsche. I had to admit, I was impressed.

Three blocks east of the main drag, in a slightly

rundown industrial area, I turned onto one of the side roads, scanning my surroundings as we went, and wondered if she was taking this opportunity to let someone know where she was before she followed a complete stranger into the industrial park. I could see her lips moving in my mirror, but couldn't tell if she was talking or singing along with the radio. I wouldn't blame her for wanting to have a failsafe if I turned out to be a psycho, but I hoped I'd done enough to put her at ease so that she didn't feel the need.

I pulled into a parking space in front of my pride and joy, and hoped she could appreciate that it looked much better kept than the ones we'd just passed. She pulled in and parked next to me, studying the small black sign hanging over the door, before she slid out of her truck and came to stand where I waited for her.

"Obsidian, huh?" she asked. "Sexy."

I grinned at her and began walking toward the door. "That's exactly what I was going for."

8

Astrid

You're Not Disappointed, I'm Disappointed

I'D PUT OFF TELLING MY PARENTS I'D WITHDRAWN FROM THE university for two entire weeks, and honestly, it was both the most nerve-wracking and liberating thing I'd ever done. I was an adult, there was no real reason why I even needed to let them know, it wasn't like they were paying my bills or tuition. But, somewhere inside me, I knew I needed to fess up eventually.

The very real urge to just keep up with the lie and enjoy the way they'd been looking at me since I'd been accepted to Redding University was hard to overcome, but I knew I couldn't continue the farce indefinitely. The trouble was that I had always been their problem child, the one who "never finished what she started" and it was so fucking exhausting to constantly reinforce their sad opinion of me, that sometimes a lie felt like the easier path.

I shook off the melancholy that thought brought about and climbed out of my truck in front of the sprawling ranch home that my brothers and I had grown up in. It was a single story that stretched out to the right and left of the front door, with a wide porch adorning the front of the house and huge windows along most of the back side, offering a stunning view of the mountains beyond them. The house had never felt especially like home to me, but it was familiar and I was happy to see one of my brothers was here as well. His muddy truck was parked in the drive, still ticking as the engine cooled, so he must have also just arrived.

It was Sunday, and my mother had in recent years decided that we should do more "family things" together, so she'd instated a weekly dinner and insisted that everyone come without fail. I wondered how that had been working out for her lately, because this was the first time I'd attended one since I had gleefully fled to Redding for school. It wasn't that it was too long of a drive, I simply didn't want to come.

My brother Ethan, the youngest of my three older brothers, greeted me as I walked through the front door. He was sitting on the bench just inside the door taking off his boots and offered me a big grin. "Hey, little sister! Long time no see."

Ethan and I were four years apart in age, and at the ripe old age of twenty-three, he reveled in reminding me as often as possible that he was my elder. Personally, I didn't see that big of a difference between nineteen and twenty-three, and he and I had always been the closest of the four siblings.

My other two brothers, Aaron and Ezra, were eight and ten years older than Ethan and twelve and fourteen years older than me. They'd both been graduated and out of the house by the time Ethan and I had reached adolescence, so they always felt a little more like uncles rather than brothers. But Ethan and I had been tight growing up and he was the main reason I even considered coming back home for visits, even when it gave me the hives to do it.

"E, it's only been three months, and you know where I live, right? It's not like you can't come see me." I rolled my eyes at him as I took a position on the bench next to him to take my shoes off.

He placed his muddy boots under the bench and swiveled sideways on it to face me, studying the side of my face for a moment. "Yeah, sis. I know where you live, I just never know if you want to see any of us."

I huffed at him. "E. You are an exception to the family rule, you know that. Everyone else might be an issue, but you always have an invite."

He grinned, looking relieved. "Good. Then maybe I'll take you up on it soon. There's a chick who bartends at this club in Redding that I've got my eye on, might need a place to crash if I work up the nerve to make a move."

"Ethan Scott, you are not going to bring a booty-call back to my place. I've only got one bed and I can't afford to have my sofa professionally cleaned of any Ethan Juniors." I narrowed my eyes at him, but he just tilted his head back and let out a booming laugh that echoed in the tile floored entryway.

"If I do, I'll make sure all my Juniors go in the trash, as Trojan intended." He reached out and ruffled his hand over my hair, pushing it into my face before he stood up and tugged on my hand. "Come on, let's go see what insanity the units have in store for today's get together."

I felt a flutter of nerves in my belly, but allowed him to pull me up from the bench. He threw an arm around my shoulders and steered me into the family room like he knew I was considering turning around and heading back the way I'd come. He wasn't wrong.

We crossed the length of the family room and he pushed me in front of him as we stepped into the kitchen, using the distraction of my appearance to step over and pull a beer from the refrigerator, only garnering a passing glare from my mother in response.

Most of her attention was focused on me instead. "Astrid, darling, I'm so glad you could join us." Her faux saccharine tone immediately set my nerves on edge.

To the uninitiated, it might seem like that was the joyful expression of a mother greeting her child whom she hadn't seen in over three months. What I heard, however, was the unspoken part. The part that said showing up on that day in no way made up for the roughly twelve family dinners I'd missed in the interim, including Thanksgiving, and that this wasn't the last I'd be hearing about it.

I groaned internally but pasted on my best masking smile and returned her platitude with one of my own. "I'm so sorry, you know how hectic it can be getting acclimated in a new place and all. But I've missed you guys!"

The lie literally made my stomach turn, but you'd never know it by the look on my face. I felt Ethan's presence at my back before he spoke up. "Ma, what's cooking today? And where's Dad?"

My mother graced my brother with a genuine smile, one that was full of affection and pride and succeeded in immediately pointing out the differences in the way she treated me versus the way she treated my brothers. It was a stunning contrast. "I'm making spaghetti, your favorite! And your father is down in his workshop, probably sneaking shots of bourbon from the bottle he thinks I don't know about. Go ahead down there and let him know dinner's almost ready?"

He offered her a salute and spun, beer in hand, toward the doorway that led to the basement of the house where my father had successfully hidden away from the world at every opportunity for as long as I could remember. He gave me a wink as he stepped onto the first stair, and I widened my eyes, silently begging him not to leave me alone with her, but he just snickered and pulled the door shut behind him, the sound of his footsteps on the wooden treads fading into silence.

For a few moments, the only sounds in the kitchen were the gurgling of boiling water on the stove and the slow simmer of the spaghetti sauce next to it. My mother stood at the counter with a damp cloth in her hand scrubbing the same spot over and over again and not meeting my eyes.

"How have you guys been?" I offered. Noting, not

for the first time, how incredibly sad it was that we'd never really learned how to talk to one another.

Her shoulders stiffened before she raised her gaze to meet mine, the eyes I'd inherited from her boring holes into my skull with barely contained anger. "How have we been? Astrid, you've not called or come by once since you packed your belongings and left for university. I've not gotten so much as a text from you to let me know you're alive and haven't been killed or kidnapped. Then you just waltz in here without a care in the world and you want to know *'How we've been'*?"

"I think you're being a bit dramatic, Mother. Obviously I'm fine and have not, in fact, been killed or kidnapped, as you can clearly see." I spun in front of her, my socks sliding against the hardwood floor in a satisfying way that reminded me of being a kid and pretending to ice skate across these same floors. One of the few warm, familial memories I could conjure, and it involved my brother, not either of my parents.

My mother narrowed her eyes at me and took in my outfit. Ripped jeans and a t-shirt I'd gotten at the Matt Maeson show last summer when Gen and I went to see him at Red Rocks. It had a skull on the front of it with the words "Get Happy" printed underneath, and I could practically hear her inner monologue as she took it all in. I hadn't purposefully dressed to annoy her, this was essentially my normal everyday uniform, but I knew she would take it as an intentional jab at her.

Oh well. I needed to come to terms with the fact that I was a disappointment to my mother and it was unlikely that I would ever be able to do anything to change that fact.

She turned her back to me and picked up a spoon, briskly stirring the spaghetti sauce before tapping the spoon against the side of the pot and laying it back down next to the stove none too gently. She spoke over her shoulder as she pulled the lid off of the boiling pot for the pasta. "Please grab the pasta out of the pantry." Cold. Detached. Unavailable.

I sighed and cut my eyes to the clock hanging over the sink and wished I could make it fly. "Yes, Mother."

9

Astrid

May Olde Assholes Be Forgot

IF IT WASN'T FOR ETHAN POSTED ACROSS THE TABLE FROM me, shooting me goofy looks and flipping me the occasional bird when my parents weren't paying attention, the strength to go through with my plan might have left me. I just focused on his clowning behavior and tried to ignore the glares my mother wasn't bothering to hide every time she looked in my direction. My father, on the other hand, wasn't glaring at me. But he also wasn't looking at me. And that had been the story of my life for as long as I could recall. My mother resented my existence and my father simply never noticed me at all.

As we all fixed our plates and began eating—what was admittedly very good spaghetti, as much as I hated to grant her anything—my father asked Ethan how work was going, and Ethan animatedly began telling us all a story about a fire they'd been called out on a few days prior. Ethan was a wild-land firefighter—or "smokejumper"—and I lived in perpetual fear that the one good member of my family was going to get called out to the middle of nowhere one day to fight a fire, and I'd never see him again. He loved what he did, though, and I would never in a million years project the weight of my anxiety about his job onto him. I just internalized the fuck out of it like I did everything else. So, while he regaled them with a story about jumping into a wildfire that a camper had inadvertently set in the national forest, I tried my best to look like I was engaged despite my fear for him.

Inside, I was also mentally shoring up my courage to tell them what I'd come here to confess. I had two hours before my shift and it was a thirty-five-minute drive, so I'd timed it all as close as I could to minimize how long I'd have to endure their disappointment before I would have an excuse to escape.

Obviously, my mind had drifted for longer than I'd realized, because I suddenly became aware that everyone at the table was looking at me with their brows raised. I met Ethan's stare across the table and shot him a panicked *oh shit, what did I miss* look, and he said, "Mom asked how classes were going."

Oh. Oh okay. It was go-time then. I sighed and squared my shoulders before I settled my gaze just above and to the left of Ethan's shoulder, not even wanting to see his reaction to my news. "That's actually part of what I wanted to tell you guys tonight. I...um...I actually withdrew from the university a couple of weeks ago."

Ethan's mouth dropped open and I saw him cringe a bit before my mother's fork clacked against the side of her plate with unnecessary force.

"Astrid Scott, you did no such thing. Please tell me this is some sort of ridiculous prank that you're pulling in an attempt to garner attention." Her face was screwed up like she'd taken a bite of something sour—except it was just me. I was the one who always put that look on her face.

I couldn't help the snark that flew out of my mouth in response, even knowing it would get me absolutely nowhere. "Yes, Mother, that's exactly what this is. I'm so desperate for your attention that I crafted this elaborate scenario just so I could enjoy another instance of your complete and utter disdain for me. It's been several months, after all, since I've been privy to it."

I heard Ethan snort before he grabbed his napkin and placed it over his mouth, disguising the sound with a cough.

Meanwhile, my father finally decided to acknowl-edge my presence by slamming his hand down on the table next to his plate, making everything on the table jump at the impact. "Young lady, you will not speak to your mother like that under my roof." His voice was deadly calm, but brooked no argument.

I stared at him for a beat before I nodded and slid my chair back from the table, carefully placing my own napkin next to my abandoned dinner.

"You're right, sir. My apologies. I'll take that as my invitation to leave and assume that future invitations to family dinner have been rescinded until further notice."

I walked quietly out of the room, feeling tremors begin to work their way through my body, and I hoped to god I could make it off of their property before I lost my shit. I didn't want to give them the satisfaction of seeing me hurt yet again over the way they had always treated me.

Ethan chased me to the foyer where I was frantically shoving my feet into my shoes, not even stopping to tie the laces.

"Hey, hey, hey…sis, come on, don't leave like this. I mean, fuck them, but I don't want you driving like this. Wait for me, okay? I'll meet you at the property line, I just need to see that you're calm before I let you drive all the way back to Redding. Please, sis. For me." His eyes pleaded with me before he shuffled his feet and glanced back in the house uneasily. He needn't have worried, though. Neither of my parents was coming to try and stop me from leaving. And didn't that just speak volumes?

I looked at him through the tears that were pissing me off—because those people didn't deserve my tears—nodded and snatched my keys off the hook by the door before slamming it behind me, and all but ran to the driver's side of my truck.

Something told me that was the last time for a very long time that I'd be setting foot inside that house, and, as upset and pissed off as I was, it was also a huge relief. The burden of being The Great Disappointment felt like it was being lifted from my shoulders, at least for a moment.

10

Astrid

You Can Never Go Home Again

TEN MINUTES PASSED BEFORE ETHAN'S TRUCK PULLED UP alongside mine and his passenger window rolled down. I was staring sightlessly through my windshield, wondering why the hell it was always like this between me and my parents. It was like I'd been set up for failure with them from day one, and if it weren't for the fact that I had most definitely inherited my features from my mother, I'd be tempted to believe there was some wild story about how I'd been dropped off on their doorstep and they'd been unwillingly forced to take responsibility for me. They'd treated me like a burden and a disappointment for as long as I could remember.

I turned my head to meet Ethan's sad look through his passenger window before he leaned over and popped the lock on the door and shoved it open, narrowly missing hitting my door frame with it. "Hop in, we'll go for a smoke and calm down, then I'll let you head home when I know you're okay."

I offered him a sad smile, but shook my head. "Can't tonight, E. I have to work. Raincheck?"

He raised his brows in surprise, temporarily losing his concerned expression. "Since when do you have a job, kiddo?"

"Since two weeks ago when I withdrew from university. It's not like I don't have a plan, Eth. I'm not a complete fuck up."

He raised his hands in front of him. "Hey, I never said you were a fuck up, As, don't put that shit on me."

I let my head flop back against my headrest before I answered him. "Sorry, bro. Just a little raw over here right now."

"That's fair. But I want to hear all about it, yeah? My baby sister has a job! That's great fucking news!" He injected so much enthusiasm into his voice I almost hated to tell him where I was working.

"I promise I'll tell you all about it soon, but for right now I gotta run or I'm going to be late, 'kay? I promise, I'm okay to drive. I won't take any abrupt right hand turns on the overpass tonight." I gave him a rueful grin meant to reassure, him but he met my gaze with a frown.

"Not funny, As. Not funny at all. Love you, be safe."

I waved as I pulled away, muttering under my breath, *"Really wasn't supposed to be funny, E."*

The smell of furniture polish and cigar smoke greeted me when I opened the employee door at the back of the club with my backpack slung over my shoulder. I was feeling like I'd been through the ringer before I'd even started my shift and I couldn't imagine that boded well for a good night.

I turned right at the end of the hallway into the office I shared with Liam, dropping my bag into my chair with a sigh before I turned and headed into the main part of the club to get something to drink. So far, I'd mostly worked during the day when the club was closed; Liam had taught me how to manage the inventory, make the deposits, and keep track of the bills for the club. It'd been nice to have a chance to get the hang of things before I had to come in and work a "normal" shift, but I couldn't deny that I was a little excited to see what the club was like when it was actually open.

I exited the employee hallway into the lounge and paused a minute to let my eyes adjust to the dim lighting before I crossed the length of it to the bar on the opposite wall. I took stock of the bartender who was busily mixing drinks for the handful of patrons who leaned against the surface or were posted up in the tall stools that lined the front of it. I'd met her briefly one of the days I'd been training with Liam and I liked her kind smile immediately, but couldn't really get a read on anything else about her during our brief introduction.

As I approached the bar, she nodded at me over the head of the woman she was serving, tilting her head toward one of the stools on the end of the bar that remained unoccupied. I settled into it to wait as I surreptitiously continued my study of her. She was a contradiction, physically speaking. Very petite, maybe five-foot-three, with a build like a tiny little hourglass. When I'd met her she'd been in a pair of baggy jeans and a tank top since she was off the clock, but tonight she was decked out in a what looked like a pair of men's black suit pants, complete with pinstripes, which she'd paired with an epic black satin bustier that showed off her arms and chest which were covered in tattoos.

I peered behind the bar to see she was wearing black and white wing-tip Doc Martens, and I wanted to pull out my phone and take notes. While she was this petite little thing in stature, everything else about her said she was tough as nails, and I admired the hell out of it. She was a whole vibe, and I immediately felt frumpy in my holey jeans and t-shirt next to her. Maybe I could get her to go shopping with me one of these days and let some of her style rub off on me.

When she was done serving the patrons who'd been waiting, she grabbed a rag and a glass and made her way to the end of the bar where I sat, offering me a warm smile. "First time for the night shift?"

I nodded, returning her smile. "I think I'm a little bit nervous, though." I glanced around the club briefly before bringing my attention back to her.

She studied my face with a bit of humor showing in her expression before she leaned closer to speak so only I could hear. "They don't fuck out in this room, love."

I widened my eyes at her comically. "Well, damn. I

was already having a shitty day, and now you've just killed any chances of me living vicariously through our customers too? Better make me a double before I go back there and get to work."

Rae tossed her head back and let out a riotous laugh that turned heads throughout the room, both male and female. "I knew I was gonna like you, girlie, but Liam told me how old you are so how about a Shirley Temple instead?"

I frowned at her in mock consternation. "I can handle my liquor, I promise."

She chuckled as she added a splash of grenadine to a highball glass. "I have no doubt, but while I'm on the clock, you're underage, and I'm not risking my license. After hours, though, if you ever want to talk about that shitty day, we'll sneak a bottle of Liam's best out of here and you can tell me all about it."

I grinned, unable to hang onto my bad mood in her presence. "It's a date."

I took the virgin cocktail she slid my way and, with a mock salute, headed back to the employee hallway to get to work.

When I got back to the office I stepped inside and immediately drew up short. "Oh, I'm sorry! I didn't know anyone was in here!"

The man turned to look at me over his shoulder before picking up the file he'd been leafing through and shouldered past me to get out the door.

"What the hell was all that about? Rude, ass." I rolled my eyes and went over to the desk where I'd left my backpack and grabbed my phone out of the front pocket.

I pulled up Liam's contact and sent him a text.

Astrid: Hey, not sure who the guy was that was just in the office, but can you tell him there was no need to be rude? Wtf

Liam: What guy? What are you talking about? What did he look like?

Astrid: I don't know, I've never seen him before. He looked like a villain in a bad action movie. Tall, built like a brick shithouse. Buzz cut. No neck.

Liam: Fuck! What did he say to you?

Astrid: Nothing, which is where the rude part comes in? I apologized for walking in on him and he just picked up a folder off the desk and nearly shoved me out of the way to get out the door without saying a word.

Liam: Fuck , FUCK! Ok, I'll let Jared know to come check things out. Lock the door until he gets there.

Astrid: Lock the door? What the hell is going on Liam? I'm in a busy club full of employees and customers, who am I locking out?

Liam: ...

Liam: I don't know. But I'll find out. Just lock the door, Astrid, and I'll send Jared to you.

11

Astrid

Violated

I sat at the desk staring at the locked office door. Fuming. I wondered if anyone else ever felt like no one in their life was ever completely honest with them? Like they were always the last to know whatever bit of information that the rest of the world just...got, without anyone having to explain it to them?

I, for one, was sick and tired of that feeling, and Liam's responses to my texts earlier had triggered something in me that had me ready for a fight before I heard the firm knock at the door.

I sprung out of the chair and stepped closer, pressing my ear to the door. "Who is it?"

"It's Jared," the gruff, slightly muffled, voice announced from the other side.

I stepped back and unlocked the door, crossing my arms over my chest and issuing him a glare when he stepped inside the room. "I don't suppose you're here to explain what the hell is going on?"

He offered me a carefully blank look. "No."

I huffed and flopped down on the couch as I watched him carefully look through everything on the desk and in the open file drawer next to it. When he was done with that, he inspected the two windows that lined the back wall of the office, checking the locks and sills carefully. I assumed he was looking to see if that's the way the asshole from earlier had gotten in, but his frustrated exhale led me to believe he didn't find anything conclusive.

"So that guy wasn't supposed to be here. He didn't work for the club?" I crossed my arms over my chest and leaned back into the couch cushions, fully expecting Jared to ignore my questions.

He surprised me when he answered. "I don't know who he was, but no, he doesn't work for the club."

He returned to the desk and started rifling through the papers there again. "Did you notice anything specific missing?"

I uncrossed my arms and stood to join him at the desk, shaking off my irritation momentarily. It wasn't Jared's fault. "Honestly, no. I'd only just gotten here when I found him. I don't know which files Liam had out on the desk or, really, which one that guy might have taken from the cabinet. I'm still getting the feel for things." I shrugged, chagrined.

Jared nodded and then pointed to my backpack sitting in the office chair. "That yours?"

I nodded. "Yeah. Nothing in there worth stealing, though. Just my wallet and my journal. Keys and stuff."

"Did you check it? Make sure he didn't take anything out of that?"

My eyes widened in sudden fear. Fuck. If someone got their hands on that journal… I frantically dove for my bag and opened the biggest of the compartments, my heart sinking. "It's gone."

"What's gone?" Jared stepped closer and peered down into my bag with me as I stood dumbfounded.

"My journal," I whispered. When I looked up at him I could feel angry tears forming at the corners of my eyes. "Why the fuck would anyone steal my journal?"

Jared winced and offered me an awkward pat on my shoulder. "Maybe they thought it was a ledger. Something to do with the club."

"But it's not! Any idiot could see that if they just flipped it open!" I exclaimed. I didn't even want to think about anyone reading my most private thoughts. The feeling of violation was so profound that I couldn't even form a more logical response. I wanted to throw myself down on the floor and scream. Things I'd written in that journal were for my eyes only. My way of processing all the fucked up shit that'd happened in my life. It was all so wildly personal that I felt like an integral part of myself had been ripped away and there was nothing I could do about it.

Jared pulled out his phone and hit a button before lifting it to his ear. "I'm here." He paused for a moment. "She's fine, but it looks like they took her journal from her bag. Not sure what else they took." He turned his back to me, like that would keep me from hearing his next statement. "No. Not okay. You should probably get here."

He was silent for another moment before he sighed. "Okay. I will." And then he disconnected the call and slid the phone back into his pocket. "I'm going to take you home. Liam will check on you later. He said you have the rest of the night off and that he's so sorry, he'll do everything he can to find out who took it and get it back for you."

Helpless tears poured from my eyes as I stared at him, growing numb from the shock. "Okay," I whispered.

"Come on, kiddo." He lifted my pack gently from the chair, taking care to re-zip the compartments before he draped it over his giant shoulder. He gestured to the door, and I turned that way in a fog, leading the way out to the main part of the club.

When I exited the employee hallway, I glanced up to see Rae shooting me a concerned look from behind the bar. "*You okay?*" she mouthed.

I shook my head and then nodded. Unsure if I was okay or not. In the grand scheme of things, someone stealing my journal wasn't the end of the world, but it was hard to tell my mind that. I felt exposed. Stripped completely naked in front of someone I didn't even know, who now had unrestricted access to every one of my deepest darkest thoughts.

She offered a sympathetic look and then met Jared's gaze over my shoulder. "Take care of her. Or else."

He nodded solemnly and placed his hand on the

small of my back, steering me toward the front door. "But my truck's out back," I argued weakly.

"Relax, kiddo. Someone will bring it home for you. I'm going to drive you home." He steered me toward the door and then once outside, to the passenger side of his car. I didn't have it in me to argue anymore so I just slid into the plush leather seat and stared vacantly out the windshield.

When Jared got into the driver's seat he looked at me over the console and gestured to my seatbelt. "Buckle up. I'll have you home before you know it."

———————————————

12

Astrid

———————————————

Fuckery Abounds

I STUBBORNLY REFUSED TO STAY AWAY FROM WORK FOR EVEN
the couple of days that Liam recommended after my
run-in with the rude giant. It wasn't in my nature to
cower and hide from anyone, and this time was no
different. I pulled up my big girl panties, bought myself
a new journal from a little indie bookshop not far from
my house, and still managed to slide into my spot in the
employee lot just in time for opening. I was determined
to carry on as if nothing had happened. I'd learned long
ago that fear fed upon itself, and I wasn't willing to let it
take over my new life before it had truly begun.

My job at the club mostly consisted of back office
stuff, liquor orders, and paying bills and such, and it
almost never took me a full eight hours to get it all done.
When I got bored, I'd meander out to the main part of
the club and see if anyone needed help with anything

while I got my fill of people-watching, and boy, did the people watching *never* disappoint.

As an added bonus, every time the dancers got on stage I was absolutely mesmerized at the beauty of their routines. No one could resist their pull, and every eye in the crowd stayed glued to their routine from start to finish. The sensuality and grace with which they moved was one of the sexiest things I'd ever seen. I was always awed when I got a chance to watch a set. I loved the variety in themes the dancers chose and, on a given night, you might see a light BDSM show or a scene from a book, everything from classic literature to more current (and spicy) options. It never got boring.

I was entering the liquor order for the week when I heard the distinct sound of breaking glass from behind the bar. I winced, muttering under my breath, "Wait for it…"

"Hey, Astrid," Rae yelled. "Can you add a couple extra bottles of the Reyka to that order? Brennan in here thinks he's auditioning for *Cocktail* and he just fumbled forty dollars' worth of vodka onto the floor behind the bar." Rae's voice dripped with sarcasm, and I couldn't stop the giggle that escaped me, even if I had no idea what she was referring to.

"What's '*Cocktail*'?" I called back.

Rae's face appeared in the doorway to the office, full of generational disappointment. She sighed. "I sometimes forget how young you are. Did you never get an education in the best and worst of eighties movies?"

I just stared at her blankly, intentionally egging her on.

"Oh, for fuck's sake. *Top Gun*? *Pretty in Pink*? *Some Kind of Wonderful*? *Breakfast Club*?" She placed her hands on her hips, staring at me incredulously.

"Ooo! I just saw *Top Gun* the other day! But I don't think that came out in the eighties?" I rubbed my hand over my mouth to conceal my grin, knowing I was just getting her even more revved up.

She narrowed her eyes at me before she lifted a hand and pointed at me accusingly. "You're fucking with me. Aren't you?"

I couldn't contain my laughter anymore, nodding. "Yes, Rae. I'm fucking with you. But not about the *Cocktail* part. That one I haven't ever seen."

She tilted her head, looking up at the ceiling for a moment. "To be fair, I don't think you're missing much there. Just take my word for it, Brennan wouldn't have made the cut." She offered me an impish grin and turned on her heel, heading back out to the main part of the club to finish getting ready for opening.

As Rae returned to the bar, Brennan argued in a desperate attempt to defend his honor. I rolled my eyes as their voices drifted back toward the office, before I scrolled to the end of the order and added a couple extra bottles of vodka to the list. I clicked save and sent it off to our supplier before I closed the laptop and leaned back in the chair, stretching my back out a bit. I was getting faster and faster at getting those orders done, but it still took me a couple hours of being hunched over the computer so I felt a little like a shrimp—all curled up—by the time I got done.

Once all of the office stuff was done, I grabbed a barstool in the corner so I could watch the show and chat with Rae in between customers. Liam was due to be in soon. We were due to go over the paperwork that needed to be filed with the city almost constantly to keep them from shutting us down, but until he got here I was a free agent.

The theme for tonight's show was *The Great Gatsby* and I absolutely loved the way the women on stage captured the chemistry between Daisy and Gatsby. Our "Gatsby" leaned in and chased and pined, while looking dapper in a tailored bustier coat with tails, basically the titillating version of a three-piece suit, while "Daisy" dodged every attempt at a caress from her co-star, leading her on a merry chase around the stage, offering coquettish looks over her shoulder but always staying just out of reach. By the time Daisy "gave in" to Gatsby's advances, everyone's gaze was locked onto the stage, invested in the chemistry they'd created. When Daisy pushed Gatsby into a chair and straddled "his" lap, reverse-cowgirl style, grinding to the beat of the music and leaning dangerously far forward, nearly causing a wardrobe malfunction that I was certain was 100 percent intentional, I'd have bet real money there wasn't a dry set of panties in the room.

Honestly, I was so turned on by the time the two beautiful dancers took their bow and exited the stage for the night that I couldn't stop shifting in my chair, and I caught Rae smirking at me as she mixed a drink for the man that had just stepped up to the bar.

An hour later, Liam walked into the club wearing a wrinkled shirt and sunglasses. He crossed the room and leaned against the bar next to me, waving to catch Rae's attention.

"Wow, boss, you look…tired." I offered him a droll look. He looked more than tired. He looked hungover as fuck and like he was still wearing the same clothes he'd had on the day before. "Is this what the male version of the walk of shame looks like?"

He turned toward me and briefly lifted his sunglasses up, causing me to gasp audibly. "Not exactly."

"Holy shit, Liam, what the hell happened to your face?" I cut my eyes over to Rae and raised my brows at her, jerking my head to call her over to our end of the bar.

He returned the glasses to his face, but not before Rae caught a glimpse of the damage. "Do I need to call Jared?" She pulled her phone out of her pocket, but Liam waved his hand at her.

"Nah. Nothing he can do about it. But, not for nothing, he already knows. He's the one who picked me up." He rested his chin on his hand, and I could see the exhaustion reflected in his posture.

"Do you think it's time to tell us what's going on now, boss? It seems like the odd occurrences around here are becoming more and more frequent." Rae leveled him with a pointed look.

Liam sighed. "There's not a lot to tell, but come on back to the office and I'll tell you what I can." He leaned around Rae and gestured to Brennan at the other end of the bar. "B, you got this for a bit?" he called.

Brennan saluted before returning to the long island iced tea he was making for the woman sitting in front of him who was giving *I'm going to slip you my hotel key* eyes.

Liam snorted and leaned over the bar, grabbed a beer out of the ice well, and headed toward the employee hallway.

When Rae and I joined him in the office, he was slumped on the leather couch in the corner. He'd lifted his sunglasses on top of his head and had the cold beer pressed to his very black eye.

I sat down gingerly on the other end of the couch while Rae pulled the office chair over, leaning her elbows on her knees and staring at him until he spoke.

"I've been having some trouble with the city. About the permits for the club," he began.

I snorted, because I'd picked up enough snippets of conversations here and there to know that it was a little more than "some" trouble.

He opened his good eye and looked at me, no doubt wondering how much I'd pieced together based on that reaction.

"At first, I just thought it was, well, like a legit concern from the city. This is a new business, and even though they aren't aware of what takes place in the private rooms in the back, just the fact that burlesque is a novelty around here. Well, like I said, I thought they were just being super cautious. They made me jump through all sorts of hoops to even get the license originally. So much so, in fact, that we had to delay the opening. And *that* made my investors very nervous." He cringed and closed his eye again, leaning his head back against the wall behind him.

He continued. "Fast forward a couple of months and that asshat shows up here, digging through the office and steals your journal." He lifted his head and shot me an apologetic look before resuming his position. "The file he took was a stack of emails I had printed out from my investors. A little bit of insurance, if you know what I mean. In case all of the electronic records suddenly disappeared, I wanted to have paper copies of everything we'd agreed upon."

Rae tilted her head and met my gaze for a minute before she spoke up. "Liam. Who the fuck are your investors?"

A shuddering sigh went through his body before he sat up and finally cracked that beer open, taking a long swig before he returned her look. "I can't tell you. But I'm guessing you've figured out it wasn't the Redding First Bank and Loan."

Rae groaned and threw her hands up in the air. "Liam, you dumb fuck, what the hell have you gotten yourself involved in? Not to mention us, by association!" She gestured back and forth between herself and me where I sat dumbfounded.

He looked at her and then at me, a resigned expression on his face. "It was the only way I could get it up and running. This was my *dream*, Rae, you gotta understand!"

She shook her head at him, biting out a sardonic laugh. "Your dream was to own a sex club masquerading as a burlesque club? Liam, even for you, that seems a little sad. How is that anyone's dream?"

"No. My dream was to own my own club, and for it to be a place people felt safe and comfortable coming to where they could explore the more...*alternative* aspects of their sex lives...without judgment and with as little risk as possible."

I felt like he was trying to tone down his response because of me, so I chose that moment to clear the air of any misconceptions he may have had about me. "You can stop treating me like I'm a child who doesn't know what kinks are, Liam. I'm pretty well versed in quite a few of them personally, in fact. I know exactly what goes on behind the curtain in this club and I support the fact that you've created a safe space for people to explore that for themselves. What I don't understand is exactly how we ended up here, talking around the fact that someone apparently used your face as a doorstop multiple times last night. So I, for one, would really appreciate it if you could just get to the fucking point."

13

Liam

Coming Clean-ish

I STUDIED THE TWO WOMEN IN FRONT OF ME, KNOWING they weren't going to let me off with some half-baked explanation of how I ended up in this condition, but also worried that if I told them too much they'd end up on the wrong end of a criminal organization that didn't seem to care who they hurt in order to achieve their ends.

Rae got frustrated with my internal debate and rolled her hands at me, urging me to get on with it while Astrid just stared at me, not giving me an inch to escape her demand.

"When I realized I'd sunk every penny of my savings into opening up the club and it still wasn't going to be enough I reached out to a...friend of mine." I grimaced.

"A friend." Rae's response was the definition of skeptical.

"Okay, *associate* is probably a better word," I conceded.

"An associate," Astrid repeated with a brow raised.

"Yep." I nodded. *These two parrots, gah.* "We met a few years back, before I became such a fine and upstanding citizen." I offered a winsome grin, but figured something got lost in the translation on account of the glaring black eye.

Rae and Astrid snorted simultaneously before Rae snarked back. "Yeah. *Sooo* upstanding, Liam. You're practically a boy scout."

Astrid raised a finger. "So, let me see if I've got this right." She studied me closely for a moment before she continued. "Once upon a time, in your deviant youth, you knew a guy who had some sort of…connections? And when you found yourself in a jam, you contacted him so that you could really step up your karma game by tying yourself to those connections financially?"

I flopped my head back against the wall with a thud. "That's about the sum of it."

"Jesus, Liam. And now…what? They roughed you up last night because you're behind on your payments?" Astrid's voice was incredulous and more than a little disapproving.

I shook my head without opening my eyes, not wanting to see either of their expressions. "I don't know, but I don't think so. I met a friend for dinner last night and got pulled over on my way home. I swear to god, I don't even know what I was doing to get pulled over, but as soon as the cop approached my car, I rolled the windows down and held my hands up. Like you do, ya know?"

Silence greeted my statement, so I continued. "Next thing I knew, they snatched me out of my car, threw me on the ground, and yelled at me to stop resisting. I think one of them accidentally kneed me in the face during all that, but it's a blur to be honest." I gestured at my eye.

"They took me to the station but never booked me. I called Jared to come get me a couple hours later when they finally gave me my phone call. The whole thing was so fucking weird, you just don't even know. It was like they all knew why I was there but no one was talking to me. They just threw me in a cell and every time someone walked by and I'd ask what the hell was going on, they'd just ignore me."

I finally opened my eyes to see both of them staring at me incredulously.

Rae finally spoke up again. "Dude, they can't just fucking grab you and hold you in a cell for hours without telling you why you're there!"

I shrugged. "That's what I thought too, but who exactly was going to point that out to them at that moment? All I could do was wait for them to come get me and let me have a phone call."

Astrid looked angry on my behalf, which warmed my heart a bit. "You should file a complaint."

I shook my head again. "I don't want to do anything else to draw attention to me or the club. Whatever the hell that was about last night, they obviously just wanted me out of the way for a couple of hours. Now I just need to figure out what was going on during that time that they didn't want me to see."

Rae cut her eyes to Astrid and then back to me before she spoke again. "Have you been home yet?"

"No, Jared picked me up and took me back to my car and I came straight here, worried that something had happened here while they had me detained." I looked at both of them in question but figured if anything crazy had happened while I was gone that would have been the first thing they told me when I got here.

Rae shook her head. "Nah, boss, all's been quiet here since we opened. Nothing new or unusual."

Astrid added, "She's right. It's actually been a pretty tame night, all things considered."

"Any new clients for the back of the club?" I asked.

Rae tilted her head, thinking for a moment. "There were a couple of faces I didn't recognize, but that's not really all that unusual. Jared always screens them at the door, right?"

I looked at Astrid. "Can you go get the list from Cassidy for tonight? If they wanted me out of here so they could sneak someone past me that I wouldn't have let in, maybe I'll recognize a name."

Astrid looked at me like I'd lost my mind. "No offense, Liam, but if that's what they were doing, what are the odds that they'd use their real name? What about the cameras, wouldn't that be a better way to check?"

I was so tired that hadn't even occurred to me, which was proof positive I needed a solid night of sleep and maybe a hot meal before I'd be able to function as a whole human again. "Right. Solid plan."

Astrid got up and went to the laptop on the desk, flipping open the lid and pulling up the feed from the last twenty-four hours. "What time did they pull you over?"

I thought about it for a minute and then responded. "Luke and I met for dinner at eight. We were probably there an hour and a half or so? So, sometime between nine thirty and ten?"

"Okay, I'll pull the footage from eight o'clock on then." Her fingers started flying over the keys, and I had to admit I was impressed at how quickly she'd gotten the hang of the system.

When she had the feed cued up, Rae and I gathered behind the chair to look over her shoulder as she paused the video on each new face that walked in. It was slow going, but luckily we had good cameras, so the images were clear enough that we could rule each one out confidently as they appeared. I was only looking for anyone I recognized who wasn't a regular.

A few minutes later, I put my hand on Astrid's shoulder, causing her to stop in her scrolling and look up at me. "That guy. Why does that guy look familiar? I don't think I've seen him here before, but I do recognize him from somewhere."

Astrid took a screenshot of the frame and blew it up so we could see him better, and when she did she muttered under her breath. "Mother. Fucker."

"What?" Rae and I both responded at the same time.

"That's the guy," Astrid responded.

"What guy?" Again, Rae and I answered simultaneously.

"The fucker that took my journal and your file. The one from the other night. That's him, I'm sure of it." I could hear her grinding her teeth and her hand clenched around the mouse as she studied his face. Suddenly, she gasped and looked at me over her shoulder. "You don't think he's *still* here, do you?"

I shook my head. "I doubt it. Otherwise, why would they have let me out? But let's watch the footage for the next couple of hours. See if we can catch him leaving."

Rae had backed away, seeming lost in thought and pacing behind the chair while we scanned the next hour of video. Suddenly, she rounded on a heel and asked, "Why would they want you out of here, though? You never saw that guy the night he broke in. When we went back and looked at the footage, his face was obscured."

I shook my head. "They couldn't be sure of that, though. Getting me out of the way was just insurance, maybe? To make sure I wouldn't recognize him when he walked in."

Astrid shook her head. "That doesn't make any sense, though. I definitely saw his face, and he knew it, so if they were going to try and keep anyone out of here when he came back, wouldn't it have been me?"

I closed my eyes momentarily, unable to answer that question and so exhausted I couldn't think straight. "Do me a favor, text me that screenshot and I'll ask a couple of people if they recognize him. In the meantime, I need a shower and sleep."

Astrid clicked a few times on the laptop and a chime rang out from my phone where it lay on the couch. "Sent."

"Thanks. I'll let Jared know that no one is to walk out of here by themselves tonight. Get him to walk you to your cars or walk out in pairs. If you notice anything weird, call me."

Rae stowed her snark for a moment, putting a hand on my shoulder. "Will do, boss. We'll be fine. Are you going to be okay to drive home? You look like you're about to pass out."

I nodded at her, warmed by her concern. "I'll be fine. But call me if you see anything off, okay? Day or night. And keep your eyes open."

She offered me a salute. "Okay. I'm going to make sure Brennan hasn't destroyed my bar in the last hour." She turned and looked at Astrid. "Wanna have a sleepover when we're done here? I don't think either of us is going to sleep real well tonight."

Astrid looked relieved at the suggestion. "God, yes, I'll get everything closed up in here then come find you."

I felt a twinge of guilt that I'd brought Astrid into this situation, and an even bigger twinge of guilt that I loved having her there. There was just something about her. She was tough but also so vulnerable at times that I thought I'd see her break right open in front of me. But she never did. It was like every time something fucked up happened I'd see a crack in her mask but then she'd close it right back up and slap a happy face on, trying to convince us all that nothing truly bothered her. It had been a very long time since anyone had inspired me to feel protective of them, but Astrid had wormed her way right into that part of me. I knew enough about masks to know they weren't created by anything but necessity, and a part of me wanted to know why Astrid needed hers.

It was clear to me that Rae felt the same way about my newest employee and I was secretly glad they'd grown so close. Everyone needed someone to have their back and I knew from my run-in in Boston that Astrid's closest friend was all the way on the other side of the country.

The only thing that wasn't clear to me was why I found myself more and more invested in Astrid's happiness. I was afraid it went beyond my responsibility to her as her boss. I reminded myself of my golden rule and shook off the feelings that were creeping into my subconscious. She was my employee.

In other words: *off limits*.

When I got back to my car I cranked it and pulled out my phone, taking a moment to send the picture to Key. We weren't "friends" exactly, but I had a feeling if this guy was affiliated with any of the crime organizations around here, then maybe Key would recognize him.

I got a response back almost immediately.

Key: Feckin hell. I'll be in touch.

———————————————

14

Astrid

———————————————

Falalalala, Lalala Fuck

LIAM HAD BEEN A LOT MORE PRESENT AT THE CLUB SINCE our chat the other night. He hovered over me and Rae to the point that she'd kicked him out from behind the bar twice today already. Ever since, he'd been sulking in the office like a little black cloud raining all over my parade.

"Liam. I mean this with all the love in my heart. Would you please, for the love of all that is holy, get a hobby or something?" I was trying to go through all of the bills that were due, and his dramatic sighs from the couch were super distracting.

"I did too good of a job with my staff, and now I feel like I need to be here to make sure you're all safe but there's nothing for me to do!" His tone was petulant. If he hadn't driven me to distraction, I might have felt sorry for him.

"Has something else happened since the other night?

I haven't noticed anything weird around here at all. I mean, the club itself has been pretty busy, but with the holidays coming up I assume most people are trying to get their fun in before they're forced to spend time with their families." I could hear the familial bitterness creeping into my tone, and I hoped he hadn't picked up on it.

My statement was met with silence and I turned in my chair to see Liam studying me with a question in his eyes. "What?" I asked, knowing I hadn't been lucky. Of course he'd picked up on it.

"Astrid, are you okay?" he asked. "Like…really okay?" He leaned forward, resting his elbows on his knees, his gaze intent on my face while he waited for my answer.

I forced out a laugh. "Of course. Why wouldn't I be?"

He cocked his head to the side. "Well, that's not the first time you've made a comment like that when it comes to family stuff. I might not be the sharpest knife in the cabinet but I'm getting the impression that your family life is…complicated?"

I snorted. "That's putting it mildly, boss."

"Do you want to talk about it?"

While I loved how "seen" his observation made me feel, this was not a topic I was keen to bring out in the open at work. I fell back on sarcasm, my trusty old friend. "I appreciate the offer, doc, but I'm all good."

He just continued to stare at me, those green eyes of his unblinking until he asked his next question. "Are you going to spend the holidays with them?"

Ugh. "I'll probably make an appearance. At least one of my brothers will be there and he's the one I like, so I'll show my face. Probably won't stay long, though."

"And after that? Will you be alone for the holidays?"

I was worried he was inching around to asking me if I wanted to spend the holidays with him and his family. I couldn't swear to it because that was honestly one topic he and I hadn't touched on in the last few weeks, so I didn't really have any idea what his family situation was, but I didn't need or want a pity invite from my boss because my mommy was a bitch.

"If I leave my folks' place early enough, I'll probably head to Boston?" The thought of that was honestly the only thing that made the holidays bearable for me. I'd never been a huge fan of the forced family proximity that came about this time of year, but Imogen and Hank had always given me a safe place to run to when it got too heavy at home. I'd yank that safety chord again this year in a heartbeat.

"Okay. Good." Liam looked relieved, if not still mildly concerned. "I'll be closing the club for a couple of days, just to give everyone a break, but we'll be back open by New Year's Eve, obviously. Got a big night planned that night. Think you'll be back by then?"

I tipped my imaginary hat at him. "You bet. I'm your girl!"

Liam got a weird look on his face, but he stood and headed for the door so quickly I didn't have time to examine his expression for long.

"So, I'm going to go see if Brennan needs any help out there." It was like he was running away from me, and I was honestly confused. What the fuck just happened?

"Um...okay. Good talk." I shrugged and turned back to the computer to finish up with half of my brain puzzling over Liam's suddenly strange behavior.

Christmas Day found me parked at the entry to my parents' driveway, more than 50 percent in favor of just turning around and heading to the airport. I tried to inject some steel into my spine with a little mental pep talk. *They're cunts. Just because they happen to be the cunts you were given as parents does not mean you have to stick around for them to abuse you. You can leave any time you want.*

I probably wouldn't have gone at all if it weren't for Ethan. He'd begged me to make an appearance, though probably so he wouldn't be the only kid there. God knew my two oldest brothers wouldn't show up if they didn't absolutely have to. Ethan had promised, if I showed up, that he wouldn't leave my side for a minute. While I appreciated the thought, it didn't escape me how completely fucked up it was that either of us found it necessary.

I let out an annoyed growl and shifted my truck into drive, committed to at least showing my face. Anything beyond that would depend on those people.

The house smelled like you would think a Hallmark movie would. All cinnamon spice and everything nice, combined with what was probably a roast in the oven. Holiday music played from the ancient record player in the living room. On the outside it looked…idyllic. The perfect picture of a family Christmas. A fire roaring in the fireplace and stockings hanging from the mantel.

The tree in the center of the room, posted in front of the picture windows, was the first clue that not everything was as it seemed. It took me a minute to realize, but it was completely bare.

Never, not once in my almost twenty years of life, had my mother not decorated the tree absolutely perfectly. Even when we were little kids she wouldn't let us help. She didn't want our ornaments we'd made in class hanging on her perfect tree and every single ornament and strand of lights had to be "just so" before she would call it done. I wondered if someone had died.

"Hello?" I called, wishing I could just duck right back out the door without ever having to announce my presence. But as I stood there listening, I realized I didn't hear any *people*.

Wouldn't that just be the ultimate *fuck you*? Invite me home for Christmas and then leave before I got there.

I crossed the living room and pushed through the swinging door into the kitchen. The smells grew stronger there, confirming my initial guess. A pot roast was sitting proudly in its glass dish on the counter, but still no sign of my family.

Just as I was about to turn around and go back the way I'd come, I heard muffled voices coming from the basement. Something about it set off all of my warning bells so I crept softly to the door, easing it open and holding onto the doorknob to keep it from squeaking, a trick I'd learned back in high school.

"Andrew, this is fucking ridiculous. You're piss drunk, which isn't anything new, but it's the holiday and our children will arrive any moment now. Could you please make an attempt to get yourself together so we can have a nice evening?"

I heard my father scoff at her before his slurred response nailed me to the floor where I stood. "*Our* children. What a fucking joke."

"*Andrew*! Keep your voice down, and please tell me, that today of all days after all these years, *this* is not the day that you're going to choose to be a spectacular bastard about this?" My mother's voice had devolved into a hiss.

"Funny choice of words, *Helen*." I heard the sound of glass clinking against glass and ice cubes rattling.

She gasped. "I made one mistake, twenty years ago, and God knows you've never let me forget about it for one goddamn moment in that whole time. You've never treated her like she was your daughter, and now that she's an adult and out from under your roof you've decided it's the perfect time to air out our dirty laundry?"

At some point during my eavesdropping my hand had crept up over my mouth. Holy. Fucking. Shit.

Holyshitholyshitholyshit.

My hands trembled and my emotions were swinging back and forth between "Ah-ha!" and utter disbelief. I'd spent the better part of my life wondering why the hell my parents treated me so differently than they did my brothers, but any theories I had come up with had always been so far-fetched as to be impossible. And I looked too much like my mother for either one of us to deny the other—despite the many times I'd wished I could pretend there wasn't any shared genetics there.

A glass slammed down, and I imagined my father sitting in his recliner in his man-cave glaring at my mother, but I wasn't quite brave enough to descend the stairs to see it for myself.

"I'm not entertaining this conversation today, Drew. I don't know what the hell has gotten into you, but we can talk about it tomorrow. When you're sober." She sounded defeated.

When I heard her footsteps approaching the stairs, I spun quickly, panicked, eyes searching for literally *any* place to be other than standing where I was when my mother reached the top of the stairs.

By the time she stepped into the kitchen, I was perched on one of the countertops with a roll shoved in my mouth. I'm not going to pretend it was the smoothest cover-up in the history of cover-ups, but I had to sit somewhere in case my knees decided to give out. They'd turned to jelly about halfway through my parents' exchange. I tried to cover the shaking of my hands by tucking one under my leg on the counter and shoving that roll in my mouth as fast as I could with the other.

She stopped short when she saw me and cut her eyes over her shoulder in the direction she'd just come from before she met my gaze again. Her shoulders slumped. A look appeared on her face that I was certain I'd never seen before.

"You heard." It wasn't a question.

I blinked at her, mouth still full of a yeast roll I couldn't have swallowed if my life had depended on it. I nodded.

"Well, shit," she uttered, letting her eyes close for a moment before she moved over to the hook by the door and grabbed her apron, sliding it on over her red sweater and black slacks. She was dressed like she was going to a business meeting and not hosting a family dinner.

She busied herself with pulling a casserole dish full of roasted potatoes and asparagus from the oven, opening a container of almonds and sprinkling them over the top before sliding it back into the oven. She did all of this without meeting my eyes once, all while I stared at her incredulously.

When she'd wiped her hands off on a dish towel and poured herself a glass of wine with hands that were shaking as badly as mine were, she finally turned and looked at me. Really looked at me.

"I suppose we should talk about this." She sounded resigned.

"Do you think, Mother?" I couldn't believe that was even a question.

"Astrid, I..." she started, but before she could finish what she was going to say, the front door opened and Ethan called out.

"Fam! Where's everyone at?" In a much jollier voice

than the occasion warranted—even *before* I'd overheard my parents fighting in the basement.

Ethan pushed through the door into the kitchen and came up short, eyes narrowing as he studied both our postures. He met my eyes first, scanning me from head to toe before he approached me, coming to stand against the counter where I was perched. Quietly, he asked, "You good?"

I met his gaze and cut my eyes to my mother over his shoulder before looking back at him. I could feel my pulse jumping in my neck and I wondered if nineteen-almost-twenty was too young to have a heart attack. "Not even a little bit, bro."

He wheeled around to face my mother and ground out his words. "Really? You promised."

She sighed and swallowed half her glass of wine in one go. "It's complicated."

"What the fuck is so complicated about treating your daughter with some common decency on fucking Christmas, Mom? It's one goddamn day!"

I reached out and put my hand on Ethan's shoulder, drawing him back around to look at me. "It is complicated, Eth. But for once she didn't hurt me on purpose." I looked at her again. "At least I don't think so."

She let out a slightly hysterical laugh and grabbed the bottle of wine by the neck, forgoing the glass entirely. "If I could erase the last twenty minutes from your memory, rest assured, I would."

And with that, she pushed out of the kitchen. I jumped when I heard her bedroom door slam a few moments later.

Ethan and I looked at each other for a minute before he spoke again. "What the hell happened?"

I hopped down off the counter and was delighted to find that my knees held me up. "Tell you what. Why don't we make a to-go plate, and I'll tell you on the way to the airport? I think Christmas is cancelled this year, bro."

15

Astrid

Boston

IT WAS MY SECOND TIME LANDING AT LOGAN International and, as tired as I was, I was glad it wasn't my first time trying to navigate it. I'd paid a pretty penny to catch a last minute flight out on Christmas, but Ethan had taken pity on me and put half on his credit card. He knew Imogen had been my safe place to run to since I was seven years old, and after everything that I'd told him on the way to the airport, I was pretty sure he agreed that getting me out of town for a few days was a great idea. I knew I needed to sit down and have that talk with my mother eventually.

The funny thing was, I really wasn't all that surprised. I mean…I was. But I wasn't.

I'd always felt "other" and apart from my family. Always. So, finding out that there was a legitimate reason for the way they'd treated me my entire life had actually freed up some space in my head that had previously been dedicated to *"what the fuck is wrong with me that even my parents can't love me?"*

I'd tried to call Gen to give her a heads up about my change of plans just before my plane took off, but it'd gone straight to voicemail. By the time I landed I knew she'd disown me for calling that early, so I opted for a surprise attack.

I hopped in a rideshare just outside the terminal and was at Imogen's Beacon Hill address within an hour. I was fucking beat. I'd caught a nap on the plane but hadn't really slept since the night before, and that had been restless at best.

Imogen had given me a key the last time I visited, and given that it wasn't even 7 a.m. yet, I just let myself in. My bestie would never be up this early in the morning unless she absolutely had to be.

I noted the living room looked like she'd had friends over the night before and I was glad she hadn't spent Christmas alone.

I climbed the stairs slowly, feeling exhaustion creeping in more and more with each step. When I got to the top I turned left to poke my head in her door and let her know I was there.

The sight that greeted me was…surprising? Shocking. Impressive?

I felt my eyes widen comically as I watched Imogen stretch languorously before opening her eyes, blinking up at the ceiling. She jumped a little when she sensed me standing in her doorway, and I couldn't help but whisper, "What the hell, bestie?"

Her cheeks pinkened adorably. "Hey, As, um, how's it going?"

This bitch. Next thing I knew she'd be asking me about the weather. I couldn't believe we were having a banal conversation like this in light of her bed partners.

I gestured to the men sleeping on either side of her, the surprise temporarily chasing my exhaustion away. "Both of them? Girl. You're my hero." I made a crown on top of my head with my fingers, and Imogen dissolved into giggles which jolted one of her companions awake with a start.

Key, who I remembered from the Halloween party, offered me a stiff nod and reached over Imogen to punch Auley in the arm. At least, I assumed it was Auley, but his face was buried in a pillow so I couldn't be sure.

A muffled curse erupted from the pillow but he still didn't raise his head or open his eyes. "Ow, fuck, dude. What the hell?"

Key offered me another look, rolling his eyes before he responded. "We have company, *dude*."

I stifled a giggle and only felt a little bit guilty for enjoying the view.

Auley lifted his head and cracked one eyelid to investigate and closed it again, laying his head back down. "Aye, Astrid, too early for awake times. Need more sleeps." And then he pulled Imogen closer to him, draped an arm over her, and promptly went back to sleep.

By that point I was wishing I'd brought popcorn to the sexy comedy show. Of all the things I'd expected to find when I walked into Imogen's bedroom that morning, one half-naked Scotsman and another who I would bet was all the way naked under those covers was not it. I cut my eyes back to Imogen and was immediately confronted with the fact that she looked happy. Not just dick-drunk happy, but happy, happy. I envied her at that moment.

After a few adjustments, Key made his way out of the room, offering me a grin on his way past that may have generated some palpitations against my will.

"Okaaaay then, I'm just gonna...go put my stuff in the other room, if you don't mind a surprise guest for the holidays?" Suddenly I was second-guessing if I should have hopped on that plane on a whim. I'd needed to see Imogen after everything had gone down at my folks place, but for the first time in our friendship, I wondered if she actually minded me being there.

"Girl, whatever, you're my family, you know that. You're always welcome here." Gen nudged Auley's arm but he just tightened it around her and snuggled in further. "I'll get up in a minute and come find you."

I nodded and blew her a kiss before I stepped out of the room. "Guess this explains why you haven't been answering my texts," I muttered as I pulled the door shut behind myself.

I dropped my bag on the bed in Imogen's spare bedroom, immediately unzipping it and pulling out a clean pair of sweats and a baggy t-shirt I'd stolen from

Ethan years ago. I just wanted—no, *needed*—to be comfortable.

A few minutes later, I heard Imogen's bedroom door open and Auley yelled something unintelligible, followed by Imogen cackling evilly. Gah, I loved that girl. When the shower turned on a moment later I took that to mean everyone was up for the day, so I headed downstairs to make some coffee. God knew I was going to need it.

The guys left us alone after breakfast and we settled on the couch with our coffee to catch up. I wanted to tell her then about what I'd overheard at my folks' place the night before, it would have been the right time and I knew she'd kick my ass for holding back, but the tea she had to spill was honestly so much more fun to talk about. Not only that, I could tell that whatever else was weighing on her mind was heavy, though she hadn't told me what that was yet. I guessed it was heavy-shit season. It was going around, for sure.

I kept waiting for the perfect moment to bring it up, but it just…never came. My tongue wouldn't spit out the words and then I was out of time. The guys returned and I took that as my cue to go to my room and give them some privacy since they were all giving each other significant looks and awkward sign language trying to talk around me.

I stood, stretched, mostly faking annoyance, as I headed for the stairs. "By all means, let me leave you all to your super-secret conversation. I can go…wash my hair or something." I leveled the boys with my best intimidating stare and a warning. "But if I walk into the middle of an orgy when I come back down, I won't be held responsible for my actions."

I didn't stick around to see what their response was, but I'd managed to make myself laugh. No small feat, all things considered.

I flopped onto the bed upstairs wishing I'd brought my coffee with me but not willing to poke my head back downstairs to retrieve it. I pulled my phone out of my pocket and started doom scrolling on social media when I got a text from Rae.

Rae: Hey, you around?

Astrid: Barely alive, but in Boston with the bff, why what's up?

Rae: Oh shit. Okay, no worries. Merry Christmas, A!

Astrid: Rae?

Rae: Don't worry about it. Everything will be fine.

Astrid: For fucks sake, what will be fine?

I got up and started pacing around the room while I waited for her to respond, already pulling up the airline app to book a return flight. With all the fuckery that had been going on with Liam and the club lately, something told me that everything would not, in fact, be fine.

When Imogen poked her head in the door a few minutes later, I stopped my pacing to give her a smirk. "Scooby meeting all done with?"

She sighed and flopped down on the bed next to my bag. "There have been some…new developments. It's not anything I should tell you about, and it really is safer for you not to know, but…" She met my worried gaze from across the room and she looked so tired. And scared. I knew, deep down, that whatever she was going through was bad. Really bad. And there was no way I could unpack my shit with her when she was already going through so much. She pulled me out of my thoughts when she continued. "I think I may have to take a bit of a trip soon. And I don't know how long I'll have to be gone." She shot me an apologetic look, but I was secretly relieved it wasn't just me that was going to have to cut our visit short.

I didn't know why I was so sure that whatever Rae had reached out about had to do with Liam. And I didn't understand at all why it mattered so much to me, but when she'd reached out and then gone silent, I'd had a sinking feeling in my gut. Something was wrong with Liam, I knew it. And I cared far more than I should. I'd flown all the way to Boston to find my safe place but suddenly realized that maybe the life I was building for myself, for the first time, was important enough to me that I was eager to run back to it. How… strange?

I realized, while I was entertaining my internal monologue, Imogen was staring at me with shrewd eyes, no doubt taking in every nuance in my expressions.

"Something came up for work, and I…" I started.

"Wait, you have a job? I mean, that's great, but I didn't even know you had a job. How are you managing that with classes and all?" Her question was fair, if triggering, and I winced.

"We have a lot to talk about, Gen, but I don't think now is the time." I let that sink in for a moment before I continued. "I know you've got big stuff going on, and I've got my whole double life to lead, but do you think we could take a pause for the night and just…have fun? My flight leaves at the buttcrack of dawn in the morning and it just feels wrong if I'm not hungover when I get on it."

Imogen grinned at me before she tilted her head. "Wait…double life?"

That night we danced. We drank. We dissolved on the couch into each other's arms in tears more than once. Her guys gave us the space to just absorb the comfort that could only come from someone who truly loved you unconditionally. The beauty of our friendship was that it was okay to just cry. She held me while I sobbed out years of heartache and never once demanded I tell her the whole story. I did the same for her.

I knew she felt like she couldn't explain what was going on with her, and I found I wasn't ready to tell her about my parents yet. Hopping on a plane at the last minute and running to Imogen's side suddenly felt a lot more like running away from my problems than seeking solace. Did that mean I was growing up?

When I woke up early the next morning, I found Imogen curled into herself in her bed, silent tears streaming down her face. Man, I hated leaving her like that, but I had to go.

I whispered our mantra to her before I kissed her on the forehead and left her to the care of her men. "Love you, bitch. Remember. No matter when."

She choked on a sob but finally responded quietly. "No matter what."

I kissed her on the forehead, and surreptitiously wiped my own tears on my way to the door, resolved that it was time for me to go back home and deal with my own shit.

I passed Key on the stairs and I was pretty sure he was going to take over where I'd left off. I still wasn't 100 percent sure about that guy, but he did seem to be very protective of my bestie, so I was willing to give him the benefit of the doubt. Unless he turned out to be a serial killer or something. Then all bets were off.

The screech of the landing gear withdrawing into the belly of the plane had me cringing and cradling my head in my hand, leaning against the window to my right. How I'd managed a window seat at the last minute was proof positive that the universe was trying to make up for what a shitty run I'd been having lately and I sent out a silent thank you.

I wanted to sleep through the flight but I'd really never been able to sleep on a plane for longer than a quick nap here or there. Too much anxious energy, too much brain spinning. That day was no different.

I hadn't heard another word from Rae since her last text the day before. Either I was going back to Cali to a huge clusterfuck or I was going to smother Rae in her bed for vague-texting and then dropping off the face of the earth.

Time would tell.

16

Astrid

Boundaries

I'D COME STRAIGHT FROM THE AIRPORT TO THE CLUB. IT WAS still closed, but something told me that's where I'd find the answers to Rae's vague-texting problem. The only car in the lot was Liam's, angled weirdly across two spots near the front door. I parked next to his car instead of pulling around to the employee lot, eager to get inside and see what was going on.

The smell of lemon oil and bleach greeted me when I stepped through the front door, and I paused, listening, before I pushed the curtains aside and looked around at the club, noting a lone glass sitting on the bar, but no Liam.

"Hello?" I called into the empty room. I took a few more steps inside and the utter silence in the club caused the hair on my arms to stand at attention. I crept toward the hallway, aware that danger still lurked somewhere nearby and remembered quite clearly that danger had ways of getting into the club uninvited.

As I approached the door I could see a band of light cast across the darkened hallway, and I peeked into the office before I pushed the door open, slapping my hand over my mouth to contain my gasp at what I saw.

Liam was passed out cold in the fetal position in the middle of the office floor, a half-empty bottle from the top shelf cradled in his arms like a baby. I stepped closer and stood over him with my hands on my hips before I cleared my throat.

He jerked at the sound but didn't wake fully until I nudged his stomach with the toe of my shoe.

"Nothankyou…" he slurred without opening his eyes. *"I don't like pickles."*

I snorted. "Liam, it's Astrid. Can you open your eyes?"

I waited patiently while the muscles in his face jumped and twitched like he was trying to make them do what I'd asked.

When he finally stared up at me blearily, he blinked several times before he looked even more confused. "Astrid? She left." He stared off into the distance, his gaze unfocused. "She went to Boston. It's good." He shook his head. "I can't have her."

I…what? "Liam, buddy, you need to sit up, come on. Let's get you to the couch, and I'll get you some water." I didn't have any illusions that water was going to sober him up any, but at least he'd be hydrated. I reached down and gently pried the bottle of liquor out of his embrace and set it off to the side before I squatted and grabbed his hands, trying to maneuver him into the sitting position.

"You don't understand. She had to go. Astrid…" He sighed. "I miss her."

"Liam, I'm right here. Come on, help me out, okay?" I tugged on his hands again.

Finally, he seemed to focus on my face and his whole demeanor changed in an instant. "Astrid! Hi! You's *so prettty.*" His face fell before he continued in a whisper. "*I wish you were ugly.*"

That drew another laugh out of me, unbidden. "Thanks, Liam, you're pretty too."

His eyes lit up. "You thinks I'm pretty?"

I tugged on his arms again, finally getting him upright. I met his hopeful gaze, not entirely sure what was happening here, but compelled, to be honest, even if he was unlikely to remember this conversation once he'd sobered up.

"Yes, Liam. You're very pretty." I gave him a half-smile. "But you're my boss."

He shut his eyes as I pulled him to stand in front of me, swaying a moment on his feet until I slid an arm around his back to steady him.

"I never should have hired her." He tilted his head to rest against the top of mine, giving me no help getting him to the couch, but his voice sounded so unbelievably sad that I paused in my efforts to move him.

"Why shouldn't you have hired her?" I asked, genuinely curious.

He sighed, lifting his head back up. "Because that means I can't love her."

I sat in the office chair, swiveled around to watch him sleep. My head was a mess trying to process what he had drunkenly confessed. He'd clammed up after he uttered those words and thankfully managed to shuffle the few steps to the couch with my help. I'd coaxed him to lay down on his side and thrown a blanket I found in the closet over him.

His words had shocked me. Liam had never given any indication he had feelings for me that were anything other than friendly professional. Had I ever looked at him as someone other than my "boss"? I mean…I'd have had to be blind not to see that he was gorgeous. His sandy brown hair, currently flattened on one side where he'd been sleeping on the floor, had tempted me on more than one occasion to thread my fingers through it to see if it was as soft as it looked and it turned out that the perpetual five o'clock shadow he sported was one of my *things*. Right up there with forearms and tattoos.

But, all of that aside, he was still my boss. And my friend, I thought. So I'd avoided thinking of him like that until the moment those words had escaped from his mouth.

But now? Now, it was all I *could* think about as I pulled out my phone and sent a text to Rae.

Astrid: I found our friend passed out drunk in the office.

Rae: ...

Rae: ...

Rae: You came back.

Astrid: Of course I came back, I just went to Boston to visit and get away from some family drama, not to hide forever.

Rae: Did Liam...say anything to you?

Astrid: Like what?

Rae: Oh nothing, girl. Just wondered. Gotta run, but I'll see you tomorrow for the party!

Astrid: RAE. What aren't you telling me?

Astrid: Girl. You better not be ghosting me right now.

Astrid: Dammit, Rae.

Part II

"Boiling water's in your veins
Slowly driving you insane..."
- little hurricane

17

Astrid

January. Sometimes it Creeps Up On You

I'D MADE NO PROGRESS IN PROCESSING THE LOSS OF HANK. The knowledge that he was gone was a gaping wound in my chest that hadn't subsided in the days since I'd received Imogen's call. I wavered between shock and utter devastation from one moment to the next. The situation was so fucking weird, and with the way Imogen was acting I knew something more had to be up. On top of that, regardless of how it happened, I was still grief-stricken.

Since she'd called me, I'd been trying to go on with life as normal, as much as possible, because there was nothing I could actually do about it. As long as I kept busy, I managed to keep my head above water. But I was off work tonight and sitting alone in my apartment with nothing to do but let the sheer fuckery of the past few months crash over me like a tsunami.

"This is Astrid, you know what to do."

Ethan's voice rang out through my phone speaker as I let his voicemail play. *"Hey, sis, I haven't heard from you in a while. I'm just checking on you. Let me know you're okay."*

My emotions began the familiar downward spiral, and I recognized all the signs that it wasn't going to be a good night for me.

Some days I could recognize the signs and stop the descent before it got bad, but I could already tell today was not one of those days. Like it or not, I was heading down the dark path, unable to stop.

That wicked fucking voice in my head telling me on repeat that I was a failure.

A burden.

That, even in her darkest hour, my best friend didn't want me by her side to comfort her.

My parents thought I was a failure and a disappointment.

Everyone in my life thought they had to protect me from reality, like I was too fragile or stupid to be able to handle real life.

I must be a fuck up. What other answer was there?

God, it was so loud.

I knew, on some level, that if I picked up the phone and called Imogen, or even Ethan, that they would tell me all the reasons to ignore the things that my fucking brain was telling me I was in that moment. But logic wasn't queen in those parts, and I could feel my skin beginning to crawl with the urge to run away from everything and everyone that knew me. I hated feeling like that.

But maybe I hated myself even more.

The feeling was so excruciating, like bugs crawling under my skin. Like nothing would ever be okay again.

But it also satisfied something inside me. The voice said, *"Ah-ha! You finally see yourself as you truly are!"* And that inner demon in my head rubbed its hands together. Finally, it was winning.

I shook my head violently from side to side and drew my knees up onto the couch cushion, curling into myself and let wracking sobs take over until I was soaked and dry-heaving. I didn't want to feel like this anymore. I was so tired of being a burden and a disappointment to everyone. Fuck. I just wanted to go.

Remiel

Accidentally Angel

I COCKED MY HEAD TO THE SIDE, WATCHING THE PRETTY human with long dark hair step onto the sand near the water's edge. My nose told me she was sad before my eyes registered the tears on her face.

Sadness had a distinctly acrid scent. It was unmistakable.

Without anywhere else to be, I settled onto my belly in the cold sand and kept an eye on her. She probably shouldn't be out here by herself at night, but I'd be here if needed. My ears perked up when the sound of her feet splashing through the surf drowned out the sound of my stomach growling. The leftover steak someone had offered me at an outdoor cafe hours earlier felt like it had been days ago already. It was almost time for me to make my rounds again.

I rose to a sitting position when she took another

step closer to the water. I took two steps closer to her, my huge paws soundless in the sand and my dark fur keeping me almost entirely concealed in the waning light of the moon. I crept closer, not wanting to scare her, but a whine crept up my throat at the sight of more tears streaming down her face.

She shook her head once, swiping at her cheeks before she stretched her arms out at her sides and tilted her head toward the sky. I paused my movement when a ragged scream erupted from her throat before she dove into the surf in front of her. She thrashed and fought the waves, but she was going in the wrong direction. Instead of pushing back toward the shore it seemed she was fighting to get past the break, where it would drag her out to sea.

With a feral growl, I launched my powerful muscles straight for her, haunches bunching as I leaped over the first few feet of surf in the direction she'd gone. My head went under water for a moment but I couldn't see anything in the murky dark water beneath the violent surf. I could hear her thrashing against the waves, though, and I steered my body toward the sound.

As I drew closer, I caught another glimpse of her face and another whine escaped as I could feel her distress but didn't know the cause.

Why wouldn't she fight the waves? Was she sick? Injured? I shook my head above the chop, clawing my way closer to her. Whatever it was, it wasn't happening on my watch.

I wasn't just going to sit by and let the ocean take her.

Once I was close enough I bumped my head up against her chest and raised my eyes to meet her startled gaze, unable to hear her gasp above the sound of the waves. I knew she hadn't noticed I was there before she'd walked into the waves, and her expression confirmed it.

I clamped my jaws in the material of her hoodie, trying to be as gentle as I could in the rough waves, before I began swimming back the way I'd come. She didn't fight me, and I was glad.

By the time I'd dragged her back to the sand and she flopped onto it, feet resting in the edge of the water, she just laid there, staring straight up at the nearly moonless night for a beat before she turned her head and met my reproachful gaze with a stunned one of her own.

"Well," she offered as she sat up slowly. "I suppose you're some kind of sign?"

I didn't know what she meant, but I thought maybe I'd done a good thing by pulling her out of the water. I let my tongue loll out of the side of my mouth and sat down on my haunches next to her, leaning the bulk of my body against her, offering her some of my warmth.

She studied me for a moment before she reached a hand up and rubbed it over the crown of my head, gently rubbing one of my ears between her fingers as if testing its texture. "Are you hungry?" she asked, giving me a hopeful, if tired, look.

I lifted a paw and offered it to her and she took it with a quiet chuckle. "Okay then. Let's go get you something to eat. I think you've earned it tonight." She stood and stared down at her wet sand-coated clothes for a moment before she met my stare again. "But first, maybe a shower."

I followed her back to a little bungalow on the edge of town, staying at her side the whole way, occasionally baring my teeth if anyone looked at her for too long. I didn't know why, but I felt very protective of her.

When she unlocked the door I followed her inside, the sound of my nails clicking against terracotta floors as I studied the room before me. My gaze tracked her as she made her way to a room off the main one and called back at me. "You can come in here if you want, big guy."

While she pulled off her wet clothes, I settled down on the floor just outside the bathroom door, resting my head on my paws and letting my eyes fall closed, but keeping an ear out for her or any other noises I needed to be aware of.

When she climbed into the steaming shower in the other room, I pretended not to hear her sobs, but couldn't quiet the low whine in my chest as I listened to her release her pain into the steamy enclosure.

19

Astrid

Life, and Pizza

I GRABBED A SLICE OF PIZZA FROM THE TRAY AND TOOK A big bite of the gooey goodness before I noticed my new friend had made quick work of the piece I'd just placed on the plate under the table for him and was giving me big eyes as he licked his lips and watched me eat.

"Wow, buddy, you *were* hungry, weren't you?" I slid another piece of meat lovers off the tray and placed it on the plate in front of him, noting he waited patiently for me to release it before he leaned his giant head down to grab it with his teeth.

I studied him as he ate, wondering at the very odd turn of events that had led me and my furry friend to sitting at this street cafe eating pizza at eleven o'clock on a weeknight.

Once he'd finished that slice he returned to his position laying at my feet, his front paws demurely crossed as he watched what remained of the foot traffic going past at this hour of the night. "You need a name. If you're going to stick with me, I need to know what to call you."

He raised his eyes to meet mine and cocked his head, one ear standing straight up and the other flopping adorably against his skull. His black fur gleamed in the light from the restaurant windows and his eyes looked black as he stared back at me like he understood exactly what I'd said.

I grabbed my slice of pizza and took another bite before I picked up my phone and opened my search app, thinking aloud. "Hmm. Should I name you after an angel? I mean, you did save my life after all."

He flopped down onto his side and threw a paw over his face in response, and I chuckled out loud.

"Gotcha. Not an angel." I pulled up a couple of dog name lists but neither of us seemed excited about any of them.

"What about Butch?" I swear to god, he rolled his eyes at me.

"Brutus?" He turned and offered me his haunches in response.

"Okay, something a bit more creative then."

I returned to my original train of thought—but with a twist—and pulled up a list of the archangels on the web. "No, not that one. Nope, too normal, too basic, too overused… Hey, buddy…what about Remiel?"

His ears perked and he spun to face me again with a low bark and a wag of his tail.

I laughed, despite the ridiculousness of the situation…I was having a full-blown conversation with a massive horse of a dog that had just pulled my ass out of the ocean. This night couldn't possibly get weirder.

"Remiel, huh? You like that one?"

Another bark, another wag.

"Can I call you Remy for short?"

20

William

Flesh and Bone

THE BODY HIT THE CEMENT FLOOR, AND I GAPED AT IT FOR a full minute before I lifted my eyes to meet hers in disbelief. She stood with the gun leveled at the spot where he'd been standing moments before. I couldn't contain the bark of laughter that escaped me and the sound made her jerk where she was standing, eyes coming back into focus as she lowered the gun.

I'd have expected her to be shaken after killing a man in cold blood but her voice was steady and low when she spoke. "I'm not sure which of us was owed that more, but I'm sorry if I've robbed you of something."

My bark turned into a full-bellied laugh that probably should have concerned me, given that I had a man's brains splattered on the toe of my left boot like a macabre splatter-painting. I got control of myself enough to commend her. "Ah, Imogen, remind me never to underestimate you."

I watched the group of four hobble out of the room, leaving me alone with my demons. Well, demon. Even if he was dead. The events of that night were a gift and a curse and I knew it in my bones.

I stepped away from the corpse of the man who had murdered my father and claimed the folding chair leaned against one wall of the room. I reached into the shaft of my right boot and withdrew an old metal flask. Leaning forward, I unscrewed the lid to the flask and poured a measure on the back of his head before I took a long swig of the Scotch for myself, toasting his corpse with the flask. "Good riddance, ya fecking cockroach of a man. And may the fires of hell remain well-stoked for the rest of your miserable eternity."

When I'd finished my drink I pulled my phone from my pocket and called in the cleanup. "Track my location. Bring a trash bag."

21

William

Heavy is the Head

THE DAY IMOGEN SHOT DEARIL IN THE HEAD HAD BEEN both the best and the worst day in my recent life. Dearil was a rat bastard and, just prior to Imogen pulling the trigger, had admitted to being the one who murdered my father. Something I'd always suspected but had never been able to prove beyond a shadow of a doubt.

Seeing the man who had destroyed my family, and subsequently woven a poison vein into the Organization that my father had built, lying on the floor bleeding into a drain satisfied a bloodthirstiness in me I hadn't known I possessed. And for that, I owed Imogen everything.

On the flip side, Dearil's death meant that someone had to step into his shoes, and I, as his nephew and the son of the former head of the Organization, was naturally expected to be the one. But I'd never wanted that.

Even at the age of fourteen, when my father talked to me about bringing me into the fold when I got older, I'd known that wasn't the life I wanted. We'd fought about it just before he was murdered and I'd lived with that regret ever since. The last conversation my father and I ever had ended with angry words from me I could never take back.

My father was a good man. He'd run the Organization with as much decency as one could. He had staunch rules about targets and collateral damage. He refused to peddle drugs to kids. He wouldn't harm women or children to get his point across. He was in the business to do well for himself and his family, but he had principles.

When he was murdered, Dearil had stepped up to take his place. Convenient, in my opinion. And, slowly but surely, every standard by which my father had lived had been whittled away until the Organization became little better than gangsters and bullies; throwing their weight around with no regard for who got hurt in the process.

It'd taken me fifteen years to find the evidence I hoped would prove that Dearil had murdered my father. When I did, and Imogen helped me confirm it, no one could have been more shocked than I was when she ended up being the one that pulled the trigger. I did have to admit, though, there was a bit of poetic justice to it.

I leaned back in the chair in Dearil's former office. The whole room was an ornate ode to pomposity, with over-sized, extensively carved furniture and gold knobs and gaudy drapery hung over the windows. As ridiculous as it seemed, one of my first orders of business was going to be to have every bit of this shit taken out into the parking lot and set ablaze.

I'd spent day and night for the past month trying to make sense of the paperwork haphazardly stashed in every nook and cranny in that office. As an added bonus I kept coming across deranged notes he had apparently left for himself all over the place. Tucked into notebooks, stuck to his computer monitor, plastered to the insides of the drawers. The more of those I read, the more I was convinced that he'd had multiple personalities, but instead of Jekyll and Hyde, it'd just been two variants of Hyde—and no sign of Jekyll in sight.

I knew that no one who remained from my father's time leading the Organization had willingly followed Dearil after he'd taken over, but there wasn't much, short of mutiny, that could change the circumstances. One didn't exactly retire from this profession. A few of them had approached me over the years, begging me to challenge Dearil for his seat and take back the reins before he destroyed everything my father had built, but as much as I missed my father, that was still not the life I wanted.

So I'd stood by, accepting a vanity position as Dearil's second that allowed me to still have some semblance of a life outside of all of it. And I watched from the sidelines as the poison that was Dearil slowly crept and oozed throughout the Organization until it was barely recognizable anymore. Thugs, thieves, and murderers, oh my!

Unfortunately, I didn't have a choice anymore. An absence of leadership created a vacuum, and the odds of someone as bad as, or worse than, Dearil stepping into that vacuum was terrifying enough to make me take the role.

I'd been at it for hours that day. I'd rolled my sleeves up past my elbows and loosened my tie ages ago, and I could feel the hair I'd styled that morning beginning to droop over my forehead. Just as I pulled the next file out of the stack and flipped it open, stifling a yawn, I heard wheels in the hallway outside my office. Then silence. Waiting.

"Enter," I called out.

Meredith came just inside the room but didn't approach the desk, studying the mess I'd made of what had already been complete madness. "I'm headed out for the night. Sir." She paused very deliberately before she tacked on that last part.

I knew she wasn't happy with the demotion she'd received when I took over, but I couldn't find it in myself to trust her, not knowing how closely she'd worked with Dearil. She was going to have to be patient and prove she was trustworthy if she wanted to regain anything close to the power she'd held under his leadership.

For now, she was relegated to a desk job and her displeasure was made evident by all the teeth gnashing and passive aggressive glaring she made a point of anytime we shared space.

I nodded at her, studying the stubborn tilt of her chin for a moment. I'd read her file earlier in the day and it had been eye opening for me to understand how she'd gotten where she was.

Once upon a time, Meredith had been one of the Organization's rising stars. No mission of hers ever went sideways and whatever goal she was assigned was achieved 100 percent of the time. No exceptions. She was lethal and precise and, until her last mission, had been wielded by my father with deadly accuracy. On her last mission, when something went horribly wrong, the file speculated she'd been sabotaged by someone within the Organization, but no motive or suspect was offered.

She'd been sent out to put pressure on a high-ranking official that was making things very difficult for one of our legitimate businesses. Of course, that business was a front for an illegitimate business, but that wasn't the point. She'd been sent out on a mission she should have been able to complete while blindfolded. Every time she'd checked in during the mission everything had been going like clockwork.

Until it wasn't.

All signs pointed to there being another professional in the room, but we hadn't sent anyone else in with her. In the end, she sustained an irreparable injury to her spinal cord at her L3, according to her medical records. She'd remained conscious long enough to request assistance and then gone completely dark.

The team sent in to extract her found her lying

unconscious in an empty room in a pool of her own blood. No sign of her target or anyone else.

It was inconclusive if whoever had done that to her had spared her life or just assumed she would succumb to her wounds before help could get to her. But again, it smacked of a deliberate job.

When she regained consciousness in the hospital she couldn't remember anything about the events that led up to her injury. Only that she'd reached her target without any issue and had begun the process of "convincing" him to cease and desist his harassment of our business.

The next thing she knew, she was lying on the floor, knowing she was badly injured, with just enough strength left to call for help before she passed out.

As I read through her file I'd tried to drum up some sympathy for her, but her personality made it really fucking hard. I hadn't known Meredith back then, but the woman I'd inherited who now stood in my office glaring at me was just a cunt.

I sighed. "Was there something else?"

She squared her shoulders, and I wondered if we were getting ready for a fight when she just shook her head at me. "I could help you, you know. I was present for most of those transactions."

I nodded. "I know. But the problem with that is that I don't trust you. Yet. Maybe ever. And until I do, I'm afraid you've been relegated to receptionist. But hey, it could be worse!" I offered her a sardonic grin. "I could have had you killed and dumped in the river!"

She rolled her eyes at me and spun to leave, calling over her shoulder. "We haven't done that in years. It's goddamn terrible for the environment."

22

William

And So it Begins

I SLID INTO THE BOOTH ACROSS FROM MY WAYWARD employee, taking a moment to pull off my coat and nod at the waitress to bring me my usual. I leaned back against the leather and gave him a nod.

"Long time, no see."

He quirked his mouth, dipping his chin at me. "Aye."

I studied him, noting the way he lounged on his side of the table, looking for all the world like an insouciant fuckboy out for an afternoon drink with a friend. This is why I'd asked him to stay on. Key, for all of his faults, blended right into every scenario I'd seen him in so far. He was a chameleon.

As usual, he was dressed like a dandy fresh off the pages of a men's fashion magazine, his crisp white collar sharp where it peaked above the black peacoat he still wore, in spite of the warm temperature inside the bar. His expression looked lazy from a distance, but from where I sat I could see the calculating way he studied every patron around us as well as the staff that circulated throughout.

I wondered why he was carrying, obviously the reason for the coat, and it occurred to me that perhaps I should be leery of this man, knowing what he was capable of. I knew not to ever presume he wasn't a threat to me, but my gut told me I wasn't his target for the evening. Not this time, at least.

The waitress paused briefly by our table and set a glass of scotch down at my elbow, offering me a coy grin as she did, and I noticed there were numbers written on the napkin she'd set it on, magnified through the bottom of the tumbler.

I winked at her but returned my attention to Key before she could take the interaction further. When I'd asked him to meet me today, I'd banked on his curiosity getting the best of him. It'd been radio silence since I'd asked him to stay on after the…event, but he hadn't told me "no", so I was going to assume he still worked for me until he indicated differently.

From the corner of my eye I saw the waitress's shoulders droop in defeat before she moved away to check on another table, but I just stared at Key, waiting for him to ask why I'd requested this meeting.

When he continued to silently study me and our surroundings over the rim of his glass, I raised a brow at him. "How's the family?" I inhaled the smoky scent of the scotch in my glass appreciatively.

I watched as his eyes darted left and right once more before he responded in a clipped tone. "They're good."

I tilted my head at him before taking a sip from my glass, feeling the delightful burn as it slid down my throat. "Glad to hear it. I'm sure you'll give Imogen my love, yes?"

His eyes narrowed, still a little sore about the last time we'd all been in a room together, I imagined. I chuckled low under my breath.

When he seemed satisfied that we weren't being observed by the white collar happy-hour crowd gathered there he nodded, and I leaned in, speaking low across the table between us. "Right then. I've been going through dickhead's files for the past six weeks, trying to make some sense of the chaos."

He nodded and picked up his glass, taking a healthy sip from the edge before he sat back and waited.

"I came across a communication from you that I found curious." I slid my phone across the table and waited for him to study the photo on the screen.

I mentally ran through the possibilities, and a suspicion crept into my mind, but I wanted to hear it from him before I jumped to any conclusions.

"An old associate of mine was having some trouble out in Cali. The Organization is…invested. So when he sent me a photo of that bloke and I recognized him, I sent it on for someone above my paygrade to handle. I haven't heard from him since, but I assumed it had been handled."

"Hmm." I returned my drink to its napkin and rested my elbows on the table in front of me.

"I assumed incorrectly, then?" he asked.

"It seems that your friend on the West Coast is making friends and influencing people. And no, my best guess is that this got shuffled under the rug intentionally. I saw no evidence that anyone had followed up on it. The question is…why, if we're invested, wouldn't they have wanted to nip something like this in the bud?"

Key shrugged his shoulders. "No way to know for sure, but my guess is that they didn't see that as a problem. If that's true, then it does make one wonder. Did they already know about it? And was that endorsed, unofficially of course, by them?"

I nodded, in total agreement. "I thought the same. So I did a little digging. The chatter is that he's beginning to draw the kind of attention that none of us are interested in. It's a bit out of your wheelhouse, if you catch my drift. I know as well as anyone that diplomacy isn't your strong suit." I smirked before I continued. "But I wanted to get a feel from you about what sort of guy I'm going to be dealing with when I follow up on this."

Key looked away for a moment, observing the steadily growing crowd around us before he responded. "Liam is a bit of a wild card. And an occasional dumbass, if his willingness to come to the Organization for help is any indication. But he's mostly solid. He has a bit of an ill-spent youth, which is how he and I met, but he's not a bad one."

If Key said he was solid, then he probably was. I'd rarely ever heard him say anything positive about one of his associates. "I'll look into it then." I picked up my glass, draining the remaining scotch in one gulp against all of my sensibilities.

I laid a fifty on the table between us. "Anything you need from me before I go?"

Key shook his head. "Nah. Can't think of anything else." He was studying my face intently, and if I didn't know better, I'd think he was looking for some sort of tell.

"Nothing else you want to tell me?" I inquired.

"Nope." He let the *p* roll off his tongue with a pop. "Happy hunting, boss."

I grinned. He'd answered my question without actually answering it, and as much of a pain in my ass I knew he would be, I was glad to know he'd opted to stay on. Even if it was just for now.

I stood and slid my coat back on to ward off the chill of the Boston winter that was raging outside before I reached a hand out. "Aye. I'll be in touch."

He shook my hand with a firm grip before he offered me a mocking salute as he too slid out of the booth. "Always a pleasure, sir."

I snorted, shaking my head. "Indeed."

I stepped out onto the sidewalk as I pulled my phone out of my pocket. "Get me on the next flight to Redding."

23

Astrid

The Indomitable Rae

"EXCUSE ME, MISS, THIS ISN'T WHAT I ORDERED." THE nasally voice of the douchebag leaning against the bar grated against my nerves. I slid my attention over to him momentarily, taking in his shirt open a few too many buttons at the collar, navy dress pants, and a pair of loafers—honest to god loafers—that looked like they'd probably cost what I paid for a months' rent, did nothing to alleviate my initial opinion of him. Douchebag.

He felt my eyes on him and turned his head, surveying me in a way that made my skin crawl before he offered me a lecherous wink. Fucking hell.

I stood from the stool I'd been perched on while Rae and I chatted, knowing she could handle this guy without any backup from me, and started making my way toward the hallway that led to my office. I heard

Rae firing off behind me and chuckled under my breath. Douchebag didn't know what he'd gotten himself into.

It was almost closing time when I heard a voice coming from the bar that I knew all too well. I tilted my head to listen more closely but couldn't make out his actual words. A bit of trepidation crawled up my spine. I'd never told him where I worked. So, if he was here now, then one of two things was true. Either he was stalking me, or my friend Rae was the girl he'd told me about back in December. Honestly, I wasn't sure which one of those options I preferred, but I stepped out of the office to face the music either way.

I studied his posture as I approached the bar, noting the *bad boy* lean he had going on and deduced he wasn't here for me. At least that meant he wasn't stalking me. I thought about turning around and running back to the office to delay the inevitable confrontation, but before I could, Rae caught my eye over his shoulder and rolled her eyes at me like, *would you get a load of this guy?*

I snorted, and he turned at the sound, eyes bulging and then narrowing as he put two and two together.

"*Astrid motherfucking Scott.* What the hell are you doing here? Please tell me *this* is not your fucking job you mentioned."

The amusement on my face died at his tone. "Exactly what is that supposed to mean, *Ethan motherfucking Scott?*"

Ethan and I had been scrapping with one another for

too many years for me to cower at his sanctimonious tone.

His angry expression cracked for a moment and he held a hand out to me. "Astrid, come on, this isn't the kind of place I want my sister working in. Surely you can understand that?"

Rae cleared her throat behind him, a smirk on her face. "Just a minute ago you had no problem with the fact that *I* work here, so what's changed in the last sixty seconds that suddenly makes it wrong for your sister to work here? Also..." She cut her eyes my way. "A little heads-up that this one is your brother would have been good."

I shrugged. "This is honestly the last place I expected him to appear. And how exactly do you two know each other?" I looked back and forth between the two and noticed his cheekbones getting distinctly flushed.

Ohhhhh. Oh. I felt my eyes widen.

Ethan shifted around on his feet and issued Rae an apologetic look. "I just meant...she's my sister...and the club is..." He was so flustered that I couldn't contain my laughter.

"Eth, I don't work in the back. I pay bills. Place liquor orders. Answer emails." I crossed my arms over my chest waiting for that to sink in. "*But*, if I did work in the back, there would be absolutely nothing wrong with that. It's my body, brother, and my choice. I get to decide what to do with it."

He hung his head, properly chastised. My brother wasn't a misogynistic asshole. And I understood where his heart was at that moment. I almost felt a little bad for him because I had a feeling Rae wasn't going to let him off so easily.

I wasn't sure how I felt about the two of them being…whatever they were, but what business was it of mine anyway? If I wanted him to respect me enough to let me live my life, then I had to return the favor.

Still didn't want him having sex on my couch, though.

I left Ethan and Rae to continue their conversation at the bar, giggling as I walked away as Rae gave him a lesson on double standards, while I went back to the office to finish up for the night. Or morning. My hours were getting seriously convoluted now that I worked most nights.

When closing time came Rae appeared in the doorway, looking a bit sheepish. "Hey."

I tried to keep a straight face. I really did. "Hey, yourself."

"Sooo…" She started but her voice trailed off, and I was pretty sure it was the first time in the entire time I'd known her that I'd seen her at a loss for words.

"Sooo…" I countered. "You slept with my brother."

She slapped her hands over her face and made a growling noise behind them. "I obviously didn't know he was your brother. Hell, Astrid, I don't even think I knew you *had* a brother." She dropped her hands and looked at me again. "Are you mad?"

I just shook my head, chuckling at her discomfort. "Brothers, actually. Three of them. And of course I'm not mad. I mean…objectively, he's a pretty good guy and not too bad on the eyes. Though he *is* a bit young for you, don't you think?" I bit my lip, trying to keep a straight face.

Rae's expression went from chagrined to angry in a split second, and I cracked up again.

"Girl. I'm kidding. Who the fuck cares how old he is? Or how old you are, for that matter. Age is just a number."

She looked relieved and then her eyes widened a little more. "Exactly how many numbers are there between his age and mine?"

I'm pretty sure the wait staff heard me cackling all the way out in the bar.

We were still leaving the club in pairs, or escorted by Jared, so once I had all my shit packed up, Rae and I headed out to the parking lot together. As we approached my truck she gave me a devilish look and pulled a bottle of bourbon out of her bag. "Don't worry, I threw forty bucks in the drawer for it, but it's one of the good ones. What say we have a girls' night?"

I looked at the sun starting to peek over the top of the building and squinted. "Girls' morning, you mean?"

"To-may-to, to-mah-to." She shrugged with a grin.

"Sounds like a plan. But can we do it at my place? I've got a…friend…there that I need to check on."

Rae popped the hatch of her old VW and grabbed a bag out of it. "Perfect. You drive."

I'd never had a dog before. Not surprising, I guess, considering my mother was always so particular about her house and her things, but in the last couple of months I'd realized two things. The first was that when you'd been gone for nine hours, you'd better open the door wide and step out of the way fast when you got home. The second was that as soon as his bladder had been emptied, the sheer joy a dog expressed upon seeing you was the best damn feeling in the whole world.

When Rae and I climbed out of my truck in front of my rented bungalow, I cautioned her. "Just let me open the door, you'll want to stand back a bit."

She shot me a puzzled look but did as I said. As soon as I got the door unlocked, a black bolt of muscle and fur streaked past us straight to the line of hedges that bordered my small yard. He was so tall I worried he might actually be peeing over the top of them and into the neighboring yard but fuck it, what was I supposed to do about that?

When he was done he came bounding back to me, offering me grins and kisses and big silly butt wags. A couple of bows let me know he'd like to play, please, and I grabbed his ball off the porch and tossed it as far as my tiny yard would allow. When he merrily chased after it I turned to see Rae's reaction. She looked like an emoji with big heart eyes and hands clasped under her chin.

She turned and gazed up at me with a delighted

expression. "When you said you had a friend you needed to check on, you didn't tell me you had a *pony!*"

I snorted. "Right? He might as well be, but he's such a good boy. And we have a bit of a history, so he's welcome here for as long as he wants to stay."

"Well, that's a weird fucking way to put that, Astrid, but okay. I can't wait to hear how you and the black pony currently chasing a tennis ball in your yard ended up being friends."

"It's not exactly a happy story, friend, but it has a happy ending, I guess?"

We settled in on opposite ends of my couch with Remy settled between us taking up every single inch of space not occupied by one of us, and some that was. We each had a nice stiff drink in our hand, and Rae leveled me with a curious look. "Okay, spill. I'm dying to hear this story."

Two drinks, and many tears, later she grabbed another tissue and blew her nose obscenely, causing Remy to jump and lift his face to hers, checking that she was okay. "You're such a goooood boy, aren't you, you little angel. Well, big angel." She cooed at him, letting him lick the tears from her face.

When she met my gaze over his big blocky head she just shook her head. "Girl. I had no idea. I'm so fucking sorry you were going through all that this whole time and...like, how were you just functioning and coming to work and doing the things? Why didn't you say anything?"

I shrugged, wiping at the tears on my own face since Remy was otherwise occupied. "It's just what I do, ya know? I never really had anyone in my life other than Ethan and Imogen who cared to know what was really going on with me. It served me better to slap on a mask around everyone else, including my parents, so they had less opportunity to hurt me."

"Babe. God. No! That's not..." Her voice trailed off and she gently pushed Remy off of her so she could slide over to my half of the couch. She was so much shorter than me that she had to rest on her knees to throw her arms around my neck, but when she squeezed with everything she had in her, I felt something in me snap back into place. "No more," she declared. "No more masking with me, you got it?"

I returned her hug and let the tears pour freely down my face. As if I had any choice.

"I don't think it's that easy, Rae, but I'll try, okay? I promise I'll try."

"And that's all I can ask for." Then she turned to Remy who was sitting on his haunches in front of us observing our embrace like he knew exactly what we were talking about with his tongue lolled out of one side of his mouth in a doggy grin. "Remy, I think another round of drinks is in order. What do you think?"

He woofed and jumped to his feet. I was pretty sure he didn't know the difference between one more round of drinks and anything else exciting, but he was game for whatever his new friend wanted. Such a good boy.

———————————————————————

24

William

———————————————————————

Down the Rabbit Hole

I PARKED MY RENTAL CAR IN A SPOT AT THE FAR EDGE OF the parking lot, surveying my surroundings as I climbed out. I'd declined having a driver meet me when I landed, not wanting anyone to be able to keep tabs on me while I was here.

I'd had reservations about the location for the club when I'd looked through Liam's file, but apparently he swore he could make it a success if he just had the capital to get it started up. I sure as fuck hoped he'd managed to make the inside of his establishment more impressive than the darkened industrial parking lot I stood in.

Despite the ominous location, though, there *were* a surprising number of cars in the lot, so maybe I shouldn't judge a book by its cover.

The man posted at the door was one of ours, a condition of the Organization's financial assistance for this venture. I wasn't surprised they'd placed someone there to keep an eye on our investment, and Jared was one of the best. On the surface, he checked guests for their memberships before allowing them entry, but I knew he was also visually screening them for weapons and potential problems without them even realizing what he was doing. He was former Special Ops, and I was sure he'd been selected for this assignment specifically for his particular set of skills. I knew the moment he spotted me approaching from the other side of the parking lot. His spine stiffened almost imperceptibly and he offered me a curt nod of respect once I'd reached the pool of light cast from the fixture above the door.

"Sir," he offered in a clipped tone as he opened the outer door for me. "Enjoy your visit."

I tipped an imaginary hat at him and clapped him on the shoulder as I passed. Jared was solid and I was glad to have him here, but I knew he couldn't be excited about being stuck out here in Cali indefinitely when his home base was New York. I made a mental note to send someone to relieve him soon so he could go blow off some steam.

Once inside the vestibule I was immediately impressed, despite my doubts that Liam could pull off the miracle he'd sworn he could. I'd seen the pictures of the warehouse prior to Liam's renovations. Now, though, it bore no resemblance to its origins.

The entryway was painted entirely black, trimmed with dark wood accents, creating the sense the space enveloped you the minute you stepped inside. My wingtips made a satisfying noise on the dark mahogany herringbone floor that gleamed in the low light cast from sconces mounted to the walls at regular intervals. The half-moons of light along the floor as I approached the hostess waiting there to greet me were just enough to see by without truly lighting up the space. Her face was illuminated by a small desk light positioned at the corner of her station and dark velvet curtains were draped in the corners and in the archway leading to the club, effectively blocking the view to the interior.

It was like stepping through a doorway from modern day grime into another world, another time. Like stepping into a dark fairy tale you'd only read about in books.

In spite of my irritation at having to fly across the country to investigate this issue, I had to hand it to him. I was pleasantly surprised so far.

As I studied my surroundings I could feel eyes on me and knowing that all public parts of the club were discreetly under surveillance, I glanced up into the corner and took note of the small black camera pointed at where I stood.

A throat cleared, and I turned my head to give the hostess standing in front of me my full attention, offering her a grin and a raised brow before she spoke.

"Welcome to Obsidian, will you be dining with us this evening?" She was dressed in a trim black sheath, with her hair pulled back in a severe twist. Probably late twenties, early thirties. Understated. Beautiful. Professional. A complete contrast to the true nature of the club, but very smart to have her as the first face to greet the clientele. She would throw off anyone who had doubts about the nature of the business.

She continued to stare at me unblinking with a polite half-smile on her face, and I wondered if she had any inkling of who I was.

I jerked my head in a nod and she pulled out a leather folder, passing it to me over her podium. "Would you like assistance selecting from the menu?"

I skimmed the list inside briefly, feeling my eyes widen before I could suppress the reaction. I cleared my throat. "What would you suggest?"

Her cheeks flushed but otherwise she gave no indication that my question unsettled her. "I suppose it depends on your appetite this evening, sir. Are you in the mood for a small sampling of the menu items available or would you prefer a seven-course meal?"

I glanced back down at the menu before lifting my gaze. "I don't know how long I'll be here tonight, perhaps I'll just grab a drink and watch the show for a bit before I decide."

She nodded and turned, pulling something from a small wooden box behind her. When she turned back to me she held her hand out with a white satin band in her palm. "Our mixologists can make anything you can dream up and they love to be challenged. Also, the show is just starting so you've arrived at the perfect time. If you decide you'd like to have a more…substantial…meal, just come back and see me and I'll upgrade your wristband. This one lets everyone know that you are just here to observe."

I took the band of satin and slid it over my right wrist with a nod. "Thank you."

She smiled again as she pulled back one of the curtains and gestured to the room beyond. "My pleasure, sir. Enjoy your evening."

I stepped into the darkened room beyond the curtains and paused to allow my eyes to adjust while I took in my surroundings. It was a stunning design, and my grudging respect for Liam grew a bit more as I took it all in.

The floor was inlaid with glossy black and white checkerboard tiles that gave the impression it went on forever. Plush half-moon velvet couches were placed throughout the club in rich shades of red and purple, each creating their own conversation area that gave the illusion of privacy from the rest of the room without blocking the view of the stage.

A long, low table sat in front of each one so the wait staff had a spot to deliver drinks and small plates of finger foods to the guests. The couches that were closer to the edges of the room were arranged similarly, but these had curtains that could be drawn around them to enclose them completely.

I found myself intrigued. I knew nothing *overt* was supposed to take place out here in the public spaces, but the exhibitionist in me was drawn to the idea of privacy in what was still very much a public place.

An impressive bar spanned the entire back wall of

the club. A gorgeous burnt woodwork of art with carved molding wrapped the bartop and reached all the way down the corners to the floor. The wall behind it bore expansive wood shelving which boasted an impressive collection of rare top-shelf labels from what I could see, along with all of the usual suspects. Labels from Glen Fidditch to Captain Morgan and everything in between.

Leather wrapped bar stools were spaced in twos and threes along the length of the bar and the two bartenders, one male and one female, were both dressed sharply in vests and suspenders, working efficiently mixing drinks for the customers gathered there. They spun around one another so gracefully, it almost looked like they had choreographed it. The dance of the sugar plum martini or whatever. I snorted at myself and shook my head.

Opposite the bar was a circular stage that allowed guests to be seated on all sides to enjoy a nearly 360-degree view of the show. It appeared that tonight's theme was *Alice in Wonderland,* and I stood briefly mesmerized as the dancers took the stage. A scantily-clad, very leggy Alice appeared in a tiny blue nighty with white thigh-high stockings and a red bow in her blonde hair. She made her way across the stage, twirling and bending in a display of flexibility that made me jealous, and I was only thirty. The crowd loved it and applauded raucously as she made her way to her mark.

When she reached the center of the stage, she wound herself around her co-star, the Hatter, who had appeared from the opposite side. She also had thigh-high stockings, but with garters and a bustier that cinched her waist impossibly, emphasizing the flare of her hips and ass. Fucken hell, she was the sexiest Mad Hatter I'd ever seen. The top hat she had perched precariously on top of her pinned curls just sealed the deal for me. She leaned casually on a cane as she slowly spun with her partner, never quite letting their bodies line up.

They teased and taunted one another to the beat of "Devil's Playground" by The Rigs. Their bodies brushed against the other before they separated again, circling and grazing fingertips along collarbones and shoulders and hips as the slow bass pulsed throughout the room, demanding our heartbeats slow to match it.

Alice ran a fingertip along the Hatter's thigh, the arch of her back, and the Hatter wrapped hers around Alice's throat with a little squeeze that had Alice's head falling back on her shoulders, a look of rapture on her face. As the Hatter backed her up against a four-poster bed that graced one part of the stage, Alice began to fall back onto the bed, but before she could, the Hatter spun her suddenly to bend her over the edge instead.

I heard a collective moan from the audience at the display, and the Hatter looked back over her shoulder with a devilish grin before she slid her hand over Alice's satin covered bottom, petting it slowly, the gesture so tender I could almost feel the satin on my own palm. She stroked and kneaded and swayed in time with the beat of the haunting music, making Alice's shoulders heave where her torso was pressed to the bed.

When the music reached a crescendo, the Hatter drew back and spanked Alice once, drawing a loud moan from her throat that I wasn't entirely sure was an act. Again, the Hatter petted her and soothed the burn before she drew back and offered another smack in time with the music. Another smack, another moan, another pet. By the second chorus, I could see a wet spot growing on Alice's nighty as she writhed beneath the Hatter, evidence that this wasn't all for show. Alice was enjoying this very much, and if the speed with which the Hatter was drawing in breath as she continued to punish and soothe Alice was any indication, then so was she.

25

Astrid

What Wicked Webs We Weave

"Yep. Yep. I heard you the first time. Of course, I'll be fine here. I've practically been running this place single-handed for the last six months while you've been doing who knows what, I think I can handle one night alone." I couldn't find my AirPods, so I had the phone clutched between my cheek and my shoulder as I worked on finishing up the liquor order for next week on the laptop in front of me.

Liam sighed over the line, and I could almost see his eye roll. "I know you can handle it. I just don't know if they can handle *you*."

I laughed, knowing he may be right. "I'll be on my best behavior, boss."

I heard him snort through the phone as my eyes drifted over to the cameras that tracked everything happening in the main areas of the club. There were cameras everywhere that were considered public, as well as the front and back entrances. I skimmed over them all and then snapped my gaze back to the view of the entryway.

A man was standing there, looking very out of place in his snazzy dress-pants and black button up. Our hostess, Cassidy, was handing him the menu everyone had to choose from as they came in, and I watched his eyes grow bigger for a split second as he skimmed it, before his expression returned to careful disinterest.

"Fuck me, he's pretty," I muttered under my breath.

"Who, who's pretty?"

Shit. I'd forgotten Liam was still on the line. We'd never talked about his drunken rambling when I'd come back from Boston. As much as the idea that Liam saw me as something more than just his friend and employee had made me start seeing him in a different light, I followed his lead when he'd come to his senses. Either he didn't remember anything he'd said to me, or he was a really great fucking actor. He'd gone back to being his normal "Liam" self and no mention of that night had ever come up again.

"Nobody, just scrolling Insta and came across a guy in his pajama bottoms. Eye candy." I tried to draw my eyes away from the screen, but couldn't make myself stop staring until he'd offered the hostess a smirk and stepped through the curtains into the main part of the club.

When he was gone, I saw Cassidy fan herself for a minute before she returned to her position.

Yeah, girl, I heard that. Me too.

I shook off the shiver that traveled down my spine and turned back to my laptop. "If that's all, I need to get off of here and finish this order. Nobody likes a half-stocked bar, sir."

He sighed. "Okay, just call if you need me. Or if anything weird happens. I'll be around."

"Will do! And have *fun*. That's what you're there for."

He muttered, "Yeah, yeah. Be good," and then the phone clicked in my ear.

I gratefully straightened, rolling my neck a couple of times to get the kinks out, before I picked up where I'd left off.

Maybe when I was done with the order I would make my way out to the main bar for a drink and see if the new guy was as pretty to look at up close as he had been on camera.

Probably not. After all, reality seldom lived up to my expectations.

26

William

A Case of Mistaken Identity

I GRABBED A TABLE NEAR THE BAR WHERE I COULD SIT WITH my back to the wall. Occupational hazard. When the show was over, I watched as the dancers took a bow to raucous applause from the crowd before they made their way off the stage and through a set of curtains in the corner of the room.

The lights in the main part of the club brightened marginally and most people began to get up and either grab another drink from the bar or gather their things to leave. Some opted to pass through the door at the other end of the room that appeared to only be accessible by electronic key lock.

No key? *No access.* I liked it.

I'd be lying if I said I wasn't watching that curtain in the corner to see if the dark-haired dancer was going to reappear and come mingle with the crowd. It would be a gross abuse of my position to engage with her, but I was hungry for another glimpse. I wanted to see what her face looked like when it wasn't overshadowed by the brim of her top hat.

A few minutes later I watched with rapt attention as she appeared from a different hallway. She'd changed into her street clothes, and I was hard-pressed to decide if she looked better in her costume or the denim that now lovingly hugged every curve of her ass and thighs. Her tank top exposed tan shoulders and her hair flowed down her back, no longer in the pinned curls she'd worn on stage.

She was younger than I'd first assumed, maybe in her early twenties, but the sight of her face washed clean of the stage makeup had me drawing in a quick breath. She was fucking stunning. High cheekbones and pouty lips I wanted to run my thumb over, just so I could see if they were as soft as they looked.

She stepped up to the bar and leaned over it, gesturing to the female bartender behind it, offering me a tantalizing view of just how beautifully that denim was worshiping her form. My stomach tightened and I barely controlled the urge to get up and stand at the bar next to her, just so I could be in her orbit.

The cute little bartender stepped to the end of the bar, and the Hatter—I didn't know what else to call her—said something that had the blonde cackling before shooting a look at me over her friend's shoulder then turning to pour a drink for her.

While she waited, I watched the Hatter spin until her back rested against the bar as she idly scanned the room in front of her. I waited impatiently for her eyes to land on me and, when they did, it was like a bolt of lightning struck home. I physically felt my body jolt, and when her eyes widened without wavering from my face, I knew it had the same effect on her. Holy fuck. Had I ever had a similar reaction from just one look? I couldn't remember a time that I had.

I offered her a half-smile and tipped my glass at her in hello. Flirtatious without being overbearing. In response, she pursed her lips and tipped her head. *Hello to you, too.* I was just about to stand and join her at the bar when her friend tapped her, drawing her attention and sliding her drink across the bar with another sly look at me.

When the Hatter turned back to face me she tilted her head in question. I held out a hand to the vacant chair next to mine. She grinned and sauntered toward me, all feline grace. Oh yes, this one knew exactly the power she held.

She approached the table and placed her glass on the surface before taking the seat next to me, crossing one leg over the other and resting an elbow next to her glass. Her chin rested in her hand as she studied me.

Neither of us had spoken yet and it felt like sacrilege to break that silence. We were saying enough to one another without ever parting our lips. I knew I wanted her in my bed and so did she. I was fairly confident that our desires were aligned in that.

Finally, she cleared her throat, lifted her chin from her hand, and took a sip of her drink before she spoke. "First time here?"

I nodded. "Not from around here."

She considered me for a moment before a throaty chuckle escaped. "Yeah. I can see that."

"And by that, you mean…?" I leaned forward, studying her face more closely in the dim light.

"It's a pretty small town. I think I would remember if we'd crossed paths before."

I leaned back with a pleased grin. "So you think I'm memorable?"

She allowed her eyes to slide from my head all the way down to my wingtip where it rested on my knee. Her eyes lingered on my forearms where my sleeves were rolled. When she returned her gaze to meet mine, she smirked. "A bit."

I tilted my head back with a real laugh. This one was sassy. I liked it.

"I enjoyed the show you put on." I tapped my finger against the side of my glass.

A flicker of confusion swept across her face but then she laughed. "It was for you, so I'm glad you liked it."

"For me, huh? In that case, I liked it that much more." I had no idea how she'd seen me in the crowd, but I was so wrapped up in her voice and the sensuality with which she moved that I didn't stop to question it. She must have seen me when I walked in. God knows I'd noticed her the minute she'd walked on stage.

27

Astrid

The Dance

I HADN'T BEEN ABLE TO GET HIM OUT OF MY HEAD SINCE I'D seen him on the cameras. I muddled through the rest of my work for the night but it was entirely possible that I'd fucked up every single thing I'd touched since the moment he'd walked in. The distraction was real.

So when I finally called it a night, I walked to the end of the employee hallway and stepped into the women's room before I passed into the bar. I studied myself in the mirror. Long, dark hair draped down my back, bangs framing my face and highlighting my eyes. The dark eyeliner I favored mad them pop dramatically and the deep blue of my tank top made them shine even more, as if they were glowing blue. I turned my head left and right, trying to see myself as other people did, as he might, but that wasn't the way it worked, was it?

We never could truly see ourselves.

I narrowed my eyes at my reflection. *Go be a sexy bitch.*

My reflection smirked back at me. *Always.*

And with that, I spun on a heel and entered the main room of the club. I clocked his location the minute I entered the lounge and knew that when I approached the bar he would have an excellent view. Or at least I hoped so. I stepped up onto the brass toe rail at the bar and leaned further over than was truly necessary to get Rae's attention, offering her a devilish smirk when she stepped closer.

"Who are you trying to lure in with your ass sticking in the air like that, hmm?" she asked with a chuckle.

"You see the guy sitting behind me by himself? With his back to the wall?" I was careful not to pull my chin in that direction.

Rae leaned a bit and looked over my shoulder before she returned her attention to me. "Damn, honey. That man is smokin'. But don't you think he might be a little old for you?" Her smirk told me she hadn't forgotten my teasing about Ethan.

"Age is just a number when you're naked, Rae. Didn't you know?" I quipped.

Rae cackled loudly at that. "Right you are, girlie, right you are. What'll you have?"

"A bourbon, neat, two fingers." I gave her my best pout.

"One vodka tonic coming up, hold the vodka." She blew me a kiss. "But I'll add a twist of lime just 'cause I'm nice."

I rolled my eyes and spun in place, resting my back

against the bar. Pretending that I could see anyone else in the room except for him, but when I finally allowed my gaze to pan back to where he sat, the jolt that went through my body was undisguisable. Holy. Fuck.

He was better than the digital version I'd drooled over earlier. Way better. *Buck up, Astrid. This is the big time, now isn't the time to swoon. Be cool, be cool.*

Before I could make an ass out of myself I felt Rae tap me on the shoulder, and I spun back around as she slid my drink across the bar toward me, taking the opportunity to steal another look his way. "Don't do anything I wouldn't do, bitch."

I smirked at her. "Oh, do you have a brother?"

Rae shot me the bird and returned to her customers, her shoulders shaking with laughter, but the exchange had settled my nerves a bit.

Game on.

I think we both knew where our interaction was leading, or at least I hoped I wasn't completely misreading things. The problem was that I wasn't sure exactly how to proceed from the flirting and suggestive looks to the actual doing of the suggestive things. I was no virgin, but it wasn't like I had to do a lot of tempting to get a teenage boy to fuck me. Usually, all I had to do was smile at them if I wanted to get laid. Low effort, if you caught my drift.

The man sitting across from me was *not* a teenage boy. Far from it. From his intense golden eyes, with his brows seeming to be permanently drawn together above them in a semi-frown, to his banded forearms exposed by the rolled sleeves of his shirt, to his fancy shoes. No. This was no teenager. This was a full-grown man and one of the most beautiful ones I'd ever seen in the flesh. What the hell was I supposed to do next?

That question was answered for me in the next moment, silencing my inner turmoil.

"There are quite a few reasons why I probably shouldn't ask this, but I can't seem to stop myself. Are you...?" He paused as if considering how he wanted to ask the question. "Are you involved with anyone?"

I shook my head slowly, maintaining eye contact with him despite the overwhelming urge to look away so I could take a full breath for a moment.

"And...is your shift finished here?"

"It could be," I responded, eyes still locked with his.

"Then, would you like to go somewhere else with me? Maybe a walk? Or...a drive?"

I smirked at him. Honestly relieved that he seemed to be as unsure of how to proceed with this as I was. "Did you want a tour of Redding at"—I glanced at my phone—"two o'clock in the morning?"

He chuckled sheepishly then sat up straighter, something entirely different coming into his expression. "Fine. That's fair. In that case, would you like to come back to my hotel room with me so I can strip you bare and lick and kiss every inch of your delectable body until I've ensured you've come at least five times before I finally slide inside of you and ruin you for all other men?"

I felt my breath catch in my throat as I blinked at him dumbly. Holy. Hell. I was pretty sure that I was supposed to say something equally sultry in response, but all I could come up with was "Bold. But...okay?"

Thankfully, he ignored my fumble, responding with a feral grin before he pulled out his wallet and tossed a few bills on the table. With that done, he held his hand out for me to lead the way. "After you."

I pointed toward the employee exit when we passed. I'd regained enough blood flow to my brain to be at least a little bit smart. "I'll just grab my truck and meet you out front. I don't ride anywhere with strangers. Safety first and all."

He got a glint in his eye before he nodded encouragingly. "Very smart. You can also tell your friend there that I'm staying at the Gaia. Suite 402."

I took a relieved breath. "Thanks. And...um. Your name?"

He stepped closer to me, intruding on my personal space in a delicious way before sliding his hand up until he cupped my jaw. "I think we should skip those. It'll keep things simpler in the long run. Are you okay with that?" He peered into my eyes and I didn't sense any evil intent there. Maybe I was a raging idiot, but I nodded.

"Okay. No names," I agreed in a low whisper.

He pressed a kiss to my forehead before he backed away slowly. "I'll wait out front."

I pulled out my phone as I walked back down the employee hallway, texting Rae as I went.

Astrid: The Gaia. suite 402.

My phone immediately dinged with a response.

Rae: Be safe, girl. Want me to check on you in a bit? See if you need an out?

My heart fucking glowed at that response. No one but Imogen had ever shown me friendship like that. I almost turned back around and crawled over the bar to hug her neck.

Astrid: I love you. Yes, please, but if I don't answer just know that I'm probably having multiple O's and can't get to the phone.

My phone dinged one more time.

Rae: <devil emoji> <queen emoji> <water emoji>

I snorted and pocketed my phone as I pushed through the door to the employee parking lot.

28

Liam

Real Women Eat Chocolate Croissants

THE WHOLE NIGHT WAS A FUCKING JOKE.

I sat across from my date, Tabitha, watching her select pieces of lettuce from her salad that didn't have any dressing on them, complaining about how she'd asked for the dressing on the side and *did that waitress have a hearing problem?*

I couldn't help but wonder why the fuck I was picturing midnight blue eyes half-lidded in pleasure from a chocolate croissant. I heard the phantom of her voice in my head. *I think you need to revamp your type then, friend.*

Goddammit. I met Tabitha at the park. She was walking her poodle while I was out for my morning run. She'd almost killed me when her poodle darted across the path in front of me, clotheslining me with its leash. It'd seemed like one of those adorable stories people tell their grandkids years later. She was cute. Pretty even. Tall, fit, blonde. Gorgeous hazel eyes and a span of freckles across her nose that gave her a "girl next door" look.

It was the right thing. Me asking her out. So why was this date turning into the disaster of the century? Because she was a vapid bitch. So far she'd told me my car was pretentious, turned her nose up at the waitress and refused to look her in the eye when she ordered, and now she was picking through a bare salad with only oil and vinegar on it like she would spontaneously combust if a drop of dressing hit her tongue.

I looked at my watch. It'd only been an hour. Fuck. Me.

"Do you want to come in for a drink?" Her voice had taken on a sultry tone I hadn't heard all night. Did she have multiple personalities?

I stared at her with incredulous eyes. How the hell did she think that the events of the evening were going to culminate in *more* interaction between us? Hell, I was pretty sure she'd made the waitress cry at one point when she had the audacity to ask if we wanted to see the dessert menu.

I cleared my throat and considered being nice about it, but honestly, I just couldn't do it.

"Not if I'd just escaped the Sahara and you had the last glass of water on earth," I deadpanned.

It took her a minute to process my words, but when

she did, she rolled her eyes and snatched her purse from the foot well. "Whatever, asshole. I'm a fucking catch. Good luck finding better in this shithole of a town."

When she got out she slammed the door with unnecessary force that had me gritting my teeth. I clenched my hands on the steering wheel and waited until she'd unlocked her door before I pulled away with a screech. I may think she was a bitch, but I'd been raised right. For the most part.

I looked at the clock as I hit the main road. I didn't want to go home, but I knew that if I showed up at the club right now I'd never hear the end of it from Astrid. I could hear her voice in my head. *"Have fun! That's what you're there for."*

I snorted and then shook off the thoughts of her, repeating my new mantra in my head:

She's too young for you, Liam.

She's your employee, Liam.

You're using her, Liam.

Maybe I'd go grab a beer somewhere and just wait a while. If I showed up after midnight, then there wouldn't be too many questions. Maybe.

I nursed a beer for two hours. It was lukewarm and gross by the time I took the last swallow, tossing a few bills on the bartop in front of me before I called it. Right or wrong, I was headed to the club. To check on things. Not because I wanted to see Astrid.

I took the short ten-minute drive carefully, nowhere

near drunk, but still clearly remembering the night I'd been snatched out of my car and thrown on the ground. No need to give anyone an excuse to pull me over.

When I pulled into the lot I was pleased to see quite a few cars still there. Business had been doing well lately.

I pulled into my usual spot and cut the engine, sliding out of my seat and shutting my door with a quiet *snick* of sound. See? No need to slam them.

When I approached the door, Jared was deep in conversation with a man standing there. They shook hands as I got closer and the man turned toward me, drawing up short as recognition came over his expression. Who was this guy?

He studied me for a beat before he stepped closer and extended a hand. "So, you're Liam, then."

I tilted my head, offering my own hand to shake, but still not seeing anything in his features that looked familiar to me. "Have we met?"

He shook his head, a rueful grin on his face I didn't understand. "Nope. But we were bound to eventually." He shook my hand with a firm grip before he released it and slid his hands in his pockets. He leaned back on his heels a bit, staring up at the moon before he addressed me again. "I'm William."

I nodded slowly, wondering if Brennan and Rae had overserved this guy or something. "Okay. Well, it's... nice to meet you, William?"

He looked surprised for a moment before he shook it off. "I've taken over. Dearil is...retired."

Realization dawned very quickly, like a bucket of

cold water over my head, making the blood drain from my face so quickly it began to tingle. "You've...taken... oh. Okay. You're the...okay. And you're here because...?"

I'd been making my payments on time. I'd satisfied that part of my agreement with the Organization. The other part was on them. They'd made no requests of me in the past few months, so I didn't think I'd done anything to warrant a personal visit from the new head of the goddamn Scottish mafia.

"Relax, grasshopper. I'm here to help you out, not to terminate our agreement." He smirked at my obvious discomfort.

I allowed myself a deep breath. "Help me out. How?"

"Well, it's come to my attention that you've been having a bit of trouble with the local authorities?" He posed it like a question, but I got the sense there was more going on under the surface than he was letting on.

"I was. Am? But mostly it's just been harassment over the business permits. But it's been a while since the last 'incident' about that. I, uh, texted one of your employees a few months ago about it, but never heard anything back and then the issues stopped, so I just assumed it had been handled already."

"Ah, yes. You and Key go way back, I hear."

I heard Jared chuckle under his breath behind William, and I wondered what the joke was.

"Well, I wouldn't say we're bffs or anything, but we've, uh, worked together before?" I felt like I was treading blindfolded on unsteady ground with this conversation. William clearly knew more about my association with Key than he was letting on, and I was just trying not to stick my foot in it and piss off either of the men who I knew would happily take me out if I posed a threat to them or the Organization.

"He speaks highly of you. Or, as highly as Key speaks of anyone." He continued studying my face, like he was looking for some outward indication of my character.

"That warms my heart, sir. It's always nice to know the sociopath in your life thinks you're swell." There was my old friend, sarcasm, stepping up to get me killed, ladies and gentlemen.

William laughed out loud, his face relaxing briefly. "I like you, Liam. Just keep doing what you're doing, and I'll be around for a bit. Probably best if you continue *not* knowing me, as far as everyone else is concerned. For now, at least."

"Okay. Super-secret spy shit. I hear you." I just wanted to get this conversation over with so I could go to my office and hyperventilate in peace.

He chuckled again and opened his mouth to say something else when Astrid's truck rounded the building. She pulled up next to us and looked at William briefly before she offered me a big fake smile. "Boss! How was your night? Is she the *one*?"

I rolled my eyes at her. "Hardly. You're heading out early, everything okay?"

"Oh! Yeah. I...um...got everything done and Rae's pretty busy so I didn't want to distract her from her work, you know. So I was just going to go ahead...

home. Yep. Headed home. Gonna get some sleep. In my bed. Alone." She just kept nodding like a bobble head, and I found myself nodding with her for some unknown reason.

"Okayyy…that sounds like a good idea. Sleeping. In your bed. Alone." I turned and offered William a quick look, only to see him staring at Astrid with a hungry look on his face. What the hell?

"Okay then! I'll just be off!" Her too bright voice announced, jerking my attention back to her. She offered a jaunty wave and pulled out of the parking lot a little faster than was probably advisable.

I turned back to William again. "So…I guess it was nice to meet you. Sir?"

He was still staring at the spot where Astrid's tail-lights had faded from view but he nodded absentmindedly. "Likewise. I'll be in touch."

29

Astrid

Missed 'O'pportunity

"I PANICKED!" I WAILED AS I THREW MYSELF DOWN ON MY couch.

Rae's voice came through the speaker of my phone where it sat on the coffee table and Remy took notice immediately.

"Girl, Imma need you to slow down for a minute. What the hell happened again?"

I grabbed a pillow off the couch and shoved it over my face, screaming into it until Remy nudged his giant head beneath it, offering me comfort in the form of a big drooling lick straight to my face.

"When I got to the front parking lot to meet him, Liam was there. I think they were talking? But I'm not sure. Anyway, I just panicked! I rambled a bunch of bullshit about how you were busy and I didn't want to distract you and how I was coming home to sleep in my bed. Alone. And the whole time he was staring at me like he wanted to eat me, but in a good way, and Liam was looking back and forth between us like he was trying to figure out what was going on and I just... left." I let out another screech that had Remy pawing at me.

A muffled giggle came through the speaker, and I stopped short. "Are you laughing right now? This is serious, Rae! I should be on my second or even *third O* of the night by now!"

Rae coughed, obviously trying to tone down her mirth before she responded. "Obviously, this is very serious. I don't know how you're going to come back from it. You might even die."

I narrowed my eyes on the phone even though she couldn't see me. "I'm so glad you understand the gravity of the situation."

She snorted. "Babe. I hate to break it to you, but I think the good ship orgasm has sailed for the evening. Your best bet is to go to sleep and hope your lady blue-balls are gone when you wake up tomorrow. Unless Bob is there to help you out?" That statement was followed by another snort from her.

"I don't want *Bobbbbbbbbb*," I wailed. I knew I was being dramatic, but that whole exchange in the club had been the hottest thing that had ever happened to me in my entire sexual life. Turning to Bob after that was just sacrilege!

"Well then, take a shot of that bourbon I left at your place. Maybe a hot shower..." She paused. "Or a cold one." Giggle. "And call me tomorrow so I know you

didn't die from a terminal case of unfulfilled grati-
fication."

I tossed and turned all night. Well, what was left of it. For the first time since I'd started working at the club I found myself staring at the ceiling of my room at the first sign of the sun peeking through my blinds. Wide awake, but not happy about it.

I felt hot breath against my left arm and turned my head, only able to see the whites of his eyes and a long pink tongue looking back at me. "I guess since I'm awake we may as well get out of here then?"

My question was met with an enthusiastic *woof* from my furry companion. Guess that settled it.

"What do you say we grab a coffee to go and check out the park. Maybe we can get a little hike in before I have to head to work."

Another woof and a tail wag.

"Okay. I'm getting up. Scoot your big butt out of the way."

We stopped at my favorite coffee shop, and I left Remy perched in the back of the Scout, sitting pretty while he waited for me to get my caffeine fix. I watched him out the window as I stood in line, worried that maybe he'd just decide to jump out and go back to wherever he'd come from, but he didn't move a muscle. Just watched the people passing by intently. I noted with a chuckle that most of them gave him a wide berth. Couldn't say I blamed them.

When I got to the counter I got a large coffee and a chocolate croissant for myself and four big doggie biscuits for Remy, along with a couple of giant bottles of water. His happy dance when I returned to the truck healed a bit of my frustration from the missed connection the night before.

"All right, buddy, let's go touch some grass."

As Remy and I hiked up the mountain I let my mind wander to the exchange I'd had with the mysterious stranger. I wasn't sure why I cared, or why I even hoped that he might make a repeat appearance, but clearly I was obsessing about him. I replayed those moments in the club in my mind's eye until Remy nudged me with his head, adding a little whine for good measure.

"Right. Sorry. I'm back!" I assured him and added a bit more pep into my step.

That night I took special care when I got ready for work. As much as it annoyed me, I still found myself spending an extra twenty minutes picking an outfit and doing my makeup even as I rolled my eyes at my own reflection in the mirror. I'd never been one of those girls who got all weird when she was interested in someone. I'd always just treated them like I treated everyone else. And if they didn't like me the way I was normally, then I stopped being interested real quick. But this one...this one felt different.

When I was as cute as I was ever going to be, I offered Remy a scratch behind his ears where he laid sleeping on the couch and headed out.

Mystery man would make a repeat appearance, or he wouldn't. No sense driving myself crazy when I could just go see for myself.

I loved watching the club come to life each night, all the waitstaff bustling around, the dancers laughing and joking as they got ready in their dressing room, Rae and Brennan filling the wells with ice, and the clinking of bottles as they restocked the bar for the night. To me, all of those things had become the soundtrack of my new life. There was a beauty in that chaos I'd never experienced before. The club, and all its inhabitants, had become my de facto family now that Ethan was the only one of my biological family I spoke to anymore.

I still hadn't had that talk with my mother. I hadn't tried and she hadn't reached out to initiate it, which spoke volumes.

The fact that my parents had inadvertently dropped that bomb on me and then didn't even care enough to check and see how it had affected me said everything I needed to know. I wondered if they would have cared, had they truly known the discovery on Christmas had ultimately contributed to what I was referring to in my head as "the Remy event." It helped to think of it that way. I didn't like remembering what I'd almost accomplished. Or the feelings of hopelessness that had prompted it.

So, when I thought about that night, I thought of Remiel and how the universe saw fit to put him on that beach with me that night. How such an extraordinary creature saw my pain and chose to intervene when so many people in my life failed to see it at all. Or, if they did, simply didn't care enough to reach out.

Remy was the good that came out of the culmination of my pain and trauma, and I'd never forget how lucky I was that I hadn't been alone on that beach. I'd never forget that he'd saved me.

30

Astrid

Birthday Bitch

I*T'D BEEN FOUR DAYS SINCE MY MISSED CONNECTION WITH* my mystery man and I'd pretty much given up any hope he was coming back to the club. Not that I could blame him. I'd basically ghosted him right to his face in the parking lot that night. No way could he have known how incredibly awkward it was to get caught by your boss when you were about to sneak away for a night of anonymous sex with one of his patrons. I could only imagine what he'd thought as I'd driven away.

A ding from my phone roused me from my thoughts and I opened my text messages and laughed out loud as I read the text message from Imogen.

Imogen: Birthday bitch! Happy birthday to you, my sister from another mister! I'm so fucking sorry I didn't call earlier, it's been a DAY. Have fun tonight and don't do anything I wouldn't do! *winky face*

I looked up from my phone and turned a bright smile on Rae as she stood behind the bar where she was polishing glasses. One of these days I was going to get her and Imogen in the same room. They'd love each other, I knew it.

"You ready for tonight?" Rae asked, shooting me a grin.

I tapped my finger against my chin, pretending to think about it. "Ready to close down early and get drunk with some of my favorite people to celebrate the absolutely iconic moment that I graced Earth with my presence?"

She snorted. "Yeah, that. But, girl, you don't *look* very excited. Hell, before you got that text you looked bummed. Get happy! It's your birthday and your boss agreed to close the entire club in your honor so we can celebrate! We're gonna have a blast, just wait."

I shrugged. "I'm excited. Really. But I've never made a big deal about my birthday before, for obvious reasons. Last year Imogen and I snuck a bottle of liquor out of her dad's cabinet and spent the night getting puking-drunk in the camper parked in their backyard while Hank pretended not to know." I felt a twinge in my heart at the thought of him. "Don't get me wrong, it was one of the funniest nights of my life, but I've never had an over-the-top celebration in my honor before. I'm not sure it's really my vibe."

"Well, how can you know if it's your vibe if you've never had one? Give it a chance, kiddo. I promise, we're going to have fun. We'll let our hair down. Who knows, maybe we'll even get puking drunk for nostalgia's sake." She smirked at me.

"Yippee," I deadpanned.

Rae lined up birthday cake shots along the bar for everyone. We'd shut and locked the doors an hour ago, rushed through closing out the registers for the night, and then it was party time. Liam had cranked up some Matt Maeson on the sound system and it was like our own little inside joke that that's where we'd first met. Even if I didn't remember it at first.

I was posted up on one of the barstools waiting for everyone else to make their way to the bar so we could take the shot together. Shots were more fun that way.

Once everyone joined us, Rae tapped a spoon against a bottle of vodka, loudly demanding everyone's attention. "To our woman of the hour"—she lifted her own shot and gestured to me—"a toast to you on your birthday. Here's to those who wish you well and all the rest can go to hell. Bottoms-up, babes!"

I lifted the sweet concoction to my lips and tossed it back like the pro I was, licking my lips appreciatively when I returned the glass to the bar. I grinned at Rae. Maybe this party wouldn't be so bad after all.

When the music switched and "BOYTOY" came on, Rae came out from behind the bar with a beer in each hand, looped her arm through mine and dragged me onto the stage to dance. She pushed the beer into one of my hands and grabbed my other one to try and spin me around. The differences in our heights made the result hilarious, and I ended up being the one to spin her under my arm instead. We danced and laughed and sang along at the top of our lungs and, by the time the song was over, she and I were both laughing hysterically. I spun to step off the stage, a little lightheaded but stopped short when I was met with a pair of golden eyes.

Golden eyes that were locked *on me*.

I felt the breath rush out of my lungs suddenly while my face flushed even more than it already was from the alcohol.

I went down the steps carefully and crossed the room until I was standing just a few feet away from him. "You're back."

His eyes crinkled at the corners. "It looks that way."

I looked around for Jared, wondering if he'd forgotten to lock the front door, but he was nowhere to be found. "This is…a private party, sort of?" I began. I didn't want him to leave, but I also didn't want Liam to get in trouble having an outsider here. What with me being underage and all.

He lifted a shoulder. "I've got connections."

Hmm. Man of few words.

"Okay then. Can I get you a drink?" I gestured to the bar behind me.

He shook his head. "From what I hear, you shouldn't be getting anyone's drinks tonight."

My heart sank. He'd found out how old I was.

I was sure of it.

And now I was pretty certain he was about to tell me that I was too young for him. I felt the hit all the way to my marrow, which was honestly really fucking stupid. I barely knew this guy. Why should I care if he was hung up on our age difference? His loss and all that. But I couldn't quite conceal the disappointment on my face, and his scrunched up in response.

"Hey. I just meant I heard it's your birthday. I think we're all supposed to be fetching *your* drinks tonight, not the other way around." He did that thing where people lowered their head to look back up at you. It was adorable, and very disarming.

I responded with a grin. "Oh, yeah. You know what? I think I heard that rumor too. So how about I walk over there with you while you make your own fucking drink."

"You've got a deal." He laughed and held his arm out for me to loop mine through.

I could feel my ears burning. I glanced up at him and offered another grin before I looked over his shoulder to see Liam studying us intently from one of the booths that lined the edges of the room. I couldn't interpret the look on his face but, if I had to guess, it wasn't *happy*. I shot him a confused look, tilting my head. "*What's wrong?*" I mouthed.

Immediately, his demeanor shifted and he offered me his signature Liam grin, shaking his head.

Okay then. That was weird.

If you were going to play a drinking game, it was best to start it at the beginning of the night. Not partway through. Rae was learning that the hard way.

We'd pulled two of the semi-circle booths to face each other in the middle of the room with two tables pushed together in the middle. Everyone had crammed in to fit in the space surrounding them with barely any room to move. We were cramped, but I was laughing so hard at Rae's antics that I didn't even worry about having people in my bubble. We were playing some dice game, and every time you rolled the dice you were aiming for the next number up from the last roll. If you didn't get it, you kept rolling until you did. Oh, and did I mention you had to drink for every time you missed?

Rae had to be the worst dice player I had ever seen. It should have been statistically impossible to miss as many times as she had, but it just kept happening.

"Bitttttttchhhh," she cried as I kept laughing when she'd roll again, and miss. Again.

Her irritation with me just made me laugh harder and I could feel the muscles in my face starting to cramp. "Yes, dear?" I called back to her, all sweetness.

"I'm staying at your place tonight. But you're gonna have to kick Remy out of your bed 'cause I am not sleeping on that sad excuse for a couch again," she declared emphatically.

I snorted. "Honey, I couldn't kick his big ass out if I

tried. He's claimed that side of the bed, but you're welcome to climb in with us, it'll be a big party!"

"Now that's the kind of ménage I can get behind!" she yelled as she rolled again. And missed *again*.

I cut my eyes over to where Liam had joined us, at least physically, and found his expression thoughtful. Maybe even a little sad. I kicked off a flip flop and nudged his knee with my toe until he met my gaze. "I think we're going to have to bundle that one up soon and get us home. Otherwise she's definitely going to be puking in someone's car on the way."

He offered me a half-hearted chuckle. "Yeah, I think it may already be too late to escape that." He stood and put two fingers between his lips, letting out a sharp whistle that got everyone's attention. "Okay, folks, it's been fun, but the birthday girl is ready to call it a night, and I for one am tired of being the lone sober asshole in a room full of drunken idiots."

His announcement was met with a chorus of groans, but everyone got up and started scooting furniture back into place and taking their empty glasses to the bar. I chuckled at the fact that, even drunk, these people weren't going to leave themselves a mess to clean up at opening time tomorrow. I didn't blame them.

When I stood to grab my half-full beer and take it to the trash, a hand on my arm stopped me. Golden eyes gave me a reserved smile. "Well, happy birthday then. Thank you for allowing me to stay and celebrate with you."

The heat that had simmered between us from the

first moment we'd met had been dampened. The fire in his eyes…banked.

I wasn't drunk, per se, but I was definitely past the point of being able to decipher that about-face. Hell, I wasn't very good at that when I was completely sober. Definitely not after a few drinks.

"Okay," I whispered. "She's going to be a bit of a handful, but I'm sure we can handle it. Thanks for staying." I looked away momentarily before I met his gaze again. "Will I…will you be back?"

He jerked his head in a nod. Clipped. Distant. "I'll be around, I'm sure."

And then he was gone. My eyes followed his retreating form all the way until he passed through the curtains at the front entrance. I got the feeling something had changed between us in the last little while, but I couldn't put a name to it. I shook off the feeling, deciding that I'd try and puzzle that out tomorrow when my brain wasn't so fuzzy.

Liam and I had our hands full getting my friend into the front seat of the Scout. We'd decided that was the safest bet. At least then if she puked on the way to my place she could just lean out the open doorway. Liam drove, and I climbed into the back, letting my head tip back against the seat when we got on the road. I enjoyed the crispness of the early morning air as it rushed around me. I lifted an arm outside the truck and let my hand surf the air currents, taking an odd sort of joy in that act. It'd been years since I'd felt carefree enough to just…enjoy the feel of the air rushing over and under my cupped hand.

I looked up and caught Liam's gaze in the rearview mirror and, again, his expression was hard to decipher. He was staring at me harder than was probably safe, considering he was driving.

What the hell was up with these men giving me all the confusing looks tonight? I couldn't help but think again about his drunken confession. I returned his stare with a slightly fuzzy one of my own.

Liam pulled into my driveway, and I saw Brennan's headlights pull in right behind us. "You want me to help you get her inside?" he offered.

I looked at Rae who was mostly passed out in the passenger seat. "I think that might be good. I'll set her up on the bathroom floor with a blanket and a trash can. Five star accommodations!"

He chuckled as Rae grumbled something about chicken noodle soup in her sleep.

"Oh, but wait, just stay here for a second. Let me open my front door first before you get out. I don't know how he'll react to a man standing at the door." I started climbing under the roll bar, between the front seats and over Liam's lap. I looked up at him just as I was straddling him and saw he was looking straight up at the night sky with his jaw clenched.

"Shit. Sorry, boss. I didn't think. This is really fucking inappropriate, huh?" I couldn't help the giggle that bubbled up out of my throat, but I hurried to climb the rest of the way over him before hopping down onto my driveway. "Just gimme one minute!" I called as I hurried to the door.

When I opened it, Remy bolted out the door like

he'd heard my truck coming from a mile away. Hell, he probably had. Smart fucking dog.

I waited until he'd done his business and then called him over to the driver's side of the truck. I put my hand on the back of his neck reassuringly. "Remy, meet Liam. He's our friend, okay?"

Liam's eyes were bulged out of his head as he studied the 170-pound Great Dane that had his head in his lap, sniffing his crotch with enthusiasm. Careful not to make any sudden moves he spoke to me out of the side of his mouth. "Remy. *This* is Remy."

I nodded happily, oblivious to his relief. "Yep. He's the best boy, but I've never actually had a man over here since he found me, so I wasn't sure how he'd react."

Liam closed his eyes and appeared to count to ten before he spoke again. "Well, how's that going?" Remy had moved on to sniffing Liam's legs and shoes, so that his head was tucked into the footwell with Liam's feet.

"Well, I'm no expert, but he hasn't eaten you yet, so I'd say it's going pretty well?" I snuck my hand up over my mouth to hide my laughter. "Remy. Off. Let the nice man carry Rae inside so you can check her out."

Immediately Remy backed away from the truck, settling onto his haunches at my side.

"Good boy." I gave him a scratch behind his ears and he rolled his eyes up at me with his mouth parted wide, showing me all his teeth.

Liam kept one eye on Remy and those teeth as he rounded the truck and scooped Rae's unconscious form from the passenger seat. I gestured for him to follow me and Remy stayed right on Liam's heels as he toted her dead weight inside.

I grabbed a couple of blankets and pillows and laid them out on the bathroom floor and Liam gently laid Rae on top of them before straightening up and finally meeting my eyes. "Are you sure you're okay? This might get messy." He gestured at her prone form, curled on her side on my bathroom floor.

"Yeah. I got it. It's not the first time I've had to nurse a drunken friend back to life."

Liam stepped to the side at Remy's urging and the big dog walked all the way around Rae, sniffing her face and looking up at me with a whine. "She's fine, buddy," I reassured him. "Just had a little too much fun tonight."

He let out a *hmph* in his doggy way and flopped down next to her, resting his head on his paws and giving me sad eyes as he looked up at me. "I think that's a good idea. You stay with her. Come get me if she wakes up."

He gave two thumps of his tail and closed his eyes. Rae roused just long enough to grin sleepily and throw an arm over his back. "Dat's mah boy. Come snuggle with Aunty Rae." And then she was out again, snoring softly into Remy's neck.

I looked back at Liam where he still lingered in the door to the bathroom. "See? She'll be fine. We got this."

He chuckled, looking more lighthearted than he had all night. "I can see that." He stepped out of the bathroom, and I followed him to the front door. He turned before he left and handed me my keys.

I grinned up at him, wavering tiredly on my feet.

"Thanks for driving, boss. And for tonight. I had a lot of fun."

"You're welcome, kiddo. Happy birthday," he said softly before he leaned in and pressed a kiss to my forehead. He turned on his heel and climbed into Brennan's car before I could even process what he'd just done.

I stood there for a minute with my fingers pressed to the spot where his lips had touched my forehead.

Man. Tonight was *weird*.

I closed and locked the front door, peeked back into the bathroom long enough to make sure Rae was still sleeping soundly, then climbed into my bed.

I was asleep before my head even hit the pillow, and for the first time in a long time, I didn't have any bad dreams.

31

William

What Happens When You Assume

MIDDAY AT THE CLUB WAS A COMPLETELY DIFFERENT experience compared to what it was like during open hours. The only sounds were the cycling of the air conditioner and the occasional clank of ice as it dumped in the industrial maker behind the bar. The cleaning crew had just finished up so everything smelled lemony-fresh and was ready to go for another night.

Liam and I had opted to meet in his office to discuss my findings so far.

"So, do you know who that guy was?" he asked. "I mean, I haven't seen him since that night he showed up here, but Key seemed to think it was a problem when I texted him his picture."

"Yeah, I know who he is. I'm still trying to get a handle on why he would have been here either of the times you said you guys saw him. He's affiliated with another…" I paused, not knowing how exactly to phrase it. "Well, he works for a different contingent, if you catch my drift. But they don't have a stronghold in this area, so the fact that he was here at all makes me think someone invited him."

Liam's face scrunched up in confusion. "What would be the point of that?"

"Sabotage," I replied. "Or at least, that's my best guess. I've been digging around into your city officials, and while it's not entirely unusual for political parties to have invisible ties to criminal organizations, from what I can tell none of the ones here locally are tied to his particular organization. So, again, no reason for him to be here unless someone invited him."

I had a hunch, but I wasn't sure about it so I was hesitant to bring it up to Liam. That being said, I also needed to know if he had any additional information that might help me get to the bottom of this, even if he didn't *know* he had it.

"Tell me, Liam, what has your impression of Meredith been?"

"You mean, Merebitch?" he snorted.

I raised a brow at him in askance. "Not a fan, then?"

"Look. I know she works for you, but every time I've had an interaction with her it's been vaguely threatening and completely clear she's not a big fan of mine. Also, she's a bit of a cunt, if I'm being honest. Does she have an actual personality hidden somewhere deep, deep inside?"

I chuckled in agreement with him for the most part, though my knowledge of her history made me think there was more to her story than met the eye. "So, do you think she would have any reason to try and burn this deal you made with us? Anything to be gained from that?"

He thought about that for a minute. "It doesn't add up to me, man. Why coordinate the deal and then try and set me up to fail? How does that make any sense?"

I nodded. "That's the question of the hour. Another option is that it was Dearil who was playing both sides. God knows he was a rat bastard, not to mention batshit crazy, so I wouldn't put anything past him."

"So what happened to him? Because that would make sense, since the problems stopped happening around the time you said he retired. And how does that work anyway? I always kinda figured people didn't retire from your…line of work." He swallowed visibly, like maybe he was reconsidering his last question.

I offered him a feral grin. "They don't." But that's all I said.

Apparently, Liam got the hint because he launched off on another string of questions, ignoring the implication. "Okay, so Dearil the Dick is gone, Merebitch remains. Things have been quiet here since December. What is it exactly that you're trying to get to the bottom of?"

"The man in the photo you sent to Key. Like I said, he's affiliated with another group. But he's utterly unhinged. Quite literally a killing machine. The grunt work he was doing here isn't really his preferred skillset. And I've never heard of a case of him starting a job and then just dropping off the face of the earth with-out...completing it. If you get me."

Liam's eyes bulged. "So...what? You think he's still around here somewhere waiting and watching? What the fuck, William!?"

I stared over his head for a few moments, thinking, before I answered him. "My theory is that this is an inside job. I think one of my people is staging a coup, and they're using the deal with you to do it. I think the pause in activity for the last few months is because of the change in our leadership. When I took over as head of the Organization, there were a lot of changes made in a very short period of time. So, my guess is, whoever was behind it is either *retired* or is biding their time to renew their efforts when I'm not paying so much atten-tion to the daily operations."

Liam was nodding, but still looked worried. Under-standably so.

I continued. "My purpose for being here is two-fold. If I catch a glimpse of that psycho lurking around here, I'll be happy to send him back to the hell from whence he came. But I'm also hoping that my absence from New York will lead whoever is behind this to make another move. Tip their hand, if you will."

"So...you're using me, and my club, as bait? What about Astrid? She saw him with her own eyes when he broke in here to steal one of my files. He stole her journal out of her backpack that night. Do you think *she's* in any danger?"

I wondered why the dancer would have been in his

office that night and a pang of jealousy shot through me. Did they have a thing going on?

"Do your dancers often have cause to be in your office, Liam?"

He shot me a quizzical look. "Dancers? No, why?" He looked offended. "I'm not that guy, I don't fuck around with my employees, if that's what you're asking." His eyes shifted away from mine momentarily.

I was the one confused at that point. "You said Astrid was in your office that night. She's the Hatter, right?"

Liam stared at me blankly for a moment before a lightbulb went off behind his eyes. "Oh, man. Noooo. Astrid is my office manager. She doesn't dance. But she does bear a striking resemblance to Talia, who *is* the dancer that portrays the Hatter when we have Wonderland nights."

I blinked at him, trying to think back, but I didn't remember ever seeing another tall brunette wandering around the club. "But wait…where was Talia at Astrid's birthday party then?"

Liam shrugged. "She never sticks around once her shows are done. She's got a little girl at home so she leaves as soon as she's done so she can relieve the babysitter. I'd love it if she could stay and mingle with the crowd a little after her shows, but I've never pressed it. She's got more important shit going on at home. And she's such a phenomenal dancer that it's totally worth it for me. She draws a huge crowd."

Things were clicking into place in my brain, one by

one. I still had questions, but, in light of what her friend had said the other night about her man at home, I guessed it really was none of my business to ask. I wondered why she'd told me she was single, though. That stung. I fucking *hated* being lied to.

I was waiting in my new favorite spot in the club when Astrid made her appearance that night, sauntering in without a care in the world to greet Rae behind the bar. She leaned over and planted a kiss on her friend's forehead and patted her on the head, resulting in a ferocious growl from the tiny blonde, before she turned and spotted me where I sat.

She tilted her head at me, a mirror of the night we'd met, but this time she looked hesitant.

I used my foot to slide the other chair out in invitation, and she crossed the room to join me, sliding into the chair without any of the sultry energy she'd displayed that first night.

I studied her tight jaw, the confusion that shone from her eyes. I tried to tamp down my fury. In fact, I'd told myself multiple times throughout the day that there was no point in confronting her about her lie, but there we were.

"Astrid," I said in a low voice. I suppose I should introduce myself to her before I went any further. "I'm William."

She smiled, despite her obvious confusion, offering

her hand to me. "William. It's nice to meet you, officially." Her voice threaded through my subconscious, trying to burrow into my brain and make me forget how mad I was.

I briefly clasped her hand, but released it almost as soon as I did. Not wanting the soft feel of her hand in mine to sway me. "I have a bone to pick with you."

She hung her head, shaking it, before looking back up at me. "Yeah, I guess you do. I'm so fucking sorry, I panicked! I didn't know if Liam would get mad if I... fraternized? I don't know if that's even the word I mean, but you catch my drift. I just panicked and took off before he could fire me for trying to leave in the middle of my shift to go back to your hotel with you. I'm so sorry about that."

I frowned at her. "Well, that part is understandable. No harm, no foul. But that's not what I'm talking about."

Her expression turned confused again. "Okayyyy... then what?"

"You told me you weren't involved with anyone. You lied to me. And I do not like being lied to, Astrid." I leaned back in my chair and crossed my arms over my chest, feeling better already about having gotten that off my chest.

She was now gaping at me in utter confusion. "But... I didn't lie. I'm *not* involved with anyone." Her spine straightened as she spoke, her voice gaining volume.

I glanced around to see if anyone else was paying attention to this exchange and met Rae's eyes over

Astrid's shoulder. She'd narrowed them and was giving me a vaguely threatening look. It might have even been intimidating if she weren't pocket-sized.

I returned my gaze to Astrid. "The other night, that one"—I jerked my head behind her, indicating her friend—"asked about your bedmate. I'd say if someone is sleeping in your bed often enough that they've claimed their own side, then that's pretty fucking involved."

I watched her face shift from confusion, to irritation, to utter hysteria in the span of time it took me to really settle into my sanctimony. One beat. Two beats.

Astrid burst out laughing, making no attempt to keep it quiet. She laughed so long and loud that tears began pouring down her face.

I leaned forward and hissed at her. "How the fuck is that funny?"

She just shook her head, still laughing too hard to form words, but she pulled her phone out of her back pocket and unlocked it. Swiping a few times before she found what she was looking for and turned the screen to face me.

I looked down at the picture she was showing me and frowned. And then realization began to dawn on me. I felt my face flush. Fucken hell.

I looked back up at her as she sat with her lip trapped between her bottom teeth, trying to curb her hilarity.

I hung my head, uttering in a low voice. "The bed partner, I presume?"

I could feel the table shaking from the convulsions

Astrid was having, trying to regain her composure. "William." She giggled. "Meet Remy. The best boy in all the land."

Well, *fuck*. Clearly, I was an idiot. I wondered how much groveling this would require.

32

Astrid

Twenty Questions

IT TOOK DAYS BEFORE I COULD LOOK AT WILLIAM WITHOUT laughing. He'd been jealous. Of my dog.

"Stop laughing. It was an honest mistake," he grumbled where he sat at what I now referred to as "his" table. He had a laptop in front of him and was apparently working, but I had no idea what it was that he actually did for a living, so I couldn't be sure.

I was taking a break from the liquor order, which meant I was sipping another vodka tonic—hold the vodka—and watching him type. It was pathetic, but I couldn't help it. "So, you're not from around here."

He smirked without looking up from his laptop. "I believe we established that already."

"But you've been here nearly every night for the past two weeks." I raised my brow, hoping he'd give me something.

"Aye." Another smirk. More typing.

"Does your wife mind you being away for so long?"

That one earned me a glower, but at least he looked up from his laptop to do it. "You know there's no wife. We already cleared up any confusion on that topic."

I tapped a finger against my lips, deep in thought. "Fair. I retract my last question, Your Honor."

"Am I on trial, Astrid?" He was smiling again, but a line of tension had appeared in his jaw that hadn't been there a moment ago.

"Just trying to gain a greater understanding." I shrugged.

"Why don't you just ask me what it is you want to know, and if I can answer, I will." He met my playful gaze with a slightly guarded one of his own.

"Okay then. Why are you here in Redding? And is there a reason you're here, in this particular club, night after night? I mean, I'll admit the shows are amazing and the bartenders are top notch, but I've never once seen you go into one of the back rooms. So I just kinda wondered what keeps bringing you back here?"

He blinked at me and then shook his head. "I can answer part of that, but not all. I'm here, in Redding, because of my work. And I'm here, in this particular club night after night, because I'm quite enamored with one of its employees, and I find that I want to take every opportunity to spend time with them while I can."

I felt a flutter in my belly at that, but I couldn't resist the urge to tease him. "It's Liam, isn't it? He's so dreamy." I fluttered my eyelashes at him and let out a little sigh.

He snorted at my antics. "Yeah. You caught me. There's just something about him."

I cackled. "No judgment! Love is love, William."

He rolled his eyes at me. "While I agree with you on that point, you've certainly not missed the fact that my eyes follow you everywhere you go. It's not Liam I'm here to see, love, at least not in that way." His gaze turned intense in a heartbeat, and I felt my pulse jump in response.

"I may have noticed a time or two. But wait, what do you mean by *at least not in that way*?"

"That's the part I can't answer, love."

I shook my head adamantly, and he looked confused. "You should stop calling me that."

It was like his face went entirely blank from one second to the next and formal William had returned. "My apologies, Astrid."

"No, no, no…I didn't mean it like that!" I was quick to explain.

"Oh? Then what *did* you mean?"

"I just meant, if you're going to give me a pet name, it should probably be something fierce. Something with *teeth*." I bared mine at him, showing him my most ferocious expression.

He tossed his head back, a bark of laughter escaping him. "Something with teeth, you say? Hmm." He leaned forward until his face was just inches from my own, studying me closely. "From this angle, you look a bit like a demon. Your pupils have dilated until there's just the barest ring of dark blue around the edges. And your skin is glowing in this light, almost as if you were from another world."

Thud, thud went my pulse in my ears.

"A demon, huh?" My voice was barely a whisper.

"Mm-hmm." He nodded, so close now that our noses brushed together when he did. "Perhaps a succubus. Here to trap me forever with your wiles."

"Yep. My wiles. Very trappy."

He chuckled. "Yes, I think that's it. You're a demon. With *lots* of sharp teeth. I could never hope to escape."

"Why would you want to?" I asked.

He closed his eyes for a moment, drawing away from me. "Ah, lass, one day I'll have to. But I won't want to."

A throat cleared behind me and I jumped, snatched out of the spell that William had woven around us with his words. The honeyed tone of his voice. The tinge of an accent that I couldn't quite place.

When I turned, Liam stood behind me, glaring at William, his hands drawn into fists, jaw clenched as he addressed him. "Can we talk?"

William slowly raised his eyes to meet Liam's angry glare, one eyebrow hitched up in annoyance. "Can it wait?"

Liam snorted, looking up at the ceiling for a moment before he answered. "I don't think it can. *Sir.*"

My eyes were bouncing back and forth between them and I couldn't shake the idea that whatever it was they needed to talk about was *me.*

Without waiting for William's response, Liam turned

on his heel and headed toward this office, leaving a wake of startled customers and employees in his wake.

William sighed and stood. "I'll see you later. Let me go see what our friend is in a tizzy about."

I gulped. "That looked like a little more than a tizzy. And why did he call you *sir*?"

He just shook his head and walked away without answering.

I stared after him, annoyed. Once again, being kept in the dark. I was getting sick and fucking tired of always being in the dark.

Liam

Shenanigans

TWELVE STEPS TOWARD THE COUCH. TEN STEPS TO THE windows. Another ten back toward my desk. Twelve steps back to the couch. Repeat.

William walked into my office and shut the door behind him, leaning back against it with his arms crossed over his chest.

I stopped my pacing to round on him. "Astrid is off limits."

There went that fucking eyebrow again. I hadn't known him long but I was starting to recognize that was a sign that I should tread carefully. "Is that so? And why is that, Liam? Is it because you want her for yourself? Because I've seen the way you look at her when you think no one will notice. I've seen the way your eyes track her movements like a lost puppy hoping for a moment of her attention."

I huffed, shaking my head. "That's not it. I would never cross that line. Astrid is my employee. I don't date my employees."

"Yes. You've mentioned that more than once. Vehemently, I might add, but I didn't ask if you wanted to *date* her, Liam. I asked if you *wanted* her. One is something that teenage boys hope for when they're lying in bed at night thinking about the pretty girl in their history class. The other is something distinctly different."

I felt my fists clenching and unclenching, and for a moment I really thought about just fucking clocking him in his ridiculous face. Thankfully, self-preservation put a stop to the urge before I could carry through with it.

"Astrid is a beautiful, charming, funny, and smart young woman. I'd have to be blind not to see her worth."

He grinned at me but it was all teeth. "Still didn't answer my question, Liam."

I pulled out the only card I could think to pull, even if it was another deflection. "She's too fucking young for me! And, rest assured, if she's too young for *me*, then she's *definitely* too goddamn young for *you*."

He straightened against the door and took a step toward me. "So, she's daft then? Not in control of her faculties? Incapable of knowing who she does, or does not, want to spend her time with? Is that what you're saying, Liam? Because if that's the case you should have said so sooner. I'd never want to take advantage of a woman who has no control of her own choices. That's utterly horrifying."

With every question he uttered, he stepped closer to me until, by the end of his little speech, his face was just inches away from mine. Close enough for me to see the steel glinting in his eyes and to hear the grinding of his molars.

I just stared at him, feeling my stomach sink; she might never forgive me for what I was about to do, but knowing it was the right thing, regardless. "She's only twenty."

He took a step back abruptly and I could tell that information had thrown him for a loop. Good.

He turned and paced away from me for a few steps before he spun back around, shooting me a glare. "It's still her decision."

"And when she finds out who you are? Will it still be her decision then, William? Or will it be too late then? Will she be able to walk away from you safely?"

And that's when his shoulders slumped in defeat. "I'd never harm her."

"Maybe *you* wouldn't, but what about your associates? What if someone tried to use her to get to you? Did you ever think of that? Being with you is not *safe* for her. Can't you see that?"

His eyes flashed at that, but he offered me a barely perceptible nod, reaching for the door. He stopped before he opened it and tossed one more statement over his shoulder. "I'll take your words under advisement. But take note of this, Liam, because I'll not say it again. You are in no position to dictate anything to me. Going forward, you will watch your tone. My bad side is not one you wish to become acquainted with."

I just glared at his back, too angry to say anything more.

The click of the door closing may as well have been a slam.

"Way to fucking go, Liam. Now he has even less reason not to kill you and dump your body in the river."

34

Astrid

Bad Mojo

WHEN WILLIAM CAME BACK FROM HIS CHAT WITH LIAM HE gave me a half-hearted excuse about needing to go and packed up his laptop. I watched him walk out before I turned to give Rae *wtf* eyes. She shrugged and jerked her chin in the direction of the back hallway. I turned to see Liam coming out of the office, stomping his way through the club until he, too, disappeared through the curtains.

I gritted my teeth. I wasn't one to assume that everything was about me, but this whole situation was setting off all of those warning bells in my gut. I threw up my hands and gestured to the back, letting Rae know I was heading out. I'd finish the damn liquor order tomorrow. I needed to get out of there before I screamed and scared away all the clientele.

When I got home Remy greeted me eagerly at the door, and I let him out to do his business while I leaned in the doorway, staring up at the moon. It was one of those spooky ones with the clouds moving past it at what looked like hundreds of miles per hour. It reminded me of the moon on the night I'd met Remy.

I hoped it wasn't a portent of the night to come.

When he loped happily back inside, I shut and locked the door then led him down the hallway to my bedroom. I quickly stripped out of the clothes I'd worn to work and threw on an old t-shirt over my panties. I climbed into my bed and immediately felt the whole thing shake and dip as Remy hopped up on the other side. He sidled over on the bed until he was lying up against my side with his big head resting on my chest.

"You are the only man in my life that isn't fucking confusing, buddy." I rubbed one of his ears between my thumb and forefinger, loving the velvety texture of the fur there.

He thumped his tail against the bed a couple of times. I liked to believe that was his way of telling me that men were dumb and dogs were far superior anyway.

I curled onto my side facing him and he fitted his giant form into mine, somehow making himself the little spoon in spite of his size.

"G'nite, Remy. *I love you.*" I felt a tear of frustration squeeze out between my closed eyelids but I was asleep before I could wipe it away.

I woke to Remy nudging my face and whining. When I opened my eyes I realized my face was damp and the covers were tangled around my legs like I'd been thrashing in my sleep.

I sat up and blinked, trying to shake off the lingering effects of the dream. I offered him a pat against his side. "I'm okay. Just a bad dream, I guess."

I looked at the clock and realized it was already after ten in the morning. I couldn't believe I'd slept that long.

"Hey, Rem, how about we go take another hike? I could stand to burn off some of this bad mojo."

He hopped off the bed and ran to the door like he knew exactly what I'd just said.

I laughed. "Okay, okay, but I'll need some clothes first."

I started a pot of coffee and let it brew while I got dressed. By the time it beeped I was standing in front of it waiting impatiently. I needed the caffeine like I needed oxygen to get my brain going.

We took off down the highway toward Whiskeytown. The park had some good hiking trails and it was close enough that we could have a good few hours to hike and still get back into town in time for me to get ready for work.

By the time we pulled into the parking lot, Remy was dancing in the back of the truck, letting out high-pitched whines and wagging his tail so hard he was making the roll bar ring like a bell every time it struck.

"Okay, buddy, okay. Calm down, let me get your

leash and we'll go, go, go!" I climbed out and pulled his leash from the floorboard behind my seat, clicking it onto his collar before I lowered the tailgate so he could jump down. I grabbed my backpack that had some snacks and bottles of water in it and strapped it over my shoulders before turning toward one of the trailheads. "Okay, let's go!"

It was a perfect May day. Not too hot, especially in the shade of the huge trees that lined the trail, and we made good time headed toward the first vista on the trail. Remy bounded and jumped around me once I let him off his leash. It was the middle of the week, so I wasn't expecting to run into too many other hikers. I'd apologize for the fright if I did, but I knew Remy would come right to me if I called and he had way too much energy for me to make him stay on his leash the whole time.

About an hour into our hike he'd run up ahead of me around a bend, so I couldn't see him. I sped up, worried what might happen if he got out of my sight and encountered another hiker. I didn't want anyone shooting my dog because they thought he was a stray.

Around the next curve I found him, standing stock still in the middle of the trail. His hackles raised all along his back and his head dropped down. A low growl was emanating from his throat. I stepped closer to him, frantically looking around for whatever had him so riled up, but I couldn't see anything in the woods around us.

I stepped up beside him and rested my hand on the

top of his head, carefully stroking him down to his neck. "Hey, buddy," I whispered. "What is it?"

His tail gave one wag and he cut his eyes up to me briefly before he resumed his stare into the woods off the side of the trail.

I didn't try to call him off whatever it was. To be honest, I wasn't sure I could if I wanted to, but we sort of had a deal. I wasn't his master, I was his friend, so I didn't do a lot of issuing orders. He obviously knew more about survival than I did, so if his instincts were telling him there was danger there, I was going to listen.

Eventually, the ridge of fur on his back began to lower and I could feel the tension in his neck starting to release. "We okay now, Rem?" I asked quietly, still not over the panic I'd felt when I found him like that.

He hadn't stopped staring off into the same patch of trees, but he wasn't bolting over there to check either, so I wasn't sure what to make of that. Either it wasn't something truly terrifying hiding over there, or he refused to leave me unprotected to go investigate.

Whatever it was, I decided we'd better call it a day. I squatted down next to him and put my face level with his, drawing his attention for a moment. "Let's head back, okay, buddy? No need tangling with a bear today if we don't have to."

I clipped his lead back onto his collar quietly and turned back the way we'd come. Tugging gently until he followed along, eventually coming back to walk next to me with his big head on a swivel, eyes alert.

I was on high alert, but I knew better than to run if it was a bear. Our best bet was to calmly walk back out of the woods and hope Remy was big enough that nothing wanted to fuck with him.

Just before we got to my truck, still parked where I'd left it in the lot, I got the strangest sensation of eyes on me. The back of my neck burned and the baby hairs there stood on end. I whipped my head over my shoulder, but couldn't see anyone behind me. Remy's attention followed in the same direction and he let out another low growl, baring his teeth.

"Okay, well, that's enough bullshit for me today. Come on, Rem, let's get the fuck out of here." I hurried to the tailgate of the truck and lowered it, urging him to jump in and slamming it closed as soon as he was inside. I was so freaked out that I climbed over the tailgate and hopped over the back seat and into the driver's seat that way, instead of walking around. Did you ever see that movie about a guy lying under women's vehicles slicing their Achilles tendons when they went to get in their cars? No fucking thank you.

I was still a little shaken when Remy and I got back to my house. Enough that I called Rae, just to hear a friendly voice.

"What's up, babe?" I could hear glasses clinking in the background.

"Oh! Shit, are you already at work?" I looked at the clock but it was still pretty early.

"Eh, nothing better to do and I needed to do inventory anyway, so here I am!"

"Ah, okay then. Well, no big deal, get back to your inventory." I kicked off my tennis shoes and started toward the shower.

"Wait!" Rae called. "What's wrong? Your voice sounds weird."

"It's probably nothing. Really. I'll tell you about it tonight. I'm going to hop in the shower."

"Astrid, seriously. What's wrong? You know my mind is going to run wild with the possibilities if you don't just go ahead and spill it."

"Well, me and Rem went to Whiskeytown for a hike today. It's a pretty day and I needed to blow off some steam, ya know?" I put her on speakerphone and started peeling off my sweaty tank top and shorts. "We were about three miles in when we rounded a bend in the trail and Rem alerted that something was big wrong. Like…I've never seen him act like that, Rae. He was growling and glaring into the trees like he was Cujo. I figured it was just a bear. I mean…right? So I coaxed him to turn around and we headed back out to the trail-head. Nice and slow, no panic. And it was all quiet until we got almost to my truck and, girl, I swear I could feel someone's eyes on me. It made my skin crawl. But there was no one else there. My car was the only one in the parking lot. So I loaded Remy up as fast as I could and climbed over him to get to my seat and we hightailed it out of there. But it just gave me the heebie-jeebies. Like…for real."

I heard a scuffle on Rae's end of the line and then her exasperated voice returned. "Someone would like to talk to you."

William's voice came over the line and I could tell it had been switched off of speaker. "Demon, tell me exactly what you saw. Did you check your truck before you got in it to make sure no one had tampered with it? Where are you now?"

"Wait a minute, caveman, slow down. One question at a time. No, I didn't see anything, I just explained that. It was just a feeling I got. No, I didn't check my truck for tampering? What the fuck, William? I'm not fucking Jason Bourne. And I'm at home. I'm sweaty and smelly and I need a shower."

He huffed on the other end of the line. "Were you followed?"

"William, you're acting like a psycho right now so I'm going to let you go, but I will see you tonight at the club. Thank you for your concern." I hung up the phone and turned the shower on to the hottest setting, climbing in as soon as the steam started to billow out the top.

Why were men so fucking *weird*?

I dried off then wiped the towel over the mirror in the bathroom before I grabbed my robe off the back of the door, wrapping it around my still damp body. I turned back to the mirror and studied my reflection in the circle I'd cleared of steam. My eyes were still a little wild and my pulse was still jumping in my neck, but I felt better after the shower.

I could hear Remy whining outside the bathroom

door and when I opened it he flew in and sniffed every corner of the room like he was checking to make sure I hadn't been attacked while I was in there. "Hey, hey. Rem. I'm okay, see?" I knelt down and he came to me, sniffing my neck and snuffling into my ear in relief. "Sorry, buddy, I shouldn't have locked you out. I wasn't thinking." He plopped onto his haunches and lifted a paw at me. "I won't do it again, I promise. I didn't mean to worry you. Come on, I need to get dressed for work."

Just as I stepped into my bedroom I heard the doorbell, and Remy abandoned me to dart toward the front door, skidding on the tile floor as he went. The bell rang again, and he let out a loud bark in warning.

My pulse skyrocketed again before I could even reason out the fact that whatever had been out there in the woods with us was definitely not going to politely ring my doorbell.

"Remy, down. It's probably just a delivery guy." I stepped up to the peephole and looked out before I opened the door, expecting to see a package lying on the stoop. What I didn't expect to see was William, one big golden eye glaring at me from the other side of the peephole.

"Demon. You hung up on me." His growl was muffled through the door.

I felt my eyes widen and looked down at my barely covered body. *Shit.*

"Umm...*lo siento, no hablo inglés!*"

"Very. Funny." He thumped on the door. "Open up. I need to see that you're okay, and then if you're lucky, maybe I'll decide not to turn you over my knee for that stunt."

I considered his threat for a minute before I called back through the door. "What exactly would I have to do for you to carry through on that threat?"

I snickered. I couldn't resist fucking with him.

"Demon." The growl was back. "Open. This. Goddamn. Door. Right. Now. I'll kick it down, I swear. Don't test me."

"Okay, okay, don't get your panties in a twist, sir." I slid the chain off the door and cracked it open a couple of inches, keeping my body behind it as much as possible.

The look on his face was gratifying, I had to admit. I could see the worry there as plain as day.

"See? I'm just fine. Not a scratch on me." I grinned at him through the gap.

He took a deep breath, holding it for a moment before he let it back out. "Let me come in."

"I'm not dressed, sir, it wouldn't be proper!" I blinked at him innocently.

"Astrid, you have two seconds to step back from the door before I come through it and then, rest assured, I *will* turn you over my knee for this sass you keep giving me."

A low growl from behind me told me that my friend didn't take too kindly to William's tone. "You might wanna reconsider that, given present company. I don't think he likes you very much and you haven't even made it through the door yet."

William paled a little, clearly just remembering the

picture I'd shown him of Remy. He cleared his throat. "Apologies. I'm very concerned about your well-being. May I come in and reassure myself that you are of sound mind and body so I can finally take a deep breath for the first time in the last hour?"

I turned and looked at Remy where he sat just behind me. "What do you think, buddy? Give him the benefit of the doubt before you eat him?"

He flopped down on his belly in the entryway but kept his eyes glued to me. "Okay, got it. You'll be watching."

I swung the door wider, keeping myself behind it while William stepped through. When he was inside, I pushed the door shut and crossed my arms over my chest, watching as he scanned me from head to foot.

"I was worried," he stated.

"Clearly." I raised a brow.

"You hung up on me," he complained.

"Technically, I hung up on Rae. I don't even have your phone number. It'd be impossible for me to hang up on you."

He took a step closer but Remy issued a low growl that had him pausing. "Are you okay?" he asked in a softer tone.

I nodded. "It scared me, but it was probably just a bear or something. Not all that unheard of. Maybe even a cougar."

"You didn't see anyone?"

"Nope. Just that weird feeling that I was being watched. Then I panicked like a little kid and the floor was lava. I climbed over poor Remy to get into the driver's seat and we never looked back. But, as you can see, I'm perfectly fine."

His expression changed when I gestured at my body, taking a more leisurely look now that he knew I was safe.

"I do need to go get ready for work, though. I'm going to be late if I don't hurry." I stepped away from him, remembering how distant he'd been the night before. "You and Remy can hang out and get to know one another. I'm sure you'll be best friends by the time I come back." I smirked at him and darted into my bedroom, shutting the door and blocking my view of his stunned expression.

I giggled as I headed to my closet when I heard him talking softly in a cajoling tone. *"Nice doggy, you don't wanna eat me, right?"*

I came out of my bedroom, dressed and ready for work, and discovered William perched uncomfortably in the furthest corner of the couch. Remy was laid out across the rest of it just gazing up at him like he hadn't taken his eyes off of him for a moment while I'd been out of the room.

When I came into view William looked up at me with a relieved expression. "I don't think he likes me."

I snickered. "Well, you did threaten to turn me over your knee. He takes my safety and well-being very seriously, so maybe he just took offense at that."

He rolled his eyes at me before he slowly got to his

feet, not making any sudden moves. Remy issued a low, only vaguely threatening growl, at the action.

I leaned down to his eye level and pressed a kiss right between his eyes. "I gotta go to work, buddy. I'll see you later, 'kay?"

He offered me his customary tail thumps and returned his head to rest on his paws. Ah, the life of a dog.

I turned to see where William had wandered off to, and he was standing stock still in front of my bookshelf, studying the pictures I had displayed there.

"Ready to go?" I called, dragging his attention away from the trip down my memory lane.

He nodded stiffly, shoving his hands into his pants pockets and following me to the door.

"I'll see you at the club," he offered in a clipped voice, and once again I was left wondering what the fuck happened. This man was like a swinging pendulum of moods. Damned if I could keep up.

I just shook my head, locking the door behind me and walking toward my truck. "Okay, weirdo. See you there."

35

Meredith

That Wasn't Part of the Plan

"STATUS REPORT." I TAPPED THE PEN IN MY HAND impatiently against the surface of my desk. I'd been trapped at this fucking desk for the past four months, doing grunt work that a monkey could perform without any effort. And now, with William away, I finally had a chance to follow up with my contact without chancing discovery.

"I was beginning to wonder if you'd cancelled our contract without letting me know." His tone was dripping with sarcasm.

"I've been living under a microscope. Does that mean you've ceased your efforts?" I paused in my frenetic tapping, waiting for his response.

An evil chuckle travelled thousands of miles across the phone line in an instant. "Now, you know me better than that."

I felt my face split into a satisfied grin. "Indeed, I do. So tell me what you've found."

"I've been following the girl. You didn't tell me she had a guard dog, though."

"Girl? What fucking girl? What the hell are you talking about?" I switched to an incognito tab on my laptop, pulling up the file I'd stored in the cloud.

"You told me to gather everything I could that would be of use against your boss. Or did I misunderstand that?" His annoyance was evident.

"No, you didn't misunderstand, but I fail to see how those two things are connected."

"It seems he's taken quite an interest in this particular girl. I took it upon myself to get a closer look. I think she may be just what you're looking for, so I've been watching her. She was there the night I pulled the file from Liam's office. And I got a little something else while I was there, which you would know if you hadn't gone radio silent." He was chastising me right now?

"What else then? I didn't ask for your attitude."

"Her journal. I grabbed it on the chance that it had something to do with the club, which it didn't, but it's been a font of information nonetheless. She's quite the troubled one, it seems. I like it."

I shook my head, failing to see how exploiting a troubled woman was going to accomplish my ultimate goal of discrediting William and proving he was unfit to be the head of the Organization.

"I didn't hire you to stalk women, you psychopath. Don't confuse your hobbies with what I asked you to do. I hired you to tank the deal with Liam and find a way to prove that William is unfit. What would make you think I'd condone you harassing an innocent woman?"

"The locals aren't interested in a partnership with me, they have their own, and your boss is seldom seen doing anything but coming and going from the club. If you want me to draw him out and prove he's not the man for the job, I'm telling you this girl is the way to do that. But, hey, maybe you're not as committed to your original goal as you indicated. You can pay me off right now and we'll dissolve our deal."

I could hear something that sounded like anticipation in his voice when he said that.

"And if I did that, would you leave the girl alone?" I already knew the answer to that.

"I don't think I will. I find her quite intriguing. But your hands would be washed of it. I might even send you a thank-you gift. I think I'd enjoy spending some time in her company if I could get her away from that hellhound she calls a pet."

The anticipation in his voice sent a chill down my spine.

I'd started this fucking vendetta before William had taken over, when Dearil was steadily doing everything in his power to drive the organization further into the mouth of madness with each passing day.

Once William took over, I had no reason to assume he'd be any different and, ultimately, my goal remained the same. I was the one who had sacrificed everything for the Organization. It was *my* life that had been inexorably changed during my last mission.

Every moment since then had been a fight to be seen as more than someone to pity. I was still a goddamn force to be reckoned with, and I was the one who deserved to sit at the helm, not a man that was merely there by virtue of his parentage. *Reluctantly,* if I'd read him correctly.

"Fine. Keep watching her then, but don't take any further action or I'll consider it a breach of contract, do you hear me? Don't think for a moment that I won't terminate our contract if you go against my wishes. I don't think you want that."

"We'll see. She might be worth it." And then he was gone, dead air the only thing coming through the line.

"Fucking *dammit!*" I quickly packed up my things and headed toward the elevator that would take me to the garage deep in the bowels of the Organization's headquarters.

I was dialing again as the doors slid closed behind me. "I'm on my way home, but we need to take a trip. Can you start packing me a bag?"

36

Astrid

You Should Have Told Me

AS SOON AS I WALKED THROUGH THE EMPLOYEE ENTRANCE, Liam pounced. "Are you okay? What the hell happened? Are you hurt? What the fuck were you thinking, going hiking alone?" His rapid-fire questions had me backing up, throwing up a hand to stop him.

"Whoa there, Lassie. Timmy isn't down the well, why don't you calm down?"

He stopped short. "What? What the fuck are you talking about?"

"What the fuck are *you* talking about? I'm fine, as you can obviously see. Why were you waiting here in front of the door ready to pounce like you're my keeper?" I glared at him.

William joined us in the employee hallway, studying Liam and I as we squared off. "I think, perhaps, it's time we all had a chat."

His voice still sounded clipped like it had before we'd left my house, and I threw up my hands in frustration. "Yes, let's all go have a chat. Maybe for once in my fucking life everyone could stop tip-toeing around me and actually tell me why you're all in such a fucking tizzy about me going for a goddamn hike in the middle of the day!"

Liam hung his head, taking in a few deep calming breaths before he looked back up and met my gaze. "Fine." His tone was petulant.

"Very mature, Liam." I rolled my eyes and turned on my heel in the direction of the office, ready for them to finally tell me what the fuck was going on.

When the three of us were behind the closed office door, I rounded on them both, hands on my hips. "Spill. And, for the love of all that's holy, if either of you hold anything back I will know. I don't know *how* I'll know, but I will and I promise you both that there will be hell to pay."

Liam looked at William, obviously waiting for him to start, but the man in question was just staring at me with an inscrutable expression on his face.

"Anything you'd like to share with the class?" I snarked at him impatiently.

"Why don't you have a seat? We have a lot to talk about." He then turned his back to us and reached into his pocket, pulling out his phone.

"Jared." He paused. "Yes. Somewhere in the vicinity. Stay alert." Another pause. "Okay. Let me know if you see anything suspect."

I hadn't budged from my spot in the middle of the

room, declining his offer to sit until I had a better idea of what bomb they were going to drop on me. When William returned his phone to his pocket, he sighed when he noted I remained standing.

"Demon, for the love of fuck, I'm going to tell you everything, but I cannot do it with you standing there glaring at me. This is going to be a lot to take in. Just sit the hell down, and I promise, if you want to walk out of this room without looking back once I'm done, no one will stop you." He issued a warning look at Liam when the other man scoffed at that.

I rolled my eyes but reluctantly took a spot in the corner of the couch, glaring at him expectantly until he started talking.

He led with a question for me. "Do you know anything about your boss's investor?"

I considered lying for a moment, not knowing if confessing that I did, in fact, know about Liam's affiliation with the criminal organization would somehow get him into trouble, but if I expected them to be honest then I had to return the favor. "Enough."

He nodded, like he'd expected that, though he did shoot Liam an annoyed glance. "Well, I am who you would refer to, I suppose, as the man in charge of that organization."

He waited a moment for me to process that information. I studied him with my eyes narrowed before I leaned back into the cushion behind me and crossed my arms. "That tracks. I hadn't guessed it, but I should have. Go on."

It was his turn to roll his eyes at me. "Someone

within my organization has gone to some lengths to sabotage either this deal with Liam, or my authority. Or both, as the case may be. They've involved an outsider that has a fucking savage reputation but an excellent track record for completing his assignments to their fullest."

"You're talking in code, William, and while I'm not a stupid woman, I would appreciate if just this once, you could stop being so fucking enigmatic and spell it out for me." I gave myself a mental high-five for that little speech.

"In the simplest of terms, what that means, Astrid, is that someone is attempting to unseat me as the head of the Organization and they're using a goddamn psychopath as their pawn to achieve their ends. Liam and I have reason to believe he may turn to you as a target, because he knows you have seen his face. He may also have deduced that my interest in you is sufficient to warrant using you as leverage against me. Either that, or he's just taken an interest in you because he's fucking crazy and can't be trusted to stay on his leash."

I'd heard what he'd said. Every word. But it took a moment for that last part to really sink into my subconscious. "Wait…when did I see his face?"

Liam cleared his throat and issued me an apologetic look. "Because you caught him the night he broke into this office to go through my files."

My eyes widened, realization dawning. "Wait a minute. So you're telling me that the psychopath that you're worried may be coming after me in order to get to him"—I gestured at William—"is the same guy I saw in here that night? The one who stole my fucking journal?"

Liam nodded solemnly. "I'm so fucking sorry, Astrid. This is all my fault. If I'd never seen you at that concert with Imogen, none of this would be happening." He let his head fall into his hands, shoulders slumped.

"Okay, one more time for the rest of the class, Liam. What the fuck does the fact that you saw me with Imogen have to do with any of this?"

I was fuming. I was pretty sure I could feel actual smoke coming out of my nostrils, making William's nickname even more apropos.

"Insurance, Liam? What in the actual flying fuck were you thinking? What is wrong with you? And why in hell would you think it would matter to anyone if I have ties to Imogen! It's not like she holds any sway with his...employees! Again, I waved a hand in William's direction.

William interjected from where he'd taken up a spot leaned against the back of the office door. "Ah, well, actually..."

I snapped my eyes in his direction, narrowing them. "Actually...*what*?"

"Well, your friend is..." He paused before offering me an apologetic look. "She's inextricably tied to the organization, whether she likes it or not. And, as it happens, I owe her quite a substantial debt of honor, so

Liam wasn't far off the mark in thinking your association with her might offer him some indemnity, should this deal have gone south."

"Imogen is…what? How? Goddammit, William, stop talking in fucking circles for once!" I rubbed my hands over my face, frustrated at the way they were doling this information out like it was medicine.

"Imogen's father was a member of the Organization. As is her current beau, Key. A few months ago, there was an event—and no, I cannot tell you more about that —that drew Imogen into the fold in a very permanent way. She's one of us now, whether she sees it that way or not, and your tie to her does grant you, and anyone you're associated with, a very large amount of immunity."

I plopped down onto the couch. Shock had suddenly and completely turned my legs into jelly. All I could do for a moment was stare straight ahead as my brain began tying things together, one event at a time. By the time I got to the phone call I'd received from Imogen just after Christmas, my throat was beginning to close up. "Hank," I whispered, looking up at William. "That's what happened to Hank?"

William nodded solemnly.

"Was she…" I cleared my throat before I continued. "Was she there? Did she see it happen?"

William offered me another apologetic look and shook his head. "That isn't my story to tell, Demon. I think perhaps you should ask your friend."

There was more to the story, I knew it. I could see it lingering in William's eyes, but I could tell he was resolved not to tell me anything more until I'd spoken with Imogen.

They both waited in silence while I processed the information they'd provided. I could feel both of their gazes on my face, but all I could do for a few minutes was stare straight ahead, unseeing.

Once I'd gotten the lump in my throat to clear I turned back to William. "Did it ever occur to either of you that if you'd told me even a small part of all of this, that I wouldn't have been stupid enough to expose myself to that danger? That I would have been smart enough to know I needed to stay in the company of other people until this fucking psycho had been dealt with?"

His expression said it all.

"No, you didn't, did you? You thought that keeping me in the dark, completely unaware and unable to protect myself, was the better way to go. Do I have that about right?"

He sighed. "I thought we could shield you from this threat without having to involve you in it. I apologize, Astrid. It was a mistake." He did truly look sorry, but it did nothing to assuage my hurt and anger.

"But now that you know, perhaps it will make what I'm about to say easier to swallow." He stepped closer to me, and I felt, more than heard, Liam shifting his stance. "You need to quit your work here at the club. Cut off all ties to it and anyone affiliated with it. Perhaps even get out of town for a bit, until we've handled this. If, at that point, you wish to come back, I can't stop you. But for now I believe that removing you from the equation is the best thing for everyone involved, you most of all."

I stared at him incredulously. Rage beginning to bubble up in my gut. "Are you out of your fucking mind? I'm not running away. And if this guy is the psychopath you've indicated he is, then what makes you think a pesky detail like me quitting my job would stop him from coming after me?"

William's jaw clenched and I could see him trying to control his temper. "Because I won't fecking let him hurt you, *that's* why. Trust me to protect you, Astrid. *Please.*"

I shook my head at him, disappointed. "I can't."

I stood up and walked toward the door, waiting until he stepped away from it before I continued. "Now, I need to go check on Remy. Because there is every chance that a psycho knows where I live and I've left him unprotected. He deserves better than that."

When I walked out the door I could feel both of them staring. I knew we weren't done discussing any of it, but my priority at the moment was Remy. Fuck everything else.

37

William

Reinforcements with Repercussions

I WONDERED IF HE'D EVEN ANSWER MY CALL. I'D HAD TO do some serious convincing to get his contact information, but I needed backup I knew I could count on. There was no one better for this job than the man I was currently praying would answer his phone.

The call connected but all I heard on the other end was silence.

"We have a problem." I waited for him to respond, knowing I didn't need to identify myself.

"You mean *you* have a problem?" His tone was unconcerned. Fair; all things considered, the Organization's problems were no longer his.

"In this case, I stick with my original statement. This one is personal." Again, I waited.

"How so?" His tone turned suspicious.

"It's Astrid."

I heard him take a deep breath on the other end of the line. "Boy, I'd suggest you start talking—and fast. Astrid shouldn't even be on your fucking radar."

I got straight to the point. "The 'how' is irrelevant right now. The 'what' is that Dimitri has her in his sights. I need an extra pair of eyes on her. Ones that I trust. Someone I know who won't hesitate to do what's needed if she's in danger."

"*If* she's in danger? You little asshole, if Dimitri has her in his sights, she's already in danger. Where are you?" I could hear him shuffling things around on his end, probably throwing things in a bag. I'd known he'd be angry as soon I decided to call him, but I also knew he wouldn't hesitate to come.

"Redding." I sighed, knowing what was coming.

"Goddammit," he cursed quietly.

"Too close to home, I know." I really did feel bad about compromising him.

"Not anymore." He sighed. "I'll be on the next flight out. I'll call when I land."

"I'll be here," I confirmed.

"You better be. We're not done discussing this."

And then the line went dead and I was left feeling both better and worse.

Better, because I knew one of the few people on Earth that I trusted to keep Astrid safe was on the way.

Worse, because one of the few people on Earth I trusted to give me a really fucking hard time about my interest in her was on the way.

Good times.

38

Astrid

Keep Your Friends Close

I DROVE HOME WITH ONE EYE ON THE ROAD AND THE OTHER on the rearview mirror. Paranoia didn't begin to describe what I was feeling, but my panic at knowing that Remiel was trapped in my house with a psycho possibly—okay, probably—planning on taking me out, overrode it enough for me to put on my big girl panties and hop out of the truck once I parked, running to the door.

"Please be okay, please be okay," I begged under my breath.

When I opened the door, my buddy didn't come racing out like he usually did and my heart sank like a stone into my stomach. I stepped inside, quietly pushing the door shut behind me before I called out in a whisper. "Rem?"

Nothing.

More panic. I could feel my heartbeat reverberating in my eardrums.

Louder this time. "Remiel?"

The sound of his nails clicking on the tile had me dropping to my knees to greet him as he strolled out of my bedroom, doing a happy dance when he saw me.

"Oh my god, buddy, you scared the shit out of me." I grabbed onto his neck and held on for dear life as he blessed me with a slobbery kiss to the right half of my face.

I felt like I could have collapsed with the relief that flooded my veins. He was okay.

We were okay.

He let out a little whine and sat back on his haunches, pawing at me and looking toward the front door. "Okay. Okay, you can go potty, but then it's right back inside. No loitering, all right?"

I swore he must've understood what I said, because when I opened the door, he bolted right to the edge of the yard, did his business, and came right back, gluing himself to my side and looking around for the threat.

"Come on. I'll get you your dinner and we can go hide in bed for the rest of the night. I need to make a phone call anyway. May as well do it from the comfort of my bed."

I poured some kibble into his bowl and carried it into my room, smiling when he dove in like he was starving. Surely, if there were some evil lurking under the bed he wouldn't be happily munching away. I took a deep breath and released some of the tension in my muscles before I kicked off my shoes and climbed onto the bed.

I dialed the number that was as familiar to me as my own and waited, not so patiently, for her to answer.

"Hey, As, what's up?" Imogen's cheerful greeting settled something inside me, despite the sense of betrayal that lingered from my conversation with the guys earlier.

"Lucy, you got some 'splaining to do," I said.

"Huh? What'd I do now?" She sounded honestly confused.

I took a deep breath. "Does the name 'William' mean anything to you?"

Dead silence was all I heard on the other end of the line. For long enough, in fact, that I was pretty sure she'd muted me.

"Imogen Turner, if you've put me on mute so you can have yet another super-secret Scooby meeting, I am going to lose my fucking mind."

"Astrid. Fuck. I can explain?" I could almost see her facial expression in my mind.

"Lucky for you, there's quite a bit I don't need you to explain. Someone else already did that for you. I just need to know one thing, and then I'll do my best to move past this and forgive you for lying to me for months." I felt the burn of tears but pushed them back. I needed to get this off my chest. "I knew there were things you weren't telling me, things that were going on that you felt like you couldn't share, and I respected that. Because you're my best friend. My sister."

She cut me off before I could continue. "I am! As, I'm so sorry, you know how much I love you!"

I growled over the phone line, causing her to stop. "Then I just want to know why, if you love me so much, you didn't think you could trust me with this. I would never betray your trust, and I think you know that. So did you just think I couldn't fucking handle it?"

I heard the tears in her voice when she responded. "No, never. That's not it. Astrid, I thought I was protecting you. I found myself in the middle of all of this fucking danger and...*mayhem*...and I just couldn't stand the thought of you getting hurt by association. I'd never forgive myself if something happened to you because of me!"

"Well, here's the funny thing, Gen. It happened anyway. And here I am, smack in the middle of my own goddamn danger and mayhem and, lo and behold, I find out that my best friend in the entire world is tied up in all of this too, but I never knew a thing about it. I don't know how that would make you feel, but it made me feel pretty fucking shitty. Especially since I had to hear about it from someone else."

She was quiet on the other end of the line for long enough that I wondered if she'd put down the phone and walked away.

"You have every right. Not that you need me to tell you that. But I understand why you're hurt. I'm so fucking sorry, As. I never set out to hurt you. I just wanted to keep you safe." She whispered that last part and I heard another sob echo over the phone line.

I closed my eyes and leaned back against my

pillows, taking deep breaths and trying to get my anger and hurt under control, but I wasn't sure it would be that easy. I knew Imogen loved me, but I needed her to understand that I didn't need to be protected by the people who loved me. I needed to be trusted.

"I'm not helpless, Gen. I'm not a child for you to shelter from all the bad things in the world. You, of all people, know what I've been through in my life. For you not to trust me…" I choked on a sob of my own. "It's so fucking hard to swallow."

"I trust you. I swear to god, I trust you. I'm so sorry. I handled this all wrong! And you're right, I do know what you've been through in your life. You're the fucking strongest person I know, and I just didn't want to add anything else to it. I'm sorry. I'm so sorry. I'll say it as many times as you need to hear it. I'll say it for the next forty years. I'm sorry. I love you so much, and I felt like I was losing every fucking thing that mattered to me in my life, and I just wanted to protect *you*."

When I thought about snapping back at her, a thought occurred to me. I'd done the same thing to her, in a sense. Not exactly on the same scale, but when I'd had the chance to tell her about the situation with my parents? I hadn't.

When I walked to that beach, leaking my pain all over the ground as I crossed it, I never called her. I never gave her the chance to be there for me, either.

I hung my head. "I'm sorry, too," I whispered.

"No, As, you don't have anything to apologize for, this is all on me. I'm so sorry that I hurt you, I swear I never meant for this to hurt you."

"But I do have something to apologize for," I confessed. "We should talk."

Imogen and I stayed on the phone for two hours. It was the longest, most honest conversation she and I had had in longer than I wanted to think about, but there was something healing about letting every bit of ugly from the last few months come pouring out of me. Like exorcising demons. I'd begun to heal the night I confessed everything to Rae, but telling Imogen everything felt like I'd finally put it all to rest.

And then, as so often happened with us, the conversation shifted.

"Hey, As?" Imogen asked tentatively.

"Yes, Gen?" I chuckled, wondering why she was suddenly being so cautious.

"How do you know William?"

I tipped my head back in the first full laugh I'd let out that night. "Oh, girl. Have I got some tea for you."

39

Astrid

Never Trust a Drunken Gangster

THE NEXT NIGHT I WENT TO WORK, JUST LIKE I ALWAYS DID. The one difference was that I dropped Remy off at Brennan's on my way. No way would I have been able to work my shift wondering if he was safe. Brennan greeted me at his door and grinned when he saw Remy waiting patiently at my side like the good boy he was.

"Thanks, Bren. I really appreciate it. He's been…" I had to come up with something on the fly. "He's been having some separation anxiety."

"Hey, girlie, no problem! I love the doggos!" He offered me a big goofy grin before hunkering down and talking directly to Remy. "What do you say we go watch the ballgame, my man? Your mom will be back to get you before you know it."

I thanked him again and handed him the leash. "I'll be back around four, but if you want to go to bed before that, just let me know and I can come get him tomorrow."

"Ah, girlie, I'm a night owl. Hazard of the trade and all that, so I'll be up."

The atmosphere in the club was so normal that it felt weird. Like everything that was going on beneath the surface should've leaked to the rest of the club, but there were still clinking glasses and people laughing and dancing and patrons swiping their keys to the back room like it was any other night. It was oddly reassuring until I looked to William's usual table and found it vacant.

I experienced an odd sort of disappointment. I was pissed at him, but I still wanted him to be there. It didn't make sense, I knew it. But what could I say?

I scanned the room quickly before I headed to the office and stopped short when I spotted him leaning against the bar in the main room, but something definitely seemed...off. He was wearing his usual, pressed and dressed like he was headed to a meeting with a board of directors or some shit, but his hair was standing up in so many different directions that it no longer resembled whatever style he'd started his day with.

William normally appeared so in control, but now he looked totally unhinged and maybe that was the biggest thing I noticed as I approached. He wasn't surveying his surroundings and noting anyone that got too close to him. No, he looked completely lost and I wasn't even sure *he* knew where he was anymore.

I approached him slowly, like you would a wounded animal, "William?" I offered in a low, soothing voice.

His head jerked up at the sound of my voice and his eyes attempted to focus on my face, but he was obviously struggling. "As. You're here."

"Where else would I be?" I tilted my head at him, marveling at this unhinged version of him that I'd yet to encounter.

"I thought…" He stopped himself, shaking his head. "I didn't think you were coming back."

I narrowed my eyes on him. "So, what, you thought you'd scared me off to the point that I would abandon my job, my life, everything that I've worked so hard to build for myself here? Oh no, pal, if anyone shouldn't be here, it's you, *not* me."

He nodded, as if he'd already come to that conclusion himself, but I couldn't stop myself from stepping closer when he began swaying. I wrapped an arm around his waist and turned him away from the bar, toward the hallway that led to the office.

"Come on, ya lush. Let's get you out of the public before Liam catches sight of you. You can sober up on the couch in the office."

He stumbled along next to me obediently, but I could almost hear his brain working through something as we moved.

When I got the door to the office opened, I steered him toward the black leather sofa along the far wall, letting him dissolve onto the cushions with a sigh.

"I'm going to grab you some water. Don't throw up on the floor, I'm not going to clean it up for you."

I stepped out long enough to grab an ice cold bottle of water from behind the bar and returned to the office to find him with his head tilted back, eyes closed. I thought he was asleep until I moved closer to put the bottle on the table next to him and his hand reached out and latched onto my wrist.

My eyes flew to the place where we were connected and when I raised a brow and looked back at his face, I could see his golden eyes staring back at me, studying me, before he spoke in a low, tortured rasp. "I'm too old for ye. An I know it, as well as you do." His accent, which he normally smoothed out to a carefully cultured thing free of inflection, had become stronger than I'd ever heard it. My guess, it was the gallon of whisky he must have consumed to get him in this condition.

"I'm not a good man, Astrid Scott. Not a good man at all. There are so many things you don't know about me and if I was half the man I pretend to be on a day, I'd get on the first plane out of this place an never come back, ye ken? I'd stay far, far away from ye." He closed his eyes and flexed the hand wrapped around my wrist before he released me and let his hand drop into his lap, closing his eyes again.

"Is that what you want, William? To get on a plane and get as far from me as you can? Never see me again?"

He shook his head, rolling it against the wall behind him, before he opened his eyes again. "Nah. It's not what I want ta do, Demon. It's what I *should* do."

"And what is it that you want to do, then?" I heard the catch in my own voice when I asked the question. More invested in his response than I wanted to admit, even in my own mind.

He met my curious gaze with one of his own before he spoke again. His face took on a resolute expression. "I want to take you out into that bar and bend you over the edge of it, slide my hand up under that little skirt yer wearin' and tease that pussy I just know is wet for me until yer beggin' me ta pull my cock out and slam it into you until every motherfucker that's ever eye-fucked you as you walked by will know exactly who ye belong to."

One part of me wanted to let him do exactly what he'd just described. His words had created a pulse somewhere distinctly south of my heart and I could hear the blood rushing in my ears. The other part of me, the part that was just starting to come into her own? Well, that part didn't like that last part of his little speech at all.

"Belong to, William? How much have you had to drink? I'll need to take notes so I know exactly how much liquor it takes to turn you into a caveman." I snatched my wrist away and took a couple of steps back. I knew somewhere deep inside me that this was important, despite how much I wanted him. "For the record, I don't belong to anyone, William. Not you or anyone else."

I didn't want to be owned. I *didn't.*

"Is that so?" He rose off the couch to stand directly in front of me, suddenly seeming far more sober than he had mere moments ago. The scent of his cologne reached out and wrapped around me, drawing me in.

He lifted his hand and ran a single finger down the side of my face, under my chin, drawing an imaginary line down the center of my throat before barely circling his fingers around it. Never applying pressure, merely giving me a taste of the feel of his hand wrapped around that delicate column.

"So if I walked you backward"—he gently pushed me until my back hit the wall—"and leaned in, pressing every inch of my body against every delectable inch of this body that you've been taunting me with, day in and day out..." He dipped his head, placing his mouth next to my ear, whispering his next words. "And told you that I've thought of nothing except having the freedom to worship you in every way imaginable since that very first night. That I've dreamed of being able to claim this pussy for my own..." He slid his hand down my stomach, barely grazing me at the juncture of my thighs with his knuckles. "Making it so you'd never want anyone else to put their hands, their mouths, their cocks, anywhere that I had been again." He straightened to his full height and met my gaze while my eyelids fluttered and the pulse in my neck jumped. "You wouldn't like that?"

My eyes rolled back in my head with the visualization of everything he'd just described and that slow pulse between my legs urged me to do something, anything, to appease the ache he'd created.

But something in my stupid, stubborn brain wouldn't let me just agree with him. I could already tell my ladyparts were going to revolt before the words even came out of my mouth. "No. I don't think I would."

I could hear my vagina screaming loudly as he slowly took a step back, letting his hands drop to his sides as he studied me. I let out a deep breath and slumped against the wall, feeling like I'd just run a marathon with the way my pulse was racing.

"Aye. I can see that yer unaffected." He smirked before he retreated slowly, trailing his fingers down my arm until he'd removed himself entirely from my space.

He stood just out of arms' reach for a breath and then turned and resumed his spot on the couch, offering me one more searing look before he rested his head against the wall again.

Before I could retract my statement and tell him I'd changed my mind, that I definitely did want every bit of what he'd described, I heard a quiet snore escape from between his lips. He'd fucking passed out.

What in that actual fuck, Astrid? Who turns that down? Restraint is not always a virtue, you idiot!

40

Astrid

Misdirection

IT TOOK A LONG TIME TO GET MY HEART RATE, AMONG other things, under control enough that I could actually get any work done. All the while, sleeping beauty snored on the couch behind me, oblivious to the mental struggle taking place just a few feet away.

Liam appeared around 2 a.m. and took one look at the drunken man passed out on the couch and gave me an incredulous look.

"What the hell happened there?"

I felt my face flush, the memory of William's words still fresh in my mind. I was also flashing back to a similar scene with Liam. I wasn't sure how I kept winding up in the position of rescuing these men from their own self-destructive tendencies and I snorted to myself. *What a lucky girl.*

"In short? He had a gallon of liquor, turned into a

caveman, propositioned me, and then passed out cold. He's been like that for a few hours now." I gestured at his sleeping form.

Liam raised his brows at me and came over to lean against the desk where I was working.

I could feel his eyes on the side of my face, but I kept my focus on the screen in front of me. "You're not going to leave. Are you?" It really wasn't a question, and I knew he already knew the answer.

I clicked send on the order I'd been working on and closed the laptop before I slid back in the chair and met his gaze. "I've worked hard to get to this place."

"I know you have, and you've done a great job here. Better than I deserve, all things considered."

"That's not what I'm talking about." I scrunched up my face, thinking of how to say what I needed to say. "Liam, the fact that you hired me as some sort of bizarre insurance policy is utterly fucked up, and we're going to talk about that eventually, but I'm not asking for a performance review right now. What I meant is, I've been sort of lost my entire life. My childhood was pretty fucked up and my parents never won any awards for how they treated me growing up. I've wandered around for what feels like a really long time trying to figure things out on my own, never feeling like I found where I belonged."

I stared at him, hoping he could understand what I was saying. "I bounced all over the place and the only time I ever did feel like I could settle myself was with Imogen. I'm so grateful for her and Hank for giving me a bit of normalcy in an otherwise seriously fucked-up life, but there had to come a point when I found my own way. Independent of their support. And, no matter what your motivation was for it, in the end you helped me with that."

His expression was indecipherable, but I continued before I lost the words. "So, while I understand why you both think it would be best if I walked away, I'm telling you that I can't. I won't. For the first time in my life I have a *life*, not just an existence. I'm calmer. Happier. The monsters in my head I've fought day and night for so long that I didn't even know what it was like not to feel sad have gotten quieter every day since I came to work here. I met all of you and felt at home, finally. I've had something to call my own. Even with a supposed psychopath after me, I won't give it all up just to run away. Not on the off chance that *maybe* I can be safe for a little while."

He looked unbearably sad at my admission. "Astrid, I—"

I cut him off before he could continue. "Whatever you're going to say, Liam, just don't. You won't change my mind about this. I appreciate that you're worried, and I get that you feel responsible, but I feel like some of this was inevitable. I was tied to this world before you ever brought me in. So just trust me for once. That's all I've ever wanted the people in my life to do. Trust me to be able to handle life with all its ups and downs and let me *live* it instead of everyone trying to protect me all the damn time."

Finally, he nodded. "Okay. Okay, but none of that means you don't need to be careful. And we still have to deal with that asshole, so maybe you could let us protect you a little bit? If we promise not to hide things from you anymore?"

"Well, I'm not an idiot. Of course I'll be careful. And obviously, I'm not a ninja badass, so if somebody needs killing, then I'll leave that up to you two deviants." I grinned at him.

He rolled his eyes before standing to his full height and looking back toward the couch. "Maybe we should come up with a plan then?"

I heard the leather creak as William shifted. I jumped when I heard his voice, still gravelly from sleep. "I suppose we should."

"I won't put Talia in danger just to try and draw this guy out." I was adamant. Absolutely no fucking way.

"Astrid, we won't let anything happen to her, I promise. And she's not going to be doing anything she wouldn't normally be doing...with a few exceptions." Liam was really trying to sell me on the plan but I wasn't convinced.

"If she's driving my truck, wearing my clothes...it feels an awful lot like using her as bait. That's not okay with me." I shifted my gaze back and forth between the two of them, incredulous that they thought I was going to buy into this.

William was holding his head in his hands, presumably in the midst of a raging hangover. "Demon. I've got people in place to watch her back. They won't let anything happen to her, I promise. We just need to get out of here for a few days and give them a chance to catch this asshole before he makes a move and *you* get hurt."

Liam's head whipped toward William, his eyes narrowing. "When you say 'we'...?"

William raised his eyes to meet Liam's, and then mine, before he answered. "Yes. *We*. Astrid and I will leave town. I'll be obvious about it, but she'll need to be hidden until we're away from here. My guy should be in town by now to help keep an eye on things and Jared is on alert as well. Those two are some of the best I've got. And when that fucking psycho realizes I've left town, his focus is going to turn to *you* entirely, which should draw him out quicker."

"Fucking hell," Liam grumbled. "I didn't know that part of the plan."

William shed his pained grimace long enough to give Liam a smug grin. "I know."

"Why can't you just use me as bait then? You go out of town, like you suggested, but leave me here. Then Talia doesn't need to be involved." I crossed my arms over my chest, staring at William with a stubborn expression. I really didn't like this plan.

"Because. I'm not going to leave you here where I can't get to you if something happens. No, you're coming with me. This plan will work, Astrid, but I won't be able to relax if I know you're here and I'm six hours away in Mammoth. That's non-negotiable." An equally stubborn expression was on William's face.

I looked back at Liam and he was glaring at the side

of William's face with something that looked a lot like… jealousy? But that couldn't be right.

By that point it was almost four in the morning, and I was exhausted, my brain and my body spent from all the drama of the night.

I rubbed my hands over my face and let out a jaw-cracking yawn before I addressed them both. "If I agree to this, when do you propose this plan should take place?"

They answered me in stereo. "As soon as possible."

———————————————————

Part III

———————————————————

Love Travels On, Part 1: Her

> the loneliest sound I've ever heard
> is a train whistle blowing by
> miserable and melancholy
> floating on the cool crisp air
> when morning is still night
> and it's only me in this bed
> 'cause you're long gone
> like that train racing by

-Elizabeth Michaud, Five Dreams

Astrid

Mammoth

I took Remy to Brennan again, and he'd been so fucking delighted that I had no qualms that he'd care for him as if he were his own. They were bffs now apparently, and I was grateful even if it made my heart pang to leave him. I didn't know what the next few days would bring for me, but I needed to know Remy would be safe. I couldn't guarantee that if he was with me.

I left Bren's house and headed to the club. We'd decided leaving my truck there for Talia to move around periodically would be smart. I patted the hood fondly before I grabbed my bag and went inside to meet William. Whoever this psycho was, he'd better not fuck with my truck.

I'd lived in California my entire life and never knew there could still be snow on the ground this late in the year. When we reached elevation I was delighted to see patches of it here and there along the side of the road.

I was also delighted that I was no longer lying in the rear footwell of William's rented SUV covered with a blanket. I shifted in my seat, cracking my spine to try and get it back into some semblance of the shape it was before I'd spent an hour cramped in that tiny space.

"I could have put you in the trunk." He smirked.

"Careful, William, your gangster is showing," I fired back at him.

His bark of laughter was my reward. "I'm not a gangster, you little shit." But he was still chuckling a few minutes later when we pulled onto the rutted dirt road that led to our hiding place for the next few days.

I returned my gaze to the scenery outside the car, taking in the huge fir and pine trees that filled the forest around us, only letting in dappled light here and there between them. There were small patches of snow still lingering in spots there as well. The drive had been cleared at some point, so we weren't in any danger of sliding off into the woods, but it was still bouncy and slow-going with all the ruts created by runoff.

Ten minutes off the highway, we pulled into a small clearing in front of the most adorable little cabin I'd ever seen in my life. I gasped and looked at William quickly before turning back to it, reaching for the door excitedly.

He just grinned and held up a finger. "Give me five minutes. I just want to check it out before you go in. Lock these." He gestured at the door locks.

"Ugh. Fine, go be a tough guy, but if you're not back in five minutes, I'm coming in to save you." I forced my face into a frown, but the sparkle in my eyes made a liar of me, I was sure.

"It's a deal." He climbed out of the SUV and shut his door, tapping on the window to remind me to lock them. I rolled my eyes, but he refused to walk away until I hit the button.

I spent the time after he disappeared in the cabin looking around at everything I could see from my vantage point. There was a wrap-around porch that had couches and rocking chairs scattered here and there, and I was really hoping there were more on the back side of the cabin I couldn't see, because the lakeshore was just a few yards from where we'd parked, and I couldn't wait to sit outside and stare out at the water with a cup of coffee in my hand.

I knew this wasn't a vacation, per se, and I was really worried about my friends who remained back in Redding, but William had promised he wasn't going to leave them unprotected. I found that I believed him, even if I'd have liked to have heard more about his "people" he had coming in to watch over them.

In the meantime, I couldn't help but be a little excited about getting away to such a pretty spot for a few days. I'd gone camping with Imogen and Hank a few times over the years, but I'd never been on a real vacation, so it was hard to control my excitement.

I was so entranced by the scenery around me that I didn't see him approach the car. I jumped a little when he tapped on my window, causing him to grin at me.

"Wanna come see the rest?" he called from the other side of the window.

"Fuck yes, I do!" I hit the unlock button and scrambled out, not stopping to close the door behind me before I ran up the porch steps and into the cabin.

I heard the chirp of the car alarm and then he joined me a moment later, with our two bags slung over his shoulders.

"Is it cool to poke around?" I asked, looking at the two closed doors that led off of the cozy open-concept living area.

"Sure, poke all you want. I had the fridge stocked before we got here, so I'll dig around and see what's good to eat." He tossed the bags on the floor just inside the door and peeled his jacket off, draping it over a hook on the wall.

I paused my cabin exploration to watch him walk into the kitchen and open the fridge, leaning in. He wasn't dressed in his usual board-meeting attire, and I approved wholeheartedly of this version of him. He wore dark jeans that looked like they'd been cut specifically to mold to the lower half of his body and a black t-shirt that displayed his roped forearms beautifully. Another thing I noticed right away was the edge of ink peeking out above the collar and below the left sleeve. Hmm. Didn't see that coming. Definitely not mad at it.

I turned away from staring at him before he caught me mooning at him like a lovesick schoolgirl and walked over to the first of the two closed doors. It opened up into a rustic bathroom, all rough-hewn logs and a rainfall shower in the corner, surrounded on three sides by what looked like stone cut directly out of the mountain. It wasn't plush but it was really pretty, and I was ecstatic to see the toilet situated inside the tiny room adjacent to it. We'd been driving for hours and he hadn't wanted to stop, for fear of anyone spotting me with him and blowing our whole plan. I darted inside and took care of my overfull bladder before I washed my hands in the stone basin sink and continued my explorations.

Back out in the living room, I opened the one remaining door and gasped as I took in the deep green comforter, dark leather furniture, and the huge cream colored rug covering most of the wood floor. This had to be the most beautiful bedroom I'd ever seen. I gaped, trying to see it all at once. The far wall was entirely glass, granting a gorgeous view of the span of the lake and the shoreline opposite us. There were two large leather chairs set up just in front of the window with a table between; a big fuzzy blanket draped over the back of each one. In the corner there was a fireplace that obviously shared a chimney with the one in the main room because I could see straight through to the other side from where I stood.

The best part of all, though, was the bed. It wasn't huge, but it was draped on all sides with gauzy curtains strung from the ceiling on a track and the pillows and blankets draped over it looked like a fluffy cloud. I just wanted to throw myself into the center of it and let it wrap around me like a cocoon. I couldn't wait to climb into it later that night.

Back out in the living room, I went to the sliding

glass door next, stepping out onto the back porch and falling even more in love with the place as I looked around. There were more chairs scattered on this side, as well as a stairwell that led halfway down to the lake where it stopped at a circular deck that had a wooden hot tub centered on it, a cushioned bench wrapping around the edge, and fairy lights strung up in a criss-cross pattern just above it. It looked like the kind of spot you wanted to sit and sip champagne while watching the sunset.

The whole cabin was absolutely magical and it was hard to remember that we weren't a couple in love sneaking away for a romantic weekend. I felt my shoulders slump.

Ah, reality, that fucking cunt.

I turned to head back inside and found William leaned against the door frame, watching me as I approached. "You like it?"

"It's beautiful," I told him honestly. "This is exactly the kind of place I'd want to go if I were on vacation and not running from a psychopath."

He stepped toward me and lifted a hand to my face, reminiscent of how he had a couple days prior at the club. "Demon. Please try not to worry, I promise I've got everything handled. Your friends are protected. I just got off the phone with Jared and he's met up with my guy. They're keeping a very close eye on everyone, especially Talia. There's nothing wrong with enjoying this time away in a beautiful spot with someone you maybe don't mind spending a little more time with?" I'd never seen William look hesitant before. I'd seen Confident William. I'd seen Pissed-off William. Sexy William, for sure, and I'd seen more of Distant William than I'd ever wanted to. But the expression he was giving at that moment was new.

I tilted my head, filing it away as one more clue to who this man really was. "I thought I'd been pretty straight-forward about the fact that I like you. Why do you sound so unsure about it now?"

"My memories from the other night are a bit fuzzy," he admitted. "But I do distinctly recall you telling me you weren't interested in what I had to offer. Which, for the record, was way out of bounds and I apologize for drunkenly propositioning you. It had been a bad day all the way around for me and I wasn't expecting to see you that night."

I thought about that for a minute and nodded. "Apology accepted. And, since we're being so honest, I'd like to clarify my rejection of your proposal that night."

"Now who's talking in circles, hmm?" He grinned.

"Fine. Let me be clear. When I spotted you on the cameras at the club the first night you showed up, I knew right away I needed to see you up close and in person. You stole my breath and a large part of my higher reasoning capabilities. When I actually came out into the club and met you face-to-face, I knew almost instantly that I'd go anywhere you wanted me to. When you suggested we skip sharing our names with one another, I went along with it because something about you had already resonated within me, and it didn't matter to me what your name was. I wanted you."

I watched his eyes darken and intensify with every confession and I hurried to continue before he could interrupt. "So the other night, when I turned down your offer, it wasn't because I don't want you, William."

He stepped closer, until he was staring down at me, almost brushing my chest with his. "Then…why? Aside from the obvious issue, of course, of me having been piss drunk."

"Because I don't want to be owned. Not by you or anyone. I wasn't lying when I said that. You were so up in your caveman era that night that, I just couldn't give in. I didn't want to start anything we might have with you thinking I belong to you like property." I was really proud of myself for standing my ground with him leaning so close to me for the second time in a matter of days. Somebody had better crown me the feminist of the year for this shit.

His eyes were glowing, with the sun setting over the lake behind my back, and I swore they caught fire right before he spoke again. "Demon. I don't want to own you like property. In my drunken state, perhaps I failed to properly convey what it is that I do want, and for that I apologize. But hear me now when I tell you that I know you are your own woman; I know how strong and capable you are, and the more I learn about this mind of yours"—he tapped his finger against my temple —"the more I want to know. So, perhaps what I should have said that night was not that I want to own *you*, but that I want to own your time. I want to own your thoughts. When you dream at night of hands on your skin, I want it to be my hands you dream of. When you long for someone to kiss these lips, I want it to be mine you long for."

He closed the remaining distance between us, letting me feel exactly how much he wanted me at that moment. He cupped his hands around my face, tilting it up to meet his. "And when you ache? When you *need*, Astrid, I want it to be my body that sates that need. My hands, my tongue, my mouth. My cock." He punctuated every statement with a kiss to my cheek, my neck, my eyelids, until I was leaning all my weight against him and wrapping my arms around his neck to help keep myself upright.

"Yes." I blinked up at him.

He stared at me, studying my eyes for a beat. "Yes?"

"Fuck, yes, William. God. Yes."

He groaned and wrapped his big hands around my thighs, lifting me up until I could curl my legs around his waist as he carried me back through the glass doors. He went straight into the bedroom I'd just been fantasizing about a few minutes before and didn't stop until he stood next to the bed, where he released me and encouraged me to stand on my own. I frowned up at him when he took a step back.

"Before this goes any further. One thing." He looked away uncomfortably and then met my gaze again. "I'm still too old for you."

I snorted, ever the sexy temptress. "I'll tell you the same thing I told Rae. Age is just a number when you're naked."

He chuckled at that, but persisted. "Do you even know how old I am?"

I shrugged. "I really don't care, but if you're dead set on telling me then go for it, but don't expect it to change anything."

He watched me carefully, gauging my reaction. "I'm thirty. I'll be thirty-one in just a couple of months."

I gasped at him in horror. "Oh my god, William! I didn't know you were *that* much older than me. This changes everything."

His shoulders slumped, but he nodded, taking another step back. "Okay, I understand…" He stopped mid-sentence when he saw my shoulders shaking. "You're an asshole, you know that?"

I fell back onto the bed, cackling. "Yes, I believe I've been called that before."

The next thing I knew, he'd pounced on me, threading his fingers through mine and pinning them to the bed over my head. All traces of amusement vanished from his expression.

"I've been waiting weeks to feel your mouth on mine. But I'm afraid I won't be able to restrain myself once I've tasted you. Are you absolutely certain?" He was intent, committed to making sure I knew what I was getting myself into.

"Less talking, more sexing, please. Now." I grinned up at him.

Another sexy groan from him, and then his mouth was on mine, the delicious weight of him pressing me into the mattress. His lips parted and he nipped my bottom lip with his teeth until I opened up for him. He slid his hand down my thigh, wrapping it behind my knee and dragging it up so he was cradled between my thighs, both of us grinding against one another, dying for relief from what felt like weeks of foreplay.

Shit. It *had* been weeks of foreplay.

I pulled my lips away from his for a moment, trying to get enough breath to speak. "I want to kiss you all night, and I want you to worship every inch of my body like you promised to that first night, and I want every orgasm you've promised with your words and your actions since we've met. But right now, William, for the love of all that is holy, please take off your pants and fuck me hard before I catch fire."

He lifted up and gave me a feral look before he reached down and popped the buttons on his jeans. I shimmied and twisted under him, trying to get my leggings off when he put a hand on my hip to still me. "Are you overly fond of these?"

"The only thing I'm overly fond of right now is the idea of you slamming that cock inside of me as fast as is humanly possible," I panted.

All pretense gone. I needed him and I needed him right then.

He grinned a wicked grin and grabbed the seam of my leggings that ran between my legs and ripped it apart until I felt cool air on my thighs.

"Nice move." I giggled.

"Thanks, I've been thinking about doing that since you climbed over the seat in the car and put this in my face." He slid his hand over my panties and shoved them to the side, gliding his fingers over the seam of my pussy.

My eyes rolled with how good it felt. "If you're worried I'm not wet enough, please don't be. I think I'll be fine." More panting.

He grinned. "Oh, I know. Your leggings are soaked."

I groaned, grinding against his hand as he tortured me. "Are you waiting for your Viagra to kick in or something?"

He popped that hand against my flesh and I let out a little scream. "Did you just...spank my pussy?" I cried out.

"Yep. Sure did. Now watch your smart mouth and show some respect."

He lifted his hips, freed his gorgeous, slightly curved, beautiful cock from his boxer briefs and reared up until he'd seated himself inside me fully, both of us letting out a groan at how good it felt.

"That's it, it's official. You really are a succubus, because my dick just decided it never wants to be anywhere else but right"—he pulled back and thrust again—"here."

The sensation of having him filling me up was amazing, and somehow I knew it wasn't just because we'd been dancing around this for weeks. Even so, I knew my body, and I slid a hand between us.

He paused, watching me as I stroked my clit, still writhing against him, and I growled at him. "Why aren't you moving?"

"The most beautiful woman I've ever seen just parted her lips and started playing with her clit while she's stretched around my cock like a good fucking girl. I want to watch."

I grunted, shifting my hips and glaring up at him.

"Watch." Shift.

"Later." Shift.

"Fuck." Shift.

"Now."

———————————————

42

Astrid

———————————————

With Age Comes Wisdom

"Okay, just remember. You asked for it." He raised up on his knees, pulling my lower body with him. He gave me a devilish smirk before he withdrew almost completely, his hands holding my hips still, his forearms bulging with the effort, before he slammed back into me, and oh. *Oh!* He…oh, he wasn't all the way in before. Okay then.

"Holy…god, William, fuck. I can't. Don't stop." I groaned and thrashed as he absolutely destroyed me with his cock.

"I'm getting mixed signals, Demon. Can you stop talking in circles?" he snarked at me, and I didn't even need to see his face to picture his smirk.

"I think if you're going to talk this much, you should try a different tactic." I gritted my teeth, trying to hold back my orgasm while also keeping myself right there on the edge of it.

"Oh really?" His voice dropped. "Would you like it more if I said that watching you stretch and take me so well is the most gorgeous sight I've ever seen. That I can't wait to watch you shatter all over my cock so I can pull out and come all over those gorgeous tits of yours. Lift that shirt baby, let me see where I'm going to come in a minute."

I slid my right hand faster and faster against my clit, his words nearly pushing me over the edge, while I slid my t-shirt up over my bra with my right.

He groaned at the sight of my lace covered breasts. "Pull them down," he ordered, and I had to stop what I was doing to yank both of the cups down. "Yes, just like that. Now get back to playing with that clit so I can watch and make sure I know exactly how you like it. Next time, that's my job."

It only took a few more thrusts and strokes before I felt my entire body begin to tense, the telltale shivers and tingles emanating from where I was frantically rubbing my clit.

When I felt my muscles clamp down on him, he groaned. "Oh fuck, yes, god, you feel so good, you're such a good girl, coming all over my cock like that. Trying to make me come inside you, but you can't have this cum, not this time."

I whimpered, riding out the last aftershocks of my orgasm as he thrust shallowly inside of me, delaying his own orgasm until I was completely spent. When I went limp, he slowly slid out of me and climbed up until he was straddling my hips, his jeans barely affording him the room to assume that position, but he made it work.

I watched as his corded forearm reached down and grabbed his slick cock, shiny from our combined juices, and slid his hand up and down. "Is this okay?" he grunted.

"This is the hottest fucking thing that has ever happened to me," I assured him.

He grinned down at me and sped up the motion of his arm. "Good. Now, put your hand back on your clit and let me see you come one more time while I watch these gorgeous tits bounce with every gasp you let out."

I did as he said but I'd be lying if I said my focus wasn't more on what he was doing with that hand he wrapped around his cock. My efforts were half-hearted at best, but who could blame me? One of the hottest men I'd ever laid eyes on was braced above me, his eyes sliding back and forth between my face and my tits which were bouncing with our movements.

When he pulled his bottom lip in between his teeth, letting out a guttural groan, I moaned in anticipation as he shot jet after jet of cum onto my chest. His expression grew more feral with every drop he marked me with. Something told me what we were doing was more than fucking.

It was a *claiming*.

I woke up a little while later with his head between my

legs. When I shifted, he looked up at me with a grin on his face.

"Sorry, I couldn't wait for you to wake up. I've been dying to do this since the day we met."

I looked down at him in astonishment, his face shiny and eyes bright, and thought *I've never seen him look this happy in the whole time I've known him.* A man who fucked like a porn star and "couldn't wait" to get his head between my legs? I'd clearly passed on to the next life and he was my reward for all the shit I'd encountered in my previous one.

"If this is the sacrifice I have to make to put that look on your face, then call me the patron saint of cunnilingus and carry on."

He grinned and resumed his ministrations, taking so well to the cues my body gave that I'd swear he could read my mind. When I let out a low growl and clenched my hands next to my hips, he lifted his head again. "Need more?"

I stared up at the ceiling, not wanting to say anything, but also, now that I'd woken up like this, I needed to come. "I've never been able to…you know, just from that." I threw my hands up to cover my face, embarrassed.

"Hey, hey…" He patted my hip, getting me to drop my hands and meet his gaze again. "I want you to tell me what it takes to get you there. I want you to tell me so often, in fact, that by the time we leave here you never have to tell me again." He lowered his face and swiped the tip of his tongue over my clit, making me roll my hips involuntarily. "So tell me, what do you need?"

"Both," I gasped. "I need your fingers too."

"Oh, fuck yes. That's what I need to know. Now hold on, little Demon, and tell me if I'm doing it right."

He lowered his head and spread me wide, using the tip of his tongue to circle my clit while his fingers…oh, holy hell, his fingers. He slid one inside me, getting it nice and slick before he added another. He lifted his head again, and I groaned. "I'm close."

I felt, more than heard, him chuckle. "I know. But I need you to pull your knees up higher."

I'd have done anything for him at that moment. Tied myself into a knot. Learned origami. Gone back to high school and passed calculus.

Whatever he asked.

I drew my knees up, and I felt him take those fingers and slide them out of me, drag them down until he was teasing them against my ass. "Have you ever had anything back here?"

I shook my head no furiously, but only because I needed less talking and more doing.

A sound of pure male satisfaction escaped him and he dropped his head again. I heard him spit and I felt more wetness drip onto my ass while he circled that hole with his fingers one more time. He leaned forward and drew my clit into his mouth, sucking so hard that I levered my upper half off the bed at the sensation. *Yay for core strength!*

When I squealed and threw my hands back to hold me up, he eased one finger into my ass and curled it gently, rubbing against a million nerve endings—fuck, I didn't know what, but it was a sensation unlike anything I'd ever felt before.

"Fuck, William, what…I…please!"

His chuckle literally reverberated through my entire pussy and, when he added that second finger, I detonated in a way I never had before.

I blacked out.

When I came to, I laid, blinking up at the ceiling and wondering if all my limbs were still attached because I couldn't feel anything at all except a delightful throb from down below.

Both down-belows, actually.

I turned my head to find him climbing back into the bed with a towel in his hand and a look of such utter male satisfaction on his face that I almost wanted to hit him just to wipe it off.

"You're pretty proud of yourself, aren't you?" I asked.

He propped himself up next to me, using the damp towel to gently clean me up while he nodded, not even trying to hide it. "Extremely."

"Are you going to use your superior sexual expertise against me forever?" I hoped so.

"At every possible opportunity," he confirmed.

43

Astrid

What Goes Up

"Bacon is the work of the gods, you can't convince me otherwise." I hummed as I stole another piece off the plate sitting between us on the little table out back. I was curled up with a blanket draped around my shoulders and a steaming cup of coffee in my other hand. I didn't think a more perfect morning had ever existed.

He didn't respond, and I finally tore my attention away from the view to see what had kept him so quiet. He was reclined in the chair opposite mine, legs crossed at the ankles, his own cup of coffee cupped in one of his hands resting on his stomach. His expression was another new one.

"What's that look for?" I tilted my head.

He studied my face for another minute before he answered. "You look happy. And I'm ashamed to say that, until this moment, I don't believe I've seen you truly happy in the time I've known you."

I gulped. I didn't want to have deep conversations when I wasn't fully caffeinated. Or ever, really, but definitely not pre-caffeination.

"I don't think that's exactly true," I began. "But...I do feel pretty happy right now. So..." I trailed off, hoping he would let it go.

He didn't. "Why do I feel like there's something there you aren't telling me?"

I closed my eyes, counting to ten in my head and telling myself that this was bound to happen eventually. I just hadn't expected him to be so goddamn observant.

When I reopened my eyes his stare hadn't wavered from mine. He just sat, steady and quiet, and waited on me. "I have a chemical imbalance. It's nothing serious, totally manageable through diet and exercise for the most part. And occasionally I break down and go get medicated for a spell here or there, but none of the meds I've tried have felt like they worked for my particular brand of crazy."

He leaned forward. "Don't do that."

"What? Don't do what?"

"Don't downplay your pain and make it a joke. I'm asking because I care, not because I'm looking for a reason to judge and dismiss you." He stayed where he was, but I could tell he wanted to bridge the distance between us. For once, I was glad he didn't.

"Sorry. Coping mechanism." I took a sip of my coffee, hoping it would work its way through my bloodstream fast enough that I didn't fuck this up.

"Understandable. Now tell me about it."

"I'm a little bit manic depressive. A lotta bit ADHD. A little bit autistic. From the moment I got diagnosed, my parents discredited the doctor that diagnosed me and told me there was nothing wrong with me. That everybody gets sad sometimes. I just needed to try harder and stop making everything about me." The words poured out of me without my permission.

His eyebrows drew down into a v over his eyes. "I'm sorry, what?"

I shrugged. "Those two didn't win any parent of the year awards, so this was just one more instance of their complete and utter lack of care for me. Either that, or their complete and utter lack of faith in the existence of mental health issues. Either way, I learned from an early age that my problems were my own to deal with. Asking them for help never did anything but make it worse."

"Astrid. What the fuck? So, what does that mean? You've been…what, just raw-dogging it through life dealing with all of that shit on your own?"

I could feel myself shrink into the chair a little more with every angry word he spoke. "Essentially?" I said. "I'm close with one of my brothers, Ethan, and he's always tried to be there for me, but he's ridiculously well-adjusted, so it's kinda hard for him to truly understand what goes on in my head." My eyes burned.

He noticed right away and immediately adjusted his body language. "Baby. I'm sorry. I'm not upset with you, I'm upset *for* you."

I sniffled, I fucking hated crying. "Thanks. And look,

I know that's a lot to bite off. I understand if all of my issues are a deal-breaker for you. I should have told you before." I could hear my voice wavering and there was nothing I could do about it. I'd only ever talked to two people about this in my entire life but I hadn't been trying to date either one of *them*. Suddenly the gravity of what I'd done to him was weighing me down.

William stood and set his coffee down before he stepped in front of my chair. I watched as he carefully lowered himself to his knees in front of me where I'd curled into myself in my chair.

"*Demon*, you don't owe me an apology. And your 'issues' aren't a lot to 'deal with.' Your untreated mental condition is a concern for me, but that's because I care about you, not because it's too much for me to bear."

I blinked at him. I even tried to absorb what he'd said. I really did. "I want to believe you," I whispered.

He reached up and cupped my cheek, never letting his gaze waver from mine. "I'll say it as many times as it takes for you to believe me."

I wanted to believe him.

William spent the next three days showing me in every way humanly possible that he was there for me.

Somewhere in the back of my mind, I knew it wouldn't last forever, but for those few days, I let myself believe that I wouldn't have to be so alone anymore.

———————————————

44

Liam

———————————————

It Shouldn't Matter

"Fuck!" I punched at the laptop keys aggressively until I heard a snort from the doorway.

Rae leaned against the frame with her arms crossed over her chest. "How's the liquor order going, boss?" Her smirk said it was a rhetorical question.

"Fine," I grumbled.

"Something tells me that isn't the thing you're really so agitated about. Wanna talk about it?"

I glared at her, though she wasn't the source of my frustration. "Nothing to talk about."

"Mm-hmm. So, the fact that Astrid and William have run off into hiding together for an untold amount of time isn't bothering you at all? I mean, there's no telling what they could be getting up to, but I have a pretty good guess." She raised her brow at me in challenge.

I pushed back from the desk with another growl.

"She's a grown woman. It's her choice to make. It's not like I have any right to her."

"Of course you don't. Because you're a chickenshit who never told her how you feel."

"I don't know what you're talking about." I busied myself with packing up the laptop and shoving it into my bag. I'd finish the damn order at home.

When I turned to the door to leave Rae was staring at me incredulously. "You don't remember talking to me the day after Christmas, do you?"

I stopped in my tracks. There was a fuzzy memory nagging at the back of my brain, but when I tried to grab hold of it and remember exactly what we'd talked about it disappeared into the ether.

I shook my head at her slowly, equal parts afraid that she would and afraid that she wouldn't tell me what we'd talked about.

She rolled her eyes at me and stepped into the office, pushing the door shut behind her. "Boss. You called me pissed out of your gourd, whining and moaning about how Astrid had left and you never got to tell her that you loved her and you were going to lose her to 'that dickbag William'." She paused. "Please note those last words were yours, not mine."

I slowly let my bag slip from my fingers, wincing when it hit the floor harder than I'd intended. I made my way to the couch and flopped onto the cushions, leaning back until my head hit the wall behind me. "Oh."

"Yeah. *Oh.*" She came closer and spun the office chair to face me before she sat down.

"Anything…uh, else?" I asked without averting my gaze from the ceiling.

"Yep." She let the *p* roll out of her mouth with a popping noise. "After I talked to you I texted Astrid."

That made me snatch my head forward so hard that I wondered if you could give yourself whiplash. "You *what*?"

"Look. You were in really bad shape. I was worried about you and I couldn't get here. I had a…uh, thing. So I texted her to see if she was in town." She shrugged.

"And?" I widened my eyes at her impatiently.

"And she was in Boston, so I wished her a Merry Christmas and told her I was sure everything would be fine."

I gaped at her for a moment before I let my head fall back again. This was a fucking disaster.

"I really thought that was the end of it, but then she texted me the next day." She held her hand up in front of her face, studying her manicure like she was suddenly a girl who cared about cuticle health.

I groaned. "What did she say?"

My question was met with silence. When I opened an eye to see what was taking her so long to answer, she was smirking at me again. "She said she'd found you passed out drunk in here. But that's all she said. I asked her if you'd said anything to her in your compromised state, but she was oddly close-lipped about that." Rae was clearly taking a great amount of joy from my pain and it was pissing me off.

"Rae!" I flopped over onto the other half of the couch, laying on my back and staring at the ceiling.

"I think you'd better talk to her, buddy. And, this time, maybe try doing it sober?" She snickered and stood to leave. "In all seriousness, Liam, if you have feelings for her, you have to tell her." Her face took on a somber expression. "It's not fair to hold shit like that back. And she's had a pretty fucking rough go of it." She held up her hand. "Before you ask, no, I will not tell you what I mean by that, but just trust me when I say that she deserves to have you be honest about your feelings. If she chooses to pass, then that's her right, but I've never known anyone more deserving of love who's been on the receiving end of so little of it."

With that, she left me to my crisis and shut the door behind her with a click.

Now what was I supposed to do?

45

William

Tell Me, If I Run Away, How Long Will I Bleed?

I WATCHED HER SLEEPING, HER HAIR A DARK SPILL AGAINST the white pillowcase. Her face was peaceful in sleep in a way it seldom was when she was awake. "Demon," I whispered, placing a kiss against her forehead, butterfly soft.

She groaned and shifted but didn't open her eyes.

"Baby." I placed another gentle kiss, on her parted lips this time. God, she was so fucking beautiful, I didn't want to wake her.

Her eyelashes fluttered against her cheeks before she finally opened her eyes and saw me sitting there. Her lips parted in a smile. "G'morning."

I waited for her to reach full consciousness, and I knew she had when her eyes narrowed on me. "You're wearing a suit."

I reached my hand out to touch her but she slid

away from me, pushing herself until she sat up against the headboard, out of my reach.

"Why are you wearing a suit? You wear jeans and t-shirts here. Or nothing at all." Her tone was accusatory, and I couldn't fault her instincts.

"I have to go." I hung my head. God knew that last fucking thing I wanted to do was leave her, but the call I'd just received left me with no choice.

I waited for her to yell at me. What happened was worse. She just...closed up. I watched every single door slam shut as if she'd never opened up to me. "Okay. Have a safe trip. This was fun."

"Demon. It's not like that...something's happened back in New York. I have to go. But I'll be back." I didn't promise. I knew better than to do that in my line of work.

"Okay, sure. I get it. You have to go. No big, I'll just rent a car or something and head back to Redding."

"Stay here. Please, stay here. You're safe here. I'll check on everyone back in Redding again before I take off, but they're fine. I've been getting regular updates from Jared,"

She was already shaking her head. "I won't. Not if you're gone. I can't stay here." Her shoulders shook.

"I'm begging you, Astrid. This is the safest place for you right now. They still haven't located Dimitri. I won't be able to do what I need to do if I know you're back there where he can get his hands on you."

"Dimitri," she said in a dead voice. "That's his name then?"

I sighed. "Yes."

She pushed me out of her way and started toward the bedroom door, giving me her back for a moment before she paused. "I'll think about it."

I breathed a sigh of relief. "Thank you. I have to go now, but I've left you the keys to the rental on the counter in the kitchen. My ride is waiting for me."

"Okay." Her shoulders were curved in on themselves. "Have a safe flight."

And then she walked out of the room. I heard the door to the bathroom close with a click a moment later. The lock slid home.

I wished she would have slammed it.

"Thank you for flying with us today, sir. Can I offer you a beverage?" My attention was jerked toward the flight attendant when she touched my shoulder.

"Scotch. Neat. Two fingers, please." I barely made eye contact before I returned to staring out the window, not seeing the tarmac stretched out below the wing of the plane. Instead, I saw water-drenched lashes blinking up at me as we floated in the lake. Her arms and legs wrapped around me as I kept us afloat, the midnight blue of her eyes gazing at me for all the world like I was the only man she ever wanted. She looked so happy.

It'd been my intention to keep making her that happy, for as long as I could.

I'd just hoped it would be for longer than three days.

I walked into my loft, dropped my keys on the table by the door, and immediately began peeling off my suit jacket. I tossed it over a chair in the dining room and loosened my tie before I paused.

"I don't remember giving you access to my loft, dear. How'd you get in?"

"What can I say? I didn't want to wait for your call, so I bribed your doorman. By the way, you might want to consider a new doorman. He didn't charge me nearly enough."

I sighed, and made my way to the wet bar in the corner to pour myself a drink. I held up the bottle without looking over my shoulder.

"No thanks, *dear*. I've already got one."

I chuckled. Annoyed and amused in equal measures.

Glass in hand, I turned and he reached over to turn on the lamp next to the couch.

"Have a nice trip?" His tone dripped with sarcasm.

I took the seat opposite him and lifted the glass to my lips. "Parts."

"So I heard."

"What did you hear?" I raised my brows at him.

"Well, my girlfriend called me flipping her shit because her best friend told her all about her new boyfriend, William." He raised an eyebrow at me. "Now, I'm not one to meddle in anyone's personal affairs, especially my boss's, but I'm far more scared of her right now than I am of you, so I think it's best if you come clean."

"Best for me? Or best for you?" I smirked.

Key rolled his eyes at me. "Stop dancing around the issue. Did you, or did you not, involve my girlfriend's best friend in the whole of the goddamn world in Organization business, thereby putting her life in danger and making my life a living hell in the process?"

"First of all, I think you're being a bit dramatic. I've met Imogen. Living hell? She's a delight." I couldn't help tweaking his nerves, it had been a hell of a day and I needed to find joy where I could.

"She's fucking pissed, William. She spent the last year doing everything in her power to keep Astrid out, and you're there for two months and now she's so deeply embroiled in our world that an assassin now has her on his radar? Trust me. Living hell doesn't begin to state it." He tossed back the rest of the liquid in his glass.

I let my head fall against the back of the couch. "I didn't bring her in. That part was already done before I ever arrived. And, from what I can tell, he already had her on his radar before I ever stepped foot in Cali. Everything I've done since then has been to try and protect her from him."

"If you didn't bring her in, then who the fuck did?"

I raised my head and met his gaze again. "Fucking Liam."

Key closed his eyes and appeared to be counting to ten. "*Fucking Liam.*"

I nodded and returned to staring at my ceiling.

"Well, that's not the only problem you've got. I hate to break it to you, but Meredith has gone off grid. Told someone at headquarters that she needed a vacation or some shit and hopped on a flight that same night."

"Do we know where?" My suspicions about Meredith were becoming more and more solid by the minute.

"According to the flight records? Nevada."

"God-fucking-dammit, Key. You didn't think I needed that bit of information before you called me back here?" I stood up and headed into my bedroom, my brain racing. "I have to go back."

"Calm your tits, *dear*. I didn't have that bit of information until you were already in the air. Hence my appearance here. We needed to talk and I didn't want to pass that information along over the phone and have you go off half-cocked and get yer arse killed."

I stopped and turned to him, glaring. "What else is there to talk about?"

"She knows." His mouth settled into a grim line.

"She knows *what*?" I barked, impatient to get this conversation over with and get back on a plane as fast as possible.

"Meredith knows about Dearil. Who was there that night. Who pulled the trigger. And who walked out of the room that night."

"*Fuck!*" I swung out and my fist connected with the wall in my hallway, leaving an impressive hole in the drywall that I'd have to fucking fix if we all survived this shit show.

"Indeed. She sent a handwritten letter. She's threatening to out us all to the rest of the Organization, in hopes it will cause mutiny, if I had to guess. But that's not the worst part."

"It gets fucking worse? Come on, asshole, stop doling information out like I'm a bairn." I continued on into my bedroom, knowing he would follow.

"She sent it to Imogen directly. The letter stated that if you didn't immediately reinstate her to her former position and step down as the head of the Organization she'll go to the feds with what she knows. Imogen will go to prison for murder, William. You know as well as I do that I'll not stand for that."

He stood in the doorway to my bedroom watching me frantically throwing clean clothes in a bag. He made a noise, drawing my attention to him. His expression wasn't one I thought I'd ever seen on his face.

"Mate. If anything happens to Imogen there will not be a chain that could hold me back from turning this whole goddamn thing on its arse to get her free. I'll implicate you, me, and any goddamn other person I can to make sure that she doesn't carry the weight of a crime that *you* led her to by the hand."

He got up in my face, but didn't move to swing. His eyes had gone cold. "My loyalty is to Imogen *first*. Do not mistake that."

For the first time in my life, I knew how he felt. And I didn't disagree with him. "I'll fix it. You have my word."

"See that you do. I'll be on the lookout for word from you that this whole mess has been fucking resolved. And then I'm taking Gen and Auley on a long vacation from which I may never return. Consider this my notice."

I nodded. I didn't blame him for that either.

"I'll fix this."

He met my gaze, unblinking, for a beat before he nodded and left, leaving me to figure out how I was going to clean up this mess and keep everyone safe.

46

Meredith

If You Want Something Done Right

"When you said we were going to Nevada, I thought you meant Vegas, babe." Topher glared out the windshield at Highway 395 winding in front of us.

I looked up from my phone. "Oops?" I blinked big innocent eyes at him that I didn't think he was buying. "But, hey, this is scenic, right? Definitely vacation worthy."

I knew it didn't matter how scenic the highway was, this had the potential to backfire in a big way when he figured out why we were there, but I needed him. His presence was calming. And I'd need the cover story if this whole plan went tits up.

"And Mammoth is considered one of the most beautiful parts of California. You're gonna love it, I promise," I continued, trying to sell it.

He shot me a dubious glance from the driver's seat and grumbled. "Would have loved Vegas more."

I knew that. But, unfortunately, my plan wasn't in the process of falling apart in Vegas. It was, however, potentially falling apart in Mammoth.

So, to Mammoth we went.

I looked back down at the flip phone I'd pulled out of the safe in my desk. Untraceable, unhackable. Working for a criminal organization did occasionally have its perks.

I'd texted Dimitri hours ago, informing him I was on my way and not to do anything until I arrived.

He hadn't answered. *Asshole.*

I'd worked so hard to gather every bit of information I needed in order to be able to force William's hand. I was so close to forcing him to hand over the reins to the Organization that I could almost taste it. And Dimitri was going to fuck it all up because he had *poor impulse control.*

Fuck me.

It was after three in the morning by the time we arrived at the cabin I'd booked, conveniently only a few hundred yards from the location he'd sent the last time he'd texted me. Which had been more than twelve hours prior.

There were a lot of things he could have gotten up to in the last twelve hours, and I had very little confidence that he was still following my orders. I just hoped we weren't too late to keep him from completely imploding my plan in pursuit of his...hobbies.

Topher eased our rented SUV carefully over the rutted road that the GPS had us turn onto from the highway, grimacing as the frame scraped. "They're probably going to charge us for that, you know that, right?" He was grumpy, and I didn't blame him. We'd been travelling for the last eleven hours. We were both tired, hungry, and he was understandably pissed that I'd dragged him on a spontaneous "getaway" to the other side of the country under the pretense of exploring "The Great Outdoors."

We were New Yorkers. We didn't do the great outdoors.

"I'll cover it. Don't worry." I patted his leg, appreciating the band of muscle under my hand. He was no outdoorsman, but he kept himself fit in other ways and I loved that about him. He was also usually a pretty easygoing guy. Down for just about anything. I'd just pressed him a little too far this time.

We finally arrived at the end of the drive, pulling up in front of a charming little cabin situated by a lake. I could see the moon reflecting off the water from where we sat. "See? It's pretty. Wait until you see it in the daylight, you're going to love it."

That got me another dubious look from him, but he just sighed and climbed out of the car, circling around to the back to grab my chair.

I opened my door and maneuvered myself so I was ready to slide into it as soon as he had it situated next to the vehicle. I shot him a grateful look. I'd almost rented a vehicle that would have provided me with greater mobility, but the woman at the rental place had taken one look at our destination and pointed out that we'd need something more rugged if we had any hope of not getting stuck. If the road we'd just come down was any indication, she hadn't been wrong.

Topher stood by while I got myself into the chair, knowing better than to step in if I didn't ask for his help. He really was a gem. Once I was settled, he gestured to the stairs leading up to the front porch. "Want some help with those?"

I frowned, looking around to see if there was another way in. I thought all rentals were accessible these days, but apparently these were the exception. I gave him an apologetic look. "Yeah, thanks, babe."

He just nodded and lifted me and the chair up the three steps, barely straining as he did, and set me down on the porch. See? Fit.

"I'll go get the bags." He trotted back to the car and started pulling our hastily packed overnight bags out of the back.

I entered the digital code into the keypad on the door and went inside to get a feel for the place. It was… quaint. Was that a word people still used? Hell if I knew.

He joined me a moment later and let out a low whistle as he surveyed the space. "You take me to the nicest places."

I rolled my eyes at him. The sarcasm was strong with this one.

Topher slept like the dead, sprawled out across the bed with the sheet pulled up to his waist. I'd gotten out of bed hours ago, after having slept just enough to allow my brain to come back online. I was in the living room working on my laptop when he lifted his head and patted the bed next to him before looking through the open door and spotting me.

"I thought this was a vacation." He yawned.

"About that…" I grimaced.

"Whatever you're about to say," he stopped me. "Please don't. At least wait until I've had coffee."

I nodded. "Okay. Deal."

"Dammit. Mere, you should have told me." He was pacing back and forth in front of me, shooting me occasional glares mid-stride.

"I know. I'm sorry. But you wouldn't have come, and I need you!" I really did feel bad about lying to him.

"You need an alibi. Not a partner. Anyone could have done that for you, but you chose to involve me in your *business*." He made air quotes with his fingers. "And now I'm here and what choice do I really have but to help you? That's gross. Really fucking gross."

"I'll make it up to you, Toph, I promise. We'll go on a *real* vacation once this is done." That earned me another glare.

"Your choice?" I offered.

He looked slightly mollified by that, but not much.

"Fine. What do you need me to do?" He crossed his arms over his chest where he stood in front of me.

"Maybe take a little walk along the shoreline? See if

you meet any neighbors?" I had my fingers crossed that William's girl wouldn't want to stay cooped up in a cabin by herself all day long. If Topher could befriend her, it would make my job that much easier. He was very disarming, after all. He was a fucking middle school science teacher. Nobody was scared of a middle school science teacher.

He rolled his eyes and held his hand out for my phone. "What does she look like?"

I pulled up the one picture I had of her, though it was grainy and taken from a distance.

He studied it before handing my phone back. "She looks young. Are you sure that's the right girl?"

"I'm sure." I nodded.

Topher leaned into my space, placing his face so close to mine that I could feel his breath as he exhaled. "You are going to owe me so fucking big for this."

I grinned, relief swimming through my veins. "Anything."

His eyes lit up at that and he stood, pointing a finger at me. "Gonna hold you to that." And then he put on his tennis shoes and walked out the back door of the cabin, jogging down the steps that led to the shoreline.

Now I just needed to figure out what Dimitri had been up to in the last twenty hours.

"You haven't been answering my calls." I made no attempt to temper the irritation in my tone. I was past the point of trying to cajole him into behaving.

"I don't think I want to anymore, Meredith. I'm bored with your agenda." He sounded distracted.

"And I think you have lost the plot," I snapped back. "The girl doesn't need to be involved and your obsession with her has nearly cost me everything. If you blow up this deal, rest assured I'll make sure you regret it for the rest of your life."

Perhaps threatening him wasn't the best course of action, but I was so fucking close to getting everything I wanted and I could see it all slipping through my fingers like grains of sand. All because of *him*.

"But I like her. And she looks so pretty when she cries. I want to know what she looks like when she screams." His voice had taken on a sing-song quality that sent chills down my spine. I was a fucking idiot for ever thinking I could involve him in my plan without something like this happening.

"What have you done?" I waited, holding my breath.

"Oh, me? Nothing yet. But soon, very soon."

The phone went dead and I tossed it onto the coffee table in front of me with a frustrated growl.

William

S.O.S.

"I need you in Mammoth."

"What now?" I could hear frustration in his voice. I understood it. He'd been hunting elusive prey with absolutely no luck.

"I think Meredith is there and I left Astrid at the cabin alone. I thought she'd be safer there."

I heard an engine roar to life on the other end of the line before he replied. "Where are you?"

"I'm on my way, but you're closer by about twelve hundred miles."

"Fuck, kid. I'm going now but I'm hours out."

"I'll call when I land. Get to her. Please." I wasn't above begging if I thought it would help.

The line went dead and I ran for my gate, praying I wasn't too late.

Astrid

It Comes and Goes in Waves

"How's my boy doing?" I was curled up in a chair on the back porch with my knees drawn up to my chest and my phone cradled between my shoulder and my ear. I missed Remy so fucking much, especially trapped at the cabin by myself. Technically, I knew I could leave, but the thought that returning to Redding could potentially put my friends in more danger held me in place. But fuck was it lonely.

Brennan chuckled on the other end of the line. "Honey, this dog is so fucking spoiled now, I don't know if he's gonna want to come back home with you when you get back."

I sniffled. I was glad Remy was okay with Brennan, but the thought that he was happier there than he was with me hurt.

"Hey, hey. I'm just kidding, Astrid. He misses you. I can tell he does. He's gonna be so fucking happy to see you, bet. But he's well taken care of, so don't worry about him, okay? Just take care of you. Enjoy your vacation."

"Thanks, Bren. I owe you one for taking such good care of him. Give him a kiss for me, okay?"

"You got it, girlie. Take care."

"Okay. Bye, Bren." I hit the end call button and felt more tears inexplicably begin to stream down my face. Why the fuck couldn't I stop crying?

I'd taken to going for walks along the shoreline. There wasn't much else to do except go hiking and I hadn't packed for that. William had left enough groceries in the kitchen that I could have fed myself for a month. It had me wondering exactly how long he'd intended for us to stay hidden.

I walked along in the sand, letting the waves lap at my ankles but I could barely look at the water without remembering being wrapped around him, grinning at him happily as he joked about me trying to drown him.

I'd never considered myself a pessimist in the truest sense. Maybe more of a realist. But even in that moment, I'd wondered when I would wake up and discover it had all been a dream.

I missed him viscerally. But, even more than that, I missed the feeling of finally being at home. I wasn't alone. Someone was there for me, and I was so happy for that brief moment in time.

When I'd woken to see him watching me sleep, already dressed like he was back in the real world, it hadn't shocked me. Somehow, I'd known he would leave. I just hadn't expected it to hurt so badly when he did. And when he said he would be back, I didn't let myself believe him.

Once he got on that plane, he wouldn't be back.

Getting lost in my memories was probably really fucking dumb, and when I almost walked right into a man walking toward me on the beach I jumped, realizing I'd walked much farther from the cabin than I ever had before.

"I'm sorry, I didn't mean to startle you. You looked so lost in thought that I wanted to check if you were okay?" His voice was a soothing balm in my ears when the only other voices I'd heard in the last couple of days had been over the phone. I realized suddenly I was starved for human companionship.

I offered him an apology, even as I studied him. "No, that's on me. Sorry for almost plowing over you." I turned my head toward the lake for a moment before I looked back at him. He offered me a friendly smile. "Memories are a real bitch sometimes, ya know?"

He gave me an understanding nod. "Yeah, I get that. They definitely can be."

He offered a hand. "I'm Topher. My girlfriend and I are staying just past that inlet." He gestured behind him to a cabin partially obscured by giant firs and pines.

I met his palm with mine, offering him a smile.

"Astrid. I'm in that one over there for…a little while. TBD, if I'm honest. I don't know how much more of this solitude I can handle."

He laughed and it was a comforting sound. "Believe me, I get it. She wanted to come and see the great outdoors, but she's been working since we got here. I'd be surprised if she even comes outside while we're here. Do you mind if I join you on your walk? I promise not to talk your ear off."

"I think I'd like that, Topher."

We walked in silence for a few paces, the lapping of the water and chirping of birds the only sounds, before he spoke again. "I know I said I wouldn't talk your ear off…"

I laughed. I could hear the "but" coming.

"But, do you mind if I ask what had you looking so sad when we bumped into each other?" He looked at me sideways as we walked.

I considered for a minute how odd it was to tell him anything, but what could it hurt? He was a stranger, it was broad daylight, and he was just about the most non-threatening man I'd ever met.

"I lost someone," I started. "Well, that's not exactly right. I found myself, with a little help from a friend, but now that he's gone I'm wondering if it was all an illusion, if any of it was real. I guess you could say I'm floundering. A crisis of faith?"

"And what is it that you've lost faith in, Astrid?" he asked gently.

"Everything, Topher. I think I've lost faith in everything." Another tear tracked down my face and I let it go. I was tired of wiping them away.

"Ah. I see." He continued walking beside me quietly for a moment before he continued. "Do you think that a moment of happiness is less valuable for its brevity? Like, if you eat a piece of chocolate, but it's just the one piece, do you enjoy it less for knowing the taste will only linger in your mouth for so long? Or do you savor it, knowing you'll have another one day and it will be that much more enjoyable for the wait?"

I considered his question. "I think there's been so little…chocolate…in my life that I don't have any faith that there will ever be another bite. Does that make any sense?"

He smiled at me sadly. "It does. But, if you don't mind a little wisdom from someone with a few more years under their belt, I think you're still at the beginning of your story. So, while it seems bleak now, one day you'll look back and realize that the parts of it you've already lived at *this* point are just a fraction of the whole. Better things can still come."

I took a deep shuddering breath, trying to believe what he'd said. "I hope you're right about that."

"Trust me. This is just the beginning." He grinned.

"What do you think about joining me and my girlfriend for dinner? If we have company, I think she might stop working for long enough to actually see the scenery for a minute."

Topher and I had walked the entire stretch of the shoreline and circled back toward both of our cabins. The sun was beginning to set and I realized that I was hungry, truly hungry, for the first time since William had left.

"Are you sure she won't mind?"

"Nah. She's cool. A little intense from time to time, but she'll love you, don't worry."

"Okay then, I think I'd like that."

"Mere! You in here? I brought company for dinner!" Topher gestured for me to follow him in through the glass doors on the back deck.

"In here! Be right out." I heard a woman's voice call out from the other room and shifted nervously, hoping she really wasn't going to mind that her boyfriend had brought home a stray for dinner.

When she came into the room I tried to temper my surprise, but apparently I sucked at that.

She laughed good naturedly. "Everyone does that at first. Topher didn't tell you, I'm guessing."

I glanced at Topher who was chuckling under his breath as he headed into the kitchen.

"I'm sorry!" I grimaced.

"Don't be! They're just wheels, it's not like I have a terminal illness. I just have to remain seated for the rest of my flight." She stared at me for a beat before I got the joke.

"Jesus, Mere, maybe don't lead with the wheelchair jokes right off the bat," Topher called from the kitchen.

I giggled. "I think I'm going to like you, Meredith." I stuck my hand out for her to shake. "I'm Astrid, I'm staying in the next cabin down, just a couple hundred feet that way." I hooked a thumb in the direction of my cabin.

She shook my hand with a firm grip, smiling in welcome. "Nice to meet you, Astrid. I love that Topher managed to make friends when we've been here less than a day. Leave it to that man."

"It's a gift!" he said. He'd pulled a bottle of wine out of the fridge and grabbed some glasses off of a floating shelf just next to it. "Astrid, would you like a glass of Pinot Grigio? It's Mere's favorite, so I'm afraid it's all we've got on hand."

"I'd love one. Thanks."

The three of us enjoyed a quick dinner, prepared by Topher, of pan-seared salmon filets and a cheesy orzo dish that he swore was the easiest and best thing he'd ever learned how to make. I didn't know how easy it was, but I had to agree it was one of the best things I'd tasted in a long time.

"It's the gruyère cheese. It makes all the difference. That's why it's so gooey." He grinned at me before shoveling another spoonful in his mouth.

Meredith watched him indulgently before she turned

to me. "So, Astrid, what brings you here? Are you having some sort of sabbatical?"

I dropped my eyes to my plate before picking up my wine glass and taking a sip. "I came with a friend but he had to leave suddenly. I'm honestly not sure how much longer I'll be able to stand the solitude and the quiet, but he told me to stay as long as I wanted." A tiny little bend of the truth, but they didn't need to know every little detail. "I guess I'll stay until I can't stand the sound of my own voice anymore."

"And where will you go then?" she asked.

"Back to Redding. That's where my…" I paused before I realized it was true. "That's where my real life is."

She nodded. "Ah, real life. I find that it's overrated." She lifted her glass and tapped it against the rim of mine. "Here's to sabbaticals!"

I nodded and took another sip of wine but the truth was, I was actually looking forward to getting back to my real life. As soon as it was safe, that is.

"So how long have you two been together?" We'd moved to the living room, and I watched Topher lift Meredith out of her chair so they could curl up on the couch together. It was cute even if it did cause a pang to go through my chest.

Meredith smiled up at Topher before she answered. "Five years, give or take."

Topher laughed. "We have different ideas about when we started dating."

I tilted my head and waited for him to explain.

"I basically stalked her for weeks trying to get her to take me seriously, so we kept bumping into one another at random places by 'accident,' until I finally just had to announce in the middle of a packed restaurant that I wanted to date her and she was breaking my heart by constantly blowing me off."

"Oh my fucking god, it was so embarrassing, Astrid. You have no idea." She was laughing, a tinge of pink darkening her cheekbones.

"But you agreed to go out with me finally." He sounded smug.

"I did." She rolled her eyes.

"So where's the discrepancy?" I asked, charmed by their story.

Topher answered first. "I say it started that day. The day she agreed to go out with me."

"And I say it didn't start until we actually went on that date," Meredith argued.

"How long was it between the two?" I laughed.

Topher offered me a huge grin. "Three days."

I rolled my eyes. "I can see how that makes a huge difference then."

They both laughed good naturedly. I glanced at the clock over the stove in the kitchen and felt my eyes widen. "Oh shit, you guys, I'm so sorry, I didn't realize it had gotten so late."

I stood from my spot on the couch and carried my empty glass to the sink. "Thank you so much for dinner and the company, it's been nice to have people to talk to."

"We're glad you joined us!" Meredith said. "Let Topher walk you back to your cabin. It's dark as hell out there, I don't want you getting eaten by a bear."

Topher hopped up and agreed with her. "Absolutely, my mother would beat my ass if she knew I let a woman walk home in the dark alone, even if it is just a few hundred feet."

William

Delayed

G: Where are you?

William: stuck in salt lake. Two hour layover. You?

G: Getting close. But i think i have a tail.

William: lose it

G: what the hell do you think i'm doing? It's going to add some time tho.

William: do what you have to. Keep me posted.

Astrid

No Idle Threats

I LAID IN BED, UNABLE TO SLEEP UNTIL THE WATER OUTSIDE the windows started glowing red with the sunrise. I'd tossed and thrashed so much that the bed looked like a war had been waged during the night. I'd hoped that the couple glasses of wine and the company would quiet my mind enough that sleep would come easy, but that hadn't happened.

I finally gave up and decided to make a pot of coffee. Maybe I'd call Imogen and talk for a little while.

With a fresh cup in my hand, I stepped out onto the back deck and settled into my new favorite chair. I pulled out my phone and dialed her number, smiling when she picked up on the first ring.

"I was just thinking about you."

"Did you have another one of those dreams about

me?" I asked. "It doesn't mean you're bi. I'm a sexy bitch."

Imogen cackled. "Shut up. And I'm pretty sure we're all bi. But no, that's not why. I was just wondering how you were doing, but didn't want to call this early. The time difference is a bitch."

I sighed. "I'm okay. I mean, I'm sad and really fucking tired, but I'm okay."

"Have you heard from him since he left?" Her tone was cautious.

"No. Not a word. But I honestly didn't expect to, so I'm not surprised."

"I'm sorry, babe. I wish I knew what to tell you. I really don't know him all that well, but if it's worth anything, I can't imagine anyone being able to walk away from you so easily. Maybe there's more going on that he didn't tell you?"

"Is there something more going on that you aren't telling me?" Something in her tone had set off my bestie senses.

"It's Organization shit. But the gist of it is that there's someone in the Organization, a woman, who's trying to blackmail William into stepping down as the head. And somehow she knows about what happened last winter. Something I did that could get me in big trouble."

"What kind of trouble, Gen?" I asked in a low voice. Knowing that we probably shouldn't even be having this conversation over the phone.

"The kind that comes with a permanent outfit change." She sighed.

"What the fuck? Who is this bitch? I'll take her out

myself." I got up and started pacing, angry energy shooting through my veins.

"We're handling it. Or I think we are. William knows about it. Maybe that's why you haven't heard from him? He's too busy trying to figure out what to do about Meredith."

I stopped cold. "What did you say?"

"I mean, I don't know if that's why, I'm just saying that he might be preoccupied with that right now."

"Not that part, Gen. The part about her name," I gritted out, realization coming at me like a freight train.

"Meredith? Apparently she was the old head's right-hand woman. That's pretty much all I know about her, other than that she's a real fucking piece of shit. She doesn't give a shit about what I did, she's just using me to get William to do what she wants." Imogen sounded angry but not particularly worried.

"And you don't think she'll go through with it?" I was pacing again.

"Oh, according to Key, she definitely would, but something tells me William isn't going to let it get that far, so I'm trying to keep calm about it. At least, now I am. When she first reached out I flipped the fuck out, but Auley and Key talked me down. It's going to be okay. But, if it's not, I'll see if I can get you on the list for my conjugal visits." She cackled, and I rounded my eyes, unable to believe she was joking about this.

"I'd love to know how they talked you down from that because you are way too damn zen about this right now."

"I'll draw you a picture." She cackled again.

"Look, I need to run for now, but I'll talk to you soon, okay? I have something I need to take care of." I was staring at the small break in the trees that afforded me a glimpse of the next cabin over. Fuming.

When I stormed up the back steps to their deck Topher was stretched out in one of the lounge chairs with his sunglasses on and an arm curled behind his head. I kicked his chair, causing him to jump. He slid his sunglasses up on top of his head and stared at me like I'd lost my mind for a beat before his face fell.

"Well, that didn't take long." He sighed.

"Where is she?" I snarled. I hadn't been 100 percent sure when I'd hung up the phone with Imogen, but Topher's response confirmed my suspicion.

He rose to his full height and offered me an apologetic look. "Come on, she's inside."

He opened the door to the cabin and called out. "Mere. Astrid is…here."

When Meredith came out of the bedroom I charged at her. "You fucking manipulative bitch. What the hell are you doing here anyway? Did you just come to see if you could fuck up my life like you're threatening to fuck up Imogen's?"

She stared at me blankly, all traces of the genial woman from last night gone like she'd never existed.

"Quite the opposite. I'm here to save your life."

"What?!"

51

Astrid

Always Feel Like Somebody's Watching Me

I PULLED OUT ONTO THE HIGHWAY AT SPEED, TIRES screeching and gunned the engine, pointed back toward Redding.

I looked up to the rearview mirror just in time to see a truck pull out behind me, gaining on me fast.

I smiled grimly and wrapped my hands tighter around the steering wheel.

I felt the front of the truck tap my rear bumper just as I turned the SUV into the next curve.

Part IV

Come out, come out, wherever you are
I know where you're hidin', I know who
you are

-"Hide and Seek" Klergy, Mindy Jones

52

Astrid

In Time

HIS LIPS HOVERED JUST ABOVE MINE, HIS BREATH COMING out in gasps as he spoke. "Are you okay?" His golden gaze leveled me with the sheer panic and adoration he showed me without his usual reservation. "Demon, please say something before I scoop you up and carry you straight to the hospital."

I stared at him for a beat, struggling to catch my breath. "I...think I'm okay." I blinked, taking careful inventory of every bump and scrape I could feel, but not discerning any mortal wounds. That was great news, but my brain still felt like it'd been shaken, not stirred, and I just kept blinking up at him in confusion.

"What are you doing here?"

A slow smile spread across his face. "Told you I was coming back, didn't I? And just in time, from the looks of it."

At the sound of squealing tires on wet asphalt William's head whipped around, his arms pulling me closer to his chest as if he intended to protect me from whatever fresh hell was headed toward us with nothing but the bulk of his body.

I heard a car door open and booted feet hit the blacktop, running toward us before William released the breath he'd been holding on a harsh exhale. "About damn time, where the fuck have you been?"

The man standing over his shoulder studied me with worried eyes before he replied. "I told you, I got delayed. I handled it. Is she okay? God, Imogen'll have my hide."

I stared over William's shoulder at a ghost, not believing what I was seeing. Scared to believe what I was seeing.

"Hank?" My voice was incredulous as I studied the man I'd mourned so completely that it had almost undone me. Unbidden tears escaped from my eyes. *"Hank?"*

He shot me a sorrow-filled look. "Garen now, love." He looked away and surveyed the area around us. When he met my gaze again he looked worried, but resolute. "I promise I'll explain, but first let's get you out of here in case he decides to come back and make sure you're well and truly dead. Or worse. Can you walk?"

William's arms tightened again before he began to rise to his feet with me cradled between them. "I've got her."

Hank—no...*Garen* shot him a speculative glance,

narrowing his eyes a bit before he shook his head. "All right then. Let's move."

53

Astrid

Vanquish

WILLIAM BOLTED TO HIS VEHICLE WITH ME GRIPPED IN HIS arms, ignoring my protests that I could walk. His head looked like it was on a swivel, and I could hear the other vehicle cranking up behind us as he loaded me into the car and slammed the door, running to the driver's side in a flash. "Buckle up, Demon, I don't know where the fuck he went, but I'm betting he didn't go far."

"William," I said.

"I know, baby, I'm glad to see you too, but we can talk about all this later." He threw the vehicle in drive and peeled away from the side of the road with tires spinning and rocks flying.

"*William,*" I said again.

He didn't take his eyes off the road but I needed him to hear me. "Where are we going?"

He never stopped checking his mirrors as he

answered me distractedly. "Garen has a safe house somewhere up here. He's taking us there."

I shook my head, throwing it back against the headrest in frustration. That wouldn't work.

"No. Take me back."

He did look at me then. "*What*? No. Why the hell would you want me to do that?"

"Because," I said. "You're fucking up our plan."

I couldn't talk him out of taking me to Garen's safe house. In fact, once I'd made that last statement he locked his jaw and refused to talk to me at all until we'd gotten there.

He still wasn't talking to me, but I could see his gaze follow me as I paced back and forth in front of them, explaining everything that had happened in the past twelve hours.

I took a break in my pacing to point a finger at Hank. *Fuck*. Garen. "Don't think for one minute that we aren't going to have it out as soon as all this drama is done with. I'm so mad at you, old man." I walked over and threw my arms around him. "But I'm so fucking glad to see you," I whispered, allowing myself a brief moment of weakness before I stepped away.

He gave me a sheepish grin and a nod, but I noticed a light in his eyes that I hadn't seen before. "So, you're working with Meredith. Explain again how that happened?"

William was sitting with his arms crossed, glaring at

me. Under different circumstances I'd have found it funny. Boy, he *really* didn't like it when he didn't get to be the knight in shining armor.

"I spoke with Imogen early this morning. She filled me in a little on the most recent issue. Of course I lost my fucking mind when she told me, and while she was trying to explain that she thought William had it under control she let a name slip. Meredith. I immediately thought about how very odd it was that I'd met a woman named Meredith just the day before."

I sent Garen a grateful look. "You always said there were no coincidences."

He nodded. "And you listened. *Good.*"

"So I confronted her."

William's eyes almost bugged out of his head. "You did *what*? Are you insane? You confronted a former assassin for the Organization, unarmed and without backup. Do you have a goddamn death wish?" He'd risen to his feet and was leaning into my space, his face red with his anger.

I narrowed mine right back at him, but didn't back down. "And who left me there unarmed and without backup, hmm? I did what I had to do. Nobody fucks with Imogen on my watch, and if you'd paid attention at all over the last few weeks, you'd know that about me."

Garen stood and slid a hand between us, pushing against William's chest until he backed up a step. "I'd suggest you refrain from screaming at her. I'd also suggest letting her finish before you fly off the damn handle. I basically raised this girl. She's no fool."

I shot him a grateful look.

"I spent the entire evening prior at their cabin. We had dinner, some wine, and good conversation. It was all very neighborly. And her boyfriend is there, so I was pretty sure she hadn't brought him with her to a murder party. I'm no assassin, but that just seems fucking dumb."

Garen snorted. "Not wrong."

"So I stormed over there, kicked the door in…"

Garen looked impressed. "Really?"

"Okay, no. I kicked a chair and Topher let me in."

William rolled his eyes. "Please, get to the part where you decided to work with the woman who is actively blackmailing me and your friends."

"Well, I think we bonded over dinner. Don't get me wrong, she's clearly fucking unhinged about this whole Organization thing, but I saw the way she was with Topher. There's a human in there somewhere and she confirmed it when she told me why she's here."

Garen looked thoughtful. "And that is?"

I shrugged. "To save my life."

William threw his hands up in the air and spun away from us. I could hear his teeth grinding with how hard his jaw was clenched.

Garen just waved a hand at him. "Ignore him. Tell me the plan."

54

Astrid

Finally, Astrid

"YOU HAVE TO TAKE ME BACK."

"Absolutely fucking not," William snarled.

Garen *tsked*. "That's not your call to make."

I rounded on him, but he wasn't looking at me, he was looking at William.

William clenched his fists. "It's insanity. She's going to get herself killed."

Garen tilted his head thoughtfully. "It's a solid plan. Honestly better than the one you had. We can watch and wait forever, but until something draws him out, we can't even think about dealing with Meredith and her threats. As Astrid proved today, he already knows she's here. Your diversion in Redding probably never threw him off. He's been toying with you."

"Look, I get it," I said to William. "I know you don't want me to get hurt, but I can't hide from him forever. I have a *life* to get back to, William. Hiding out here isn't doing any good, and eventually, he's going to get tired of this cat and mouse game we've been playing. We need to force his hand so that happens on our terms, not his."

He stared at me for so long I didn't think he was going to answer. "You're wearing a tracker. And I'll never be more than a hundred feet from you."

I shook my head. "He'll see you. This won't work if he knows it's a trap. I'll agree to the tracker, but you're going to have to back off farther than that."

The savage grin that spread over William's face was a sight to see. "He won't see me. I have skills you don't even know about yet, Demon."

Unbidden, images of the skills he had that I *did* know about came to mind. I felt my cheeks flush and Garen groaned. "No, no, no. That is not a conversation I'm going to take part in." He leveled a glare at William. "And I still have words for you about this." He gestured between me and William.

I snickered. "Aw, Pops, I missed you." I felt my heart jump at the show of paternal love.

He wrapped his arms around me, squeezing me tight. "Missed you too, kiddo."

They took me back to the wrecked SUV. It wasn't totaled, but I imagined the rental company wasn't going to be thrilled when they got a look at the damage. I hoped William had good insurance.

Just before we got there I looked at Garen. "You'll be watching?"

"Got your back." He tapped a rifle with a scope draped over his lap.

I looked at William next. "You won't interfere until you're sure we've got him?"

He reached over and grabbed my face, pressing his so close that we were sharing air. "You stay alive. I'll keep my distance, but I'll intervene, even if it means we lose him again, if he lays a fucking hand on you."

Fair enough. I nodded. "See you soon."

I climbed out of the truck and watched him do a slow three-point turn, pointing back the way they'd come, running without lights.

I approached the vehicle cautiously, keeping my eyes open. Peering underneath and in the backseat before I climbed in. When I went to crank the engine I noticed something on the passenger seat that hadn't been there before.

It was a knife. A large, jagged, curved knife with a bone handle. It rested on top of a note.

I THINK YOU WANT TO PLAY. DO YOU THINK YOU CAN BEST ME? ENJOY MY GIFT, CONSIDER IT A FREEBIE.

I'LL BE WAITING.

My hands shook as I read it and I locked the doors belatedly, realizing he could be watching me at that moment.

Probably *was* watching me at that moment.

I put the key in the ignition and turned it, eager to lead him to the spot we'd all agreed on for our trap.

Nothing happened. The interior light shut off. The doors unlocked of their own accord.

When I looked to my right toward the darkened forest, I could see a word written on the window:

RUN

55

Astrid

That's a Real Dick Move

I SNATCHED THE KNIFE OFF THE SEAT AND FLUNG THE driver's door open, trusting with every inch of me that, when they said they'd be watching, they meant it.

This plan just went to shit.

My only options were to stick to the road and head up the mountain, or go back down it. Or into the forest to my right. The only thing on the left side was a steep drop off that wouldn't lead me anywhere but straight into traction or dead.

My hands were shaking so bad I wondered if I'd even be able to keep hold of the knife.

I could see lights through the trees in the distance and something told me that's where I was supposed to be headed, but fuck that. I wasn't going to make this easy.

I stepped off the asphalt into the forest like in that

part of the horror movie where everyone starts throwing popcorn at the screen, yelling "go back!" but I kept going. This ended tonight.

The lights from the highway faded from view about fifty yards into the forest and I was walking blind, afraid to turn on my flashlight for fear of making myself too easy of a target.

I stepped as carefully as I could, the way Hank had taught me and Imogen, but even so my progress through the forest wasn't quiet. I stopped to listen periodically, but couldn't hear anything but forest sounds.

"*Come out, come out, wherever you are…*" I sang under my breath, trying to calm my own nerves.

I stood still, a tree at my back, listening for any movement.

A branch snapped to my left, and I saw a dark silhouette appear in my peripheral vision.

"You're not playing the game right," a mechanical voice sounded off from a different direction.

"I can't run. It's the goddamn forest at night. I'll break a leg," I spat at the silhouette.

The voice came again, from a different direction this time. "But if you don't play then how will we know who wins? I even gave you a gift. Don't you like my gift?"

"It's lovely." I rolled my eyes, doubting he could see my face. "The nicest murder weapon anyone has ever gifted me."

Mechanical laughter filled the forest. Oh good. I'd made the murderer laugh. *Go, Astrid.*

"I knew you would be fun. Won't you run for me,

though? It's so much more fun if I can *chaseeeee*." That last word was hissed in a sibilant tone.

"Perhaps, if I shed some light on the subject." Another bout of mechanical laughter and flood lights came on all around me, so bright I was blinded entirely, my night vision completely shot.

This time, broken leg or not, I could feel him close to me and my adrenaline wouldn't let me remain still. I ran through the break in the trees, deeper into the forest like a goddamn idiot, but my sense of direction had never been the best and I was fucking blind from those bright ass lights.

I drew up short when I broke through the trees. I realized I was back at the shoreline, looking directly at the back of the cabin from across the lake. What the fuck?

He had been watching me this entire time. Setting this up so close to where we'd thought I was safe.

I could still hear the laughter coming from the trees. Had he been there from the start?

"I feel so alone sometimes. I wonder what it would be like if I just disappeared. I know Imogen would be sad. And Ethan. That's the only reason I stay some days. But when I think of what it might be like to close my eyes and never have to open them again all I feel is relief." The mechanical voice was reading my fucking journal.

"Wow, asshole, that's a real dick move," I shouted.

"I'm here to make your dreams come true, Astrid. We could make each other so happy. And all you have to do…"

The voice went silent and the hair on the back of my neck stood up. I could feel him right behind me.

"…is *run*." The guttural voice in my ear spurred me into action and I darted toward the shoreline, running parallel to it as fast as I could, my breath coming out in bursts as my lungs screamed at me that I wasn't getting enough fucking oxygen.

I could hear him behind me laughing and taunting me, and I knew he would have already caught me if he wanted to. He didn't because he was enjoying the chase too much.

When I curved around the inlet, passing underneath the lights from Topher and Meredith's cabin, I heard her voice.

"*Dimitri!*" Meredith screamed.

I ducked behind the boat shed, gasping for breath and wondering where the fuck William was.

Dimitri stepped into the light and offered Meredith an unhinged smile, all teeth and gums. "I can't talk right now. I'm playing."

"Yes, I see that. But I'm here to tell you I'm terminating our contract. Your services are no longer required."

He growled at her. "Do you think I give a fuck about your contract anymore? You don't give me orders. She's mine to play with. Mine to keep."

"I don't think so, Dimitri." She positioned herself so I could see her clearly in the light from the cabin and I could see the gun in her hand.

"I don't care what you think. This is my game. My rules. You weren't invited." His voice had taken on a petulant tone, and I wondered if this particular psycho wasn't operating with a full deck. This was the most bizarre exchange I'd ever seen. Why was he entertaining this conversation with her? Why didn't he just attack her?

Why didn't she just shoot him?

"Dimitri," she warned. "I will not allow this. Stand down."

He shook his head, swatting at his ears. "No."

"Yes. Stand down. Don't make me do this." She lifted the gun and pointed it at him, her hand steady.

"But…" Now he sounded confused, almost childlike. "I want her."

"You can't have her."

Dimitri took another step closer to where I was half hidden behind the storage building, and a single shot rang through the night. He looked down at his chest, a stunned expression on his face before he looked back up at Meredith.

Her face was devoid of emotion but her voice, when she spoke, said it all. *"I'm sorry, little brother."*

56

Astrid

Oh, Brother

MY LEGS GAVE OUT EVEN AS MY JAW HUNG OPEN. WHAT?
What?

My back slid down the plastic wall of the shed and my ass landed in the sand at my feet as I stared straight ahead, trying to come to terms with what I'd just witnessed.

I heard Meredith shift on the porch above me. Heard the safety click on her weapon before she rested it on the table next to her.

"You can come out. I won't hurt you."

"Brother?" I called. "*Brother?* Are you fucking kidding me?"

"Come inside. We'll talk."

I heard the glass door open and heard her go inside. I ordered my legs to resume their function, even if they were still shaky, and stood. I stepped closer to the base of the stairs and paused to look closely at Dimitri's still form, lying in the sand. I watched for long enough that I was sure he wasn't breathing.

Better safe than sorry, and all that. It took longer than I was proud of to climb the stairs to the upper level and when I walked through the back door Meredith sat in the middle of the room, unarmed and meeting my incredulous stare head on.

"I'm sorry. My brother has always been…different." She stared at me. "His therapist said he had poor impulse control when he was still a small child. As he grew up it became apparent there was a bit more to it than that."

I stared at her incredulously. "Do you *think*?"

She rubbed her hands over her face, suddenly looking exhausted. "How far are they behind you?"

"Not far at all." William's voice came from just outside.

"And the other one?" she asked without looking at him.

"Right behind you," Garen said.

"And Topher?" she asked.

"Politely detained in the bathroom," Garen said. "Unnecessary collateral damage."

She nodded. "Thank you."

William approached me and studied me from head to toe for injury. "Are you okay?"

I nodded. "I think I am. But I definitely need to start running more often if this is going to be a thing now that we're dating. I almost hyperventilated."

He snorted and pulled me to him, wrapping his arms around me. "I think I love you," he whispered into my ear.

I leaned up and put my mouth against his ear. "I think you should."

I heard Garen cough from his position behind Meredith, and I looked over, his face screwed up as he tried not to laugh out loud. I shot him a wink that he returned.

"Now what?" Meredith asked.

William released me and turned to face her, placing his body between hers and mine. I glared at his back and stepped up next to him, shaking my head at him when he gave me a disapproving look.

I replied before William could. "You've been a pretty naughty girl, Mere. I can understand some, maybe even most, of your motivations for blackmailing William, but you crossed the line when you involved Imogen."

She looked at me and, for just a moment, it was the same friendly face that had sat across the dinner table from me less than twenty-four hours prior. "I wouldn't have done it. If nothing else, don't you think my actions in the last few days have proven how I feel about collateral damage? Imogen was always safe from me." She vowed that to me, not William, and I believed her. Maybe it made me an idiot, but I trusted my gut.

"I'll hold you to that. Because now I have enough on you that I could quite easily return the favor. How do you think you'd do in federal prison, Mere? There's no pinot grigio there. No Topher. No Earl Grey. Plus, I think you'd look atrocious in orange. You're more of a winter."

Garen was making no attempt to conceal his laughter anymore. "Goddamn, kid, you've always been a riot, but I think you've gotten funnier since I died."

"Very funny, Pops. You're still on my shit list."

And he was. I was pissed as hell that they'd let me believe he was dead for so many months. I'd punched him in the shoulder when he explained it to me, but I was pretty sure it'd hurt me worse than it did him. Hank Turner had to die. And anyone who knew what really happened in that room that night was at risk. I was angry and hurt, but the joy I felt when I looked at him and saw him staring at me like a proud papa? It softened that hurt a lot.

William was still staring at Meredith—well, glaring, to be exact. "I was right not to trust you."

She met his gaze straight on, without flinching. I had to respect that. "You were."

"You were trying to undermine me from day one," he declared.

"I was," she agreed.

"But you just saved Astrid's life," William said.

"It was my fault she was ever at risk," Meredith said.

My eyes widened. Wow, that was a ballsy thing to say under those circumstances.

William considered her for another moment without saying anything, and she didn't fidget, just sat there waiting for judgment.

"I don't want to run the Organization," William declared.

"I'm aware," she said.

"But you're a bitch and I don't want to give you what you want," he stated.

She looked thoughtful for a moment. "Fair. You're not wrong, but I'd like to argue that my being a bitch makes me *ideal* for the job."

I looked back and forth between the two of them, occasionally cutting my eyes to Garen to see what he thought of this exchange but he just looked mildly amused as he leaned against the wall by the bathroom door.

I raised my hand. "I have a suggestion."

Both Meredith and William turned to look at me, one amused, the other exasperated. "Give it to her."

William's eyebrows drew together. "What?"

I rolled my eyes at him before I gestured at Meredith. "She's smart, obviously, capable, determined, devious, and manipulative enough to successfully lead a criminal organization."

Meredith returned my stare. "Thank you?"

"You're welcome. You're still a bitch, though," I reminded her.

William was still staring at me like I'd lost my mind. "Why would I do that? She's fucking blackmailing me, Astrid."

"Because it makes sense, William. She wants it. You do not. She's a criminal. You are not. Well, not for the most part. This doesn't have to be complicated. If you're worried she's not going to do a good job, then just make her your partner. But either way, you don't have to take on the role you never wanted in the first place, and she finally gets the only thing she wanted all along."

"*Um, excuse me?*"

We all turned to the bathroom door.

"It sounds like this is all going really well and that's just swell, but do you think someone could untie me? My legs are going to sleep."

57

Astrid

The Gang's All Here

WE PUT MEREDITH AND TOPHER ON A PLANE AT ONE OF the small municipal airports not far from Mammoth. Topher hugged me tight before they boarded, whispering in my ear, "Thank you. I never want to see the great outdoors again."

I returned his hug and patted him on the back. "There, there, buddy. You'll be back with the hordes of rude people and light pollution before you know it."

I watched them go, knowing there was still a chance Meredith might screw us all over in the end. But I didn't think she would.

I turned to look at Garen and William where they leaned against the hood of our recently replaced rental car. Garen was going to drop us off in Redding and then head back east. He didn't like being this far from

Imogen and his life was there now. I knew I'd see him again, but I wanted to cry at the thought of saying goodbye again so soon.

He gave me that smile again. The same one he'd given me when he told me he had my back. I stepped into his arms and he bundled me into a bear hug. "I'm proud of you, kiddo."

"And I'm still mad at you," I choked out.

He rocked me back and forth a couple of times before he grabbed my shoulders and pushed me back so he could look into my eyes. "I'm sorry, Astrid."

"I know. Still mad though." I sniffled.

"When you're not mad anymore, maybe you'll come visit? It'd be nice to have my girls together again. I have a cabin on the lake…"

"Nooooooo!" I exclaimed, my tears turning into laughter. "I don't want to see another cabin on the lake for a long, long time."

He tilted his head. "Okay, that's fair. How about Imogen's place? This Christmas?"

"Wild horses couldn't keep me away."

When he dropped us off at my place several hours later, we skipped the tearful goodbye. We'd already done it and I didn't think I had another one in me.

I leaned into the car window and gave him a peck on the cheek. "Love you, old man."

"Love you, kiddo. See you soon." And then he was gone.

William picked up our bags and waited by the door for me to open it. I expected it to be sad, coming home without Remy there to greet me, but when I opened the door a blur of black fur came streaking toward me, nearly knocking me over in his exuberance.

"Hey, buddy! What are you doing here? Oh my god, I missed you. Look at you, did you get bigger?" He danced around me lifting his front paws off the ground and grinning like a fool. It was the best welcome home I could have hoped for and I threw my arms around his neck and hung on for dear life. My Remiel. My lifeline.

"I knew you'd want him to be here when you got home." The voice came from the living room, and I widened my eyes when I saw Liam standing there with an uncertain expression on his face, his hands tucked into his pockets, staring at me like I was the best thing he'd seen in a long, long time.

I went to stand in front of him, soaking in his features, his lopsided grin. Just everything that was Liam. He fucking drove me crazy. But he was my Liam.

I threw my arms around him and he returned my hug with a grunt. "Liam?"

"Yes, Astrid?" He rested his head on top of mine.

"I quit."

He stared at me for a split second before realization dawned. *"Thank god."* And then…my ex-boss kissed me like he'd been waiting to do it for half his life.

I returned his kiss eagerly until we both broke apart when a throat cleared behind me.

Liam's eyes widened when he looked over my shoulder, meeting William's gaze. "Shit."

I slapped my hand over my mouth, but I couldn't stop the giggles. I looked back at William and he rolled his eyes at me. "I'm not gonna stop calling him Fucking Liam."

Liam looked back and forth between us like we'd both lost our minds. "What is happening right now?"

I shrugged. "William and I had a lot of time to talk while we were away. A *lot* of time."

I looked at William to see if he wanted to add anything to that. "Mate, if you think I'd missed the way you looked at her, you must think I'm a fucking idiot. Lucky for you, she seems to return your affections. As far as I'm concerned, as long as you don't do anything stupid like putting her in mortal danger, *again*, what Astrid wants, Astrid gets."

Liam still looked shell-shocked so I took him by the hand and pulled him to the couch. We sat down and I smiled at him. "Liam? Do you like me?"

"Of course I like you, Astrid." Poor Liam still looked confused, but at least he was honest.

"And do you want to date me?" I asked.

He cut his eyes to William again but I caught his chin and pulled him back to me. "Don't worry about him."

He nodded. "Yes."

"And do you have an issue with me dating both you *and* William?" I asked.

He thought about it for a minute before he shook his head. "Much less likely you'll say the wrong name in bed."

I stared at him for a beat and then burst out laughing. "Well, okay then. I think we should give this a try."

I looked back at William and he shrugged. "I hear all the cool kids are doing it."

Epilogue 1. Astrid

Sumo Cum Laudly

The road to self-discovery looked a lot more like that show where everything you have to cross is spinning and twirling and turning, trying to knock you down into a pit of Jell-o. I didn't think that was exactly how it went, but that was the gist of it. I couldn't take credit for the analogy, my therapist was the one who said it, but it made me laugh and it stuck with me.

I still had days where I thought everyone hated me, days where I doubted every good thing in my life, and days where I didn't want to get out of bed and face the world. My therapist said I probably always would. My goal wasn't to get to the point where I never felt like that again, but to get to the point that I could fight that voice in my head with the arsenal I'd created. Me. I'd done that.

And when I couldn't? I'd learned to lean on the

people in my life that wanted to be there for me. People who I knew, without a doubt, would be there for me if I needed them. And all I had to do was ask. Magical.

"I think you're making really great progress, Astrid. I'm so proud of the work you've done." She beamed at me.

"Thanks. I know I'm not done, but it's great to have some tools to help me fight the voices in my head." I made the crazy gesture next to my face.

"Well, the key to that is remembering that the voices in your head are *you*, so you have to keep training yourself to treat yourself like you would your best friend."

I snorted. "So, call myself a bitch and remind myself I probably need to get laid?"

She laughed, shaking her head. "Well, that's not exactly what I meant, but close enough. That's all our time for today, but I'll see you next week?"

"I'll be here!" I offered her a jaunty wave and left her office with a real smile on my face. It wasn't always like that. Sometimes I left so utterly ruined emotionally that all I could do was go home and go to bed, but on those days, Remy curled up right next to me and refused to leave my side until I'd cried it out.

He was the best boy.

I hurried to the Scout and hopped in, gunning the engine and heading for home with excitement buzzing in my veins. I had a date tonight, and I couldn't wait for the guys to see what I'd planned.

"Demon. Are you serious with this?" William studied the entrance with a dubious expression.

I jogged back and forth from one foot to the other, too excited to stay still. "I could literally not be more serious."

I looked to my other side to see Liam's reaction and he had his head tilted straight up at the sky like he was praying for divine intervention.

My laughter was ringing out across the parking lot, drawing stares from the other customers, but I didn't care. Let them look.

"Come on! We're gonna miss our time slot."

When I found the place online I literally cackled for fifteen minutes picturing that very moment.

William and Liam stood side by side, or as close as they could get to one another in the giant inflatable sumo wrestler costumes, with identical glares on their faces. See? Bonding. They were already agreeing with one another. They'd be crossing swords before I knew it.

"Are you ready?" I called.

"Demon, what exactly are you going to be doing while we are"—he gestured to their giant bellies—"bouncing around in this cage like two overgrown toddlers?"

I poured myself a glass of wine from the bottle I'd ordered and leaned back in my chair, crossing one leg over the other. "Oh, don't worry about me, William, I promise I am going to be *very* entertained. Now, when the bell dings, it's go time!"

I think I may have peed in my pants. But seeing the two of them trying to beat the shit out of each other without actually being able to make contact was the funniest thing I had ever seen. There'd been some lingering tension here and there, snarky comments and quite a few "fucking Liam's" in the past few months. I thought this was the perfect way for them to work out their problems. Plus, I'd recorded the whole thing on my phone.

Imogen was going to *die*.

3 a.m. had always been my witching hour. Somehow, nearly every night, that was the time I would wake up and have my previously scheduled existential crisis.

I would have loved to tell you that therapy and the love of not one, but two, good men, had healed me from that particular issue, but there were still days that found me tip-toeing out of our bedroom so I wouldn't wake my three favorite men.

That night, only Remy lifted his head from his plush Tempur-Pedic bed in the corner, a gift from William that was not without selfish motives, but I held up a finger to my lips before I smoothed my hand over his head as I passed. "I'm okay, buddy," I whispered.

He thumped his tail twice and resumed his sleeping position, but I knew if I didn't come back soon he would come find me. My good boy always did.

I stepped around a stack of boxes in the living room and crossed to the glass doors that overlooked my tiny backyard. An odd nostalgia took over for a moment, and I was sad all over again to let this place go, but one of the things I'd learned over the past few months was that the one sure thing about life was that change was the only constant. And what was coming for me was a big change. I was excited about moving in with the guys, but sad to let go of my first little place that was all my own.

I curled up in the chair and stared out at the postage sized yard and the starry night beyond it, letting myself feel my emotions as they came over me in waves. Taking the time to recognize each one before moving on to the next. My therapist said to think of them as waves in the ocean. If I tried to fight against them all the time, I would just wear myself out and, ultimately, never be able to move past them. By allowing myself the space to process what I was feeling, I could choose to hold onto those that were healthy and let the rest continue out to sea. The analogy, and its significance to me personally, was more effective than even she could have predicted.

The ocean and I went way back.

I must have fallen asleep because the next thing I knew I was wrapped in a set of arms, being carried back to the bedroom.

"Come on, love, it's a few hours yet before we have to be up." He pressed a gentle kiss to my temple, and I took a deep breath into my lungs that was all spicy man with a little bit of sunshine thrown in. I didn't know how he did it, but Liam always smelled like sunshine on a summer day to me.

He carried me into the bedroom, gently nudging the door open with his shoulder before he laid me down, ever so gently, in the middle of the considerably bigger bed that now occupied the space.

I sighed when I felt a different set of arms curl around my waist from behind.

"Mm, Demon, can't sleep?" William burrowed his face into my neck, and I heard him breathe deeply.

"Just anxious, I think." I turned toward him and returned his embrace.

I felt the bed dip behind me as Liam curled up against my back. "Let us help."

I grinned against William's chest. "If I let you two 'help' me with my anxiety every time it crept up on me, we'd never get anything done and we'd probably all die of dehydration."

I felt, more than heard, William's chuckle. "Ah, but what a way to go."

Liam's hands slid to my hip bones, dragging my sleep shorts down my thighs and I felt him follow their progress with the rest of his body, until he was dragging them all the way off and tossing them over his shoulder. A disgruntled *hmph* sounded from Remy's corner, and I giggled.

"Sorry, Rem." Liam chuckled.

His apology was met with the sound of more canine grumbling and I listened as Remy padded out of the room, presumably so he wouldn't have to be witness to the utter defilement of his mother. Smart boy.

William lifted the hem of my tank, encouraging me to raise my arms so they could divest me of all of my clothing in short order.

Once I was naked, cloaked only in the bands of shadow and moonlight that streamed through the bedroom window, Liam ran his hands up my legs gently, stroking the skin of my thighs before he settled his hands on my hips and turned me so I was straddling William.

I widened my eyes at William and he grinned in response, half his face cast in shadow, but I could still see his eyes gleaming up at me from his prone position.

He slid a hand from my navel slowly up my chest until he circled my throat with it, applying just enough pressure to make me gasp. "Demon, are you going to be a good girl for us and take what we give you?"

I nodded jerkily, my voice having escaped me. His hand tightened imperceptibly before he slid it around the back of my neck and slowly pulled me down until I was on all fours above him. I had some ideas about where they were going with this but when I felt Liam's warm exhale between my legs, I squeaked and squirmed.

"Love, your only job right now is to hold still and take this." Liam breathed against my most sensitive skin.

And while William stroked and petted my shoulders and arms and stomach, everywhere except for where I needed his hands most, I felt Liam seal his mouth to my pussy from behind and *devour*. That was the only word that came close to what he was doing to me. He consumed me, groaning and shifting to get closer, taste more of me.

"Fuck, love, I'll never get enough of your taste on my tongue," he growled before he resumed destroying me.

When I began unconsciously rocking back against his mouth, seeking even more of him, William *tsked* at me. "What did I tell you?"

I blinked at him, unable to answer in anything but gasps and groans.

"Hold still," he repeated.

When I whined at him—not my proudest moment— he chuckled and slid his hand through the curls between my legs, tugging lightly before he parted my lips and slid his index finger down to where Liam was latched onto me, stealing some of the moisture there before he slowly and methodically began rubbing maddening circles around my clit. I could feel how wet I was between their combined efforts, and when Liam speared his tongue inside me, fucking me with it, William increased his speed just enough that I could feel the beginnings of an orgasm radiating out from my center, crawling up my spine, causing me to throw my head back in a silent scream.

"Fuck, yes, come all over his face. He fucking loves it. He doesn't need to breathe; all he needs is to drink you down. Now, *come*."

There was no holding it back, but I couldn't think of any logical reason I'd want to. I worried for a minute that Liam truly couldn't breathe, but then I felt him lapping at me gently, swallowing everything I'd given him before he rose enough to place a bite against one of my cheeks before he moved and did it again on the other side.

"This ass, I could just sink my teeth into it, baby." He rose until he was kneeling behind me, pressing his back against mine. "I need you," he whispered against my neck.

His words had me mindlessly nodding. "Yes." I pushed back against him and felt the fat head of his cock breach me just barely, the feel of him stretching me had me sinking my nails into William's chest, rocking over him, getting him slick with my juices as he watched what was happening above him with a predatory smile.

"Get her nice and warmed up, Liam. I have something in mind, but she'll need to come at least once more before we can even try it."

Focusing on his face was no small effort, and before I could react to his words, Liam slammed the rest of the way inside of me, taking my breath away momentarily.

It came back on a moan. "More." I shuddered.

William smirked and then leaned over and slid open the drawer next to the bed, retrieving a small silicone toy I hadn't seen before.

He saw me watching and smirked. "I went shopping." He slid the sleeve over his index finger and hit a button at the base of it, the vibration audible even with the way Liam and I were both panting. He placed it against my clit with no mercy, and I swore I was going to come again right then and there, but he eased it back a bit.

"Can you take more, Demon?"

"More?!" I gasped.

He hit the button again.

And again.

When he placed it against my clit a second time, at full power apparently, I screamed and saw stars.

Liam groaned behind me. "Fuck, love, you're clamped down so tight on me I'm going to burst any minute now."

"No!" William barked. "Not yet."

I regained my senses when Liam pulled out slowly, teasing me with his retreat and causing secondary baby orgasms as his dick scraped along my walls deliciously. All I could manage was a pitiful whine at his absence.

"Don't worry, love, we're not done," he assured me.

William traded places with him and when Liam was stretched out on his back below me, I felt William's warm body curl around mine, one arm banded around my ribs and the other sliding back down between my legs, his new toy still buzzing away. He teased me with it for a moment before he slid home and groaned.

"I can still feel the tremors from that orgasm, your pussy is grasping at my cock. You want me to fill you up?"

I heard the keening wail coming from my throat but it wasn't a sound I'd ever made before. "God, yes. Please, sir."

He punched his hips, the slapping sound it made obscene in the darkness. When he returned the toy to my clit, I couldn't have told you if I had another orgasm or if he just restarted the one it felt like I'd been having for the last five minutes.

When I felt him drop down so that he was sitting on Liam's thighs, still inside of me, I was confused. I turned and looked over my shoulder at him, but his face was in shadow.

"I want you to take us both. Can you do that? Do you want two cocks at once?" His voice had turned guttural and the sound sent shivers down my spine.

"I don't think you'll both fit." I looked down at Liam, and he looked almost as concerned as I was.

"I don't want to hurt her," he addressed William—not me.

"We won't." His hand cupped my chin and turned my head back his way. "We stop when you say stop, Demon. But I think you're going to like this."

I nodded uncertainly, but when I felt Liam nudging against me, seeking entrance, I couldn't resist the urge to grind down on him.

"Slowly. Go slow," William coached. "Rotate your hips."

I did as he said, sliding over the head of Liam's dick, teasing us all, and when he thrust up just barely I felt him slip in alongside William.

"Wait, wait, wait. Fuck. That's…that's a lot," I panted.

"Take your time, baby. We're not going anywhere." William re-upped his efforts with the toy and before long my hips were moving of their own accord.

"Oh. Oh my god." I was so full I was scared they were going to split me in half, but when they started fucking me in tandem all while William held the toy against my clit I could feel my muscles beginning to pulse again. With every thrust they went a little deeper, a little harder, and before long they were fucking into me in earnest, while all I could do was fight to stay on all fours and not collapse into a puddle on Liam's chest.

Seeming to sense my dilemma, Liam slid his arms around me and pulled me down so I was prone on his chest with my ass in the air. William locked his hands around my hips, keeping them where he wanted them, and I shuddered again when I realized he'd been holding back until then. Liam stopped moving entirely, just staying fitted inside me like he'd always belonged there.

William fucked us both until I felt Liam jerk inside me, shoving his mouth against mine as he groaned with his release. I could feel his cum painting my insides and beginning to leak out as William mercilessly slid in and out of me until he, too, jerked and groaned, his fingers tightening on my hips in a way that would be bruised the next day, but I didn't care. I liked the bite of pain with my pleasure.

William leaned over us both, panting and jerking still with aftershocks while all I could do was try not to black out entirely.

"You did so good for us, Demon." He began to ease out of me, and I felt a pang that told me I was going to be very sore tomorrow. But, they'd done exactly what they promised they would.

I couldn't think of a single thing to be anxious about.

Epilogue 2. Astrid

Leave Your Dead Where You Bury Them

I'd put off the conversation with my mother as long as I could, but finally, in the quiet of a fall morning, I turned onto the gravel drive that led to my parents' place. My tires kicked up dust and pebbles as I went, the little pings they created as they bounced off the undercarriage of my old Scout provided a soundtrack to the usual gnawing sense of wrongness which crept under my skin the closer I got to the house I'd grown up in.

The house wasn't evil, and neither were the people who inhabited it; they didn't make it a habit to kick puppies or punch babies. But they'd never made any attempt to understand who I was as a person and, after several months of therapy, I'd come to realize that none of that was my fault. Or, I was coming to believe it. It was still a work in progress.

The infamous Christmas discovery made me realize

my mere existence had been a wound on their marriage that could never heal. And I was the one who got punished for it, time and time again.

So, I'd given up trying to bond with them in the familial way many years ago. But I'd always wanted to understand *why*. Because I'd grown up with the inherent knowledge that I was unlovable. If your own parents couldn't love you, what else were you supposed to think?

Some people might think it odd that it'd taken me nearly a year to go back and talk to my mother about what I'd discovered the Christmas prior. Some might think I was avoiding the situation in favor of other, more pleasant, distractions in my life. Some…wouldn't be wrong.

But I'd come to the realization that, in this case, while I deserved answers, the responsibility wasn't mine to reach out. So I'd waited. In vain, of course, because I hadn't heard a peep from my mother in nine months. Not one text or phone call. No passive aggressive messages sent via Ethan. Nothing.

But when I'd woken up that morning and felt whole —really truly whole, for possibly the first time in my entire life—I'd decided it was time. I got in my truck and drove the twenty-five miles to my parents' house. It might as well have been a thousand miles for how hard it seemed to bridge the gap.

When I pulled up in front of the porch I noticed a few things immediately. The flowers that normally filled the pots by the door, providing a pop of color amongst all the wood and stone, were dead and decaying. The porch was strewn with the natural debris that collected when it hadn't been swept off in weeks. If I didn't know better, I'd have thought they'd just abandoned the house to the elements and taken off for parts unknown. No forwarding address given. But something told me I wouldn't be that lucky.

And I didn't really want to be. Whatever came out of the conversation with my mother, I wanted to walk away without regrets. And I wanted to know who my father was.

My *real* father.

I rang the bell, no longer comfortable just letting myself in, and I waited. And waited. Finally, I heard footsteps in the foyer and my mother's face appeared in the glass. We stared at one another through the pane for long enough I thought maybe she was just going to turn around and leave me standing outside the door. When I heard the lock slide free I straightened my spine and waited to face her.

When she opened the door she stepped back, but didn't invite me in. Okay then.

I crossed the threshold and she closed the door behind me, and I stopped and stared.

This looked nothing like the woman who had raised me. Her hair had grown out from her last dye job, the gray roots prominent. She wore a bathrobe with a red stain on it. Was that wine?

"Mother?" I honestly had to check.

She sighed and rolled her eyes, turning and walking into the living room where she had apparently been having a party for one. For quite some time. There were empty bottles spread across almost every surface, all except the one she was currently pouring herself a glass from. Oh wait…that one was empty too.

"What the hell happened to you?"

She stared at me with blank eyes. "Your father left me."

"Umm. Okay. He's a dick and an alcoholic, not to throw stones inside the glass house."

"Astrid, why are you here?" She wasn't even looking at me anymore. She'd turned on the television and was flipping through channels like her life depended on it, but I could see the tremor in her hands. Not as nonchalant as she was pretending.

"Well, I thought we needed to talk, but now I'm thinking we need an intervention." I gave a pointed look at all the empty bottles.

"I don't need an intervention, Astrid. I just need a nap and to know why you're here now after all this time. I thought you were done with me." She took a long gulp from her glass and turned an apathetic look my way.

Okay, clearly the conversation was not going to go any of the fifty ways I'd imagined it would. Time to get to the point then.

"I want to know who my father is."

She winced, showing for the first time that she felt anything about my presence there that day. She looked down at her glass, as if she could manifest a full one by sheer will alone.

When she looked back up at me she almost looked sorry. Almost.

"Your real father is dead."

I felt tears begin to well and I took a gasping breath. It felt like I'd been punched in the sternum.

"Who?" I whispered, broken.

"Hank Turner."

The End.

Not ready for it to end yet? Want to know what happens when Astrid gets together with Hank and Imogen for Christmas?

Ebook readers click *here* to sign up for my newsletter and get your free bonus chapter! :)

Paperback readers, go to the address below to sign up for my newsletter and receive your bonus chapter :)
https://authorlorenlee.myflodesk.com/satebonus

When I sat down to write Burn, I had zero intention of it ever becoming a duet but somehow this world just wouldn't let go of me that easily. I fell in love with these characters in my mind and, as my friend R.A. Hunter pointed out when I was in the final stages of writing Burn, Astrid simply had more to say.

I hope you've enjoyed the Burn world as much as I have enjoyed living and breathing these characters for the past year. There might even be more to come if you're very, *very* good. <wink>

I'd like to give special thanks to a handful of people and they're probably the only ones that are still here reading this so here goes:

Thank you to Megan. At some point in time you became much more than just the girl on the other end of the line that designs my covers. You are a GEM and I think I love you.

Caroline? Girl. You're a rockstar and I hope you stick

with me for many more to come. Thank you for helping these books be the best possible books that they could be and also for making sure I used *come* and *cum* correctly.

My writing pals Stacey LP and R.A. Hunter, who went from being weirdos on the internet to weirdos that I can't do without. I love you madly. Now get in my house!

As always, thank you to my amazing husband and his unlimited font of patience. You're my favorite human and you keep showing me day after day why saying "yes" was the best decision I ever made.

Last, but not least, to the team of women who show me love on a regular basis, who share and "like" and read and chat and encourage and scream and review and send me unhinged DM's in the middle of the night. I call them *The Order of Fuckery* and they are, without a doubt, some of my favorite humans on the planet. I don't know what I did to deserve you ladies, but I love you all to the moon.

Until next time, my darlings… ***dream sweet.*** ;)

Other Books by Loren Lee:

Standalone:

Tumble

Series:

Burn

Sate

The Killer & The Siren (coming soon)

About the Author

Loren currently lives just outside of Atlanta with her husband, the most adorable puppy in the world, and four succulent plants that she's managed not to kill yet. This could change before the printing of this book, however, so don't hold her to that. She's quite possibly the most awkward person you'll ever meet and she will 100% blurt out something inappropriate if given half a chance. You've been warned.

www.authorlorenlee.com/contact